The Doodled Asterisk

R.A.J. Walling

Originally published London, 1943
Hodder & Stoughton

This edition published 2023 by

OREON

an imprint of

The Oleander Press
16 Orchard Street
Cambridge
CB1 1JT

www.oleanderpress.com

ISBN: 9781915475312

Sign up to our infrequent newsletter
to **receive a free ePub** of
Fatality in Fleet Street
by Christopher St John Sprigg and get
news of new titles, discounts and give-aways!

www.oleanderpress.com/golden-age-crime

A CIP catalogue record for the book
is available from the British Library.

Cover design, typesetting & ebook: neorelix

NOTE

All the persons and incidents of this story are fictitious. I have taken some liberties with the topography of North Wales, for which I apologise to any who may find them profane. I hope that a deep, and I trust evident, admiration and affection for the scenes of Tolefree's adventures in search of a witness, and for the characters he meets, may secure my absolution.

The Doodled Asterisk

1

1

On the night of the 2nd September, 1939, Tolefree disappeared into the blue for eighteen months.

After dinner, he had walked down Whitehall with Dr. Mapperley and they had stood a minute or two watching the crowd milling at the entrance of Downing Street. Then he had shaken hands with that learned buccaneer and turned into a dark building. It swallowed him. The machine he had left twenty-one years before caught him up. Next morning the Prime Minister told the country that it was at war with Hitler...

None of his familiars saw Tolefree again till March, 1941.

On the 21st of that month, late at night, I, with my occupation gone, was doing a spell of fire-watching in Manchester Square. Huddled in my thickest coat, I leaned against a chimney breast on the roof, peering out into the sea of darkness which was London in the blackout, observing the gun flashes away in the East, tracing the searchlights, the silver pencil strokes, listening intently for the crump of bombs, watching for the sudden glow of incendiaries, speculating on the strange fate which had plunged me into two world wars before I was fifty.

My mind went back to nights of vigil in the trenches on the Western Front. Nights very much like this: the Western Front had shifted; that was all. Not quite so silent as the Pimple on Vimy Ridge, this O.P. in the middle of four hundred square miles of bricks and mortar; but nearly. Little traffic went on in the darkness below. Ten millions of people moved or slept; ate or talked; danced or made love; or, like myself, watched for fires, on this London night of March. This sort of London night had never entered any of our dreams in peace time.

During the day something had drawn my attention to the revolution which a year-and-a-half had wrought in my life and everybody else's. Not any big thing – not rationing, not State control of my business, or conscription, or a fifty percent income tax, or any of the other strange dislocations of custom and habit that all welcomed because they were necessary to cook the goose of That Man across the North Sea. A little thing – a paragraph in a newspaper about the opening of the trout season on the Avon.

Could it be possible that people still fished for trout on the Avon? Apparently they did, for the writer waxed eloquent about the deadly effect of a March Brown he had cast on the first day of the season.

It sent my mind back to the two trout fishermen I had best known, Tolefree himself and his friend Pierce of Scotland Yard. There would be no trouting for either of them this season. They were after bigger fish and with other tackle. Where and how they fished there was no deponent to say, nor would anybody else ever know.

The flicker of the gun flashes died away. The searchlights went out. I looked from my watchman's eyrie into a gloom "of Cerberus and blackest midnight born." Did anyone read Milton now?

I stirred and turned towards the hatch as the sirens shrieked their long call of "Raiders passed!" Before I reached it a shape, only seen because it was blacker than the blackness, came through.

"That you, Farrar?"

"Aye? – oh, it's you." I greeted one of my neighbours.

"You're wanted on the phone. I was going to take your place for a minute or two – but the All Clear's gone. Nothing doing tonight, was there?"

I followed him through the hatch and closed it. "Bit of gunfire way down the river – too far away to hear anything. That's all."

"Good. Well – hurry. Somebody's all het up about speaking to you. I told the commissionaire to put him through to your flat."

The next minute I was speaking for the first time in eighteen months to Tolefree.

"Hello, Farrar! Good to hear your voice. You all right?"

"Lost a spot of weight. Otherwise yes. And you?"

"Fit as a cart horse."

"Where are you, Tolefree? Not at Bridge House, I know – and Watling Street's no more."

"Never mind where I am now," said Tolefree. "It's where I'll be tomorrow that matters – and that's anywhere you can be. I've got some leave, Farrar, and I've almost forgotten how to spend it. You shall decide for me."

"It's the very devil, Tolefree," I answered dolefully. "I'm pushing off tomorrow morning for a day or two."

"Oh – rotten! Is my luck out! Where and why?"

"Where – Westport, by the ten-thirty. Why – to see a man, if you can believe it, by the name of Blenkinsop."

"Blenkinsop?" Tolefree paused. "Did I hear that right, Farrar?"

"Perfectly."

"Friend of yours? Business?"

"Neither. I had a letter from him saying that he was detained at Westport, but he had a message for me from the captain of his ship."

"Ah! – a ship captain. And he gave Mr. Blenkinsop a message for you. I suppose he couldn't write it himself?"

Tolefree seemed resentful.

"I'm afraid he couldn't, old fellow. Don't you read the papers? There was a yarn about the ship and the captain this morning."

"I read 'em sometimes – well, always," said Tolefree. "The yarn — ?"

"About the steamship *Bridgend*, torpedoed in the Atlantic. All hands lost. Only survivors two passengers, landed at Lisbon by a sardine boat."

"Yes, I read that, Farrar."

"Well, you see why Captain McPherson couldn't write his message to me."

"Sorry, Farrar. Poor chap! And Blenkinsop? – was he one of the two passengers?"

"He evidently was."

"How come he's at Westport?"

"Brought from Lisbon, of course, by – well, never mind what sort of ship."

"Of course. Not a word. Well, Farrar, I'd hate not to shake hands with you. So I'll be along in the morning. You get to Paddington tennish, and we can have half an hour. That a date?"

"Splendid, Tolefree. I'll be under the clock at ten."

"Right. Till then," said Tolefree.

When, carrying a small suitcase, I arrived under the clock on the stroke of ten next morning, Tolefree was already there. We gripped hands long and hard.

"You're a cure for sore eyes," said Tolefree. "How are the nieces?"

"Grown-up young ladies. One's a Wren, and the other's a Waaf. I don't see either of 'em once in a blue moon. Too busy beating Hitler to worry about their bachelor uncle. Also, he can't get any petrol for joy rides in his car. In fact, he's sold it. From their point of view he's on the beach."

Tolefree grinned. "Reduced, like any commoner, to riding in a train. A sad comedown, Farrar. But war's war, and this one especially."

"What have you been doing to yourself?" I asked him. "You haven't got sore eyes, but you're looking like a washed-out rag."

"I feel well enough. But you know what a job like mine is. Keeps you for ever on the stretch. First leave I've had – and the doctor's insisted on a whole fortnight. I've been thinking it over since last night, Farrar. Why shouldn't I start it by a day or two in Westport with you?"

"Could you possibly?" I exclaimed. "Cheers! I don't suppose my business with Blenkinsop will take long. We might have a look round. We may need permission to enter, though."

"I've thought of that," Tolefree answered.

"Trust you to think of everything! And I suppose you've even got your bag on the station somewhere?"

"Naturally. It's on that porter's barrow. I thought you'd take the infliction like a man. There's so much to ask and to tell. Six hours in the train and we'll tear the heart out of the last year or two, eh?"

"Splendid!" I moved up the platform. "Come and have a coffee before the train goes. We'll drink our own healths and frustration to his enemies."

2

The famous train, which stopped oftener than in peace time, and ran less fast, was pulling out of Iscaster before we'd finished with "Where were you?" and "Did you see?" We had lunched. There was an hour to go.

Tolefree had lit his pipe, I a cigar. We watched the blue water sliding by on one side and the red cliffs on the other, passing an occasional friendly smile to each other across the compartment. Tolefree said suddenly,

"So you're going to Westport to meet a man by the name of Blenkinsop, whom you've never seen before. Or heard of?"

"Not a word."

"Blenkinsop..." Tolefree mused. "Not a common name. I wonder how Mr. Blenkinsop got a permit to be in Westport?"

"I told you. A certain ship—"

"Yes, I know. But there was nobody by the name of Blenkinsop on that ship, Farrar. The two passengers were called Black and Perry."

I stared. "How — ?"

"Well, I'd known about that episode before the newspapers published it. When you mentioned it, I thought Blenkinsop was a new one on me, and I had it looked up."

I continued to stare.

"You're not surprised by my curiosity about Blenkinsop, are you?" Tolefree asked.

I shook my head. "Nothing you do in the course of your job surprises me, my dear fellow. I wasn't thinking of that."

"What then?"

"The suitcase on the barrow at Paddington." It was Tolefree's turn to stare. "I bet that Blenkinsop's no mystery to you, never mind what you say."

"You lose," said Tolefree. "Blenkinsop is precisely that – a dark mystery to me."

"Nevertheless, Tolefree, confess that Blenkinsop and not Farrar is the reason why you're in this train on the way to Westport."

"That's what's biting you? My dear Farrar, rather than miss our talk I'd have gone with you e'en unto Wigan or Skegness. But I'll confess this – that last night, when you told me on the telephone a man named Blenkinsop was breathing the air of Westport and you were going to see him, I was tickled to death."

"And that was why – but never mind, Tolefree. It's good to have had a few hours with you on any terms. Now, tell me why you were surprised to know that Blenkinsop, whoever he is, was breathing the air of Westport?"

"Because I understood that he wasn't breathing any air at all. I thought he'd gone down with the ship. If he came from Lisbon, as you say, on a certain vessel, the authorities in charge of that vessel didn't know it."

"Whew!" I exclaimed.

"And so, perhaps you might explain how you came to know it. A letter, you said?"

I nodded. "Came yesterday morning. He marked it 'Private', but I've no secrets from you, Tolefree." I drew a paper from my wallet.

"I dislike intruding on private affairs," Tolefree declared with a grin. "But in this instance, perhaps—"

"Here you are," I said, unfolding the paper and reading:

"IMPERIAL HOTEL, WESTPORT,
19th March, 1941

SIR – I am a survivor of the S.S. Bridgend, *which was torpedoed in the Atlantic.*

In conversation during the voyage, Captain McPherson had spoken of you as an old friend. Before I entered the boat he gave me a message for you which, if I got away with my life, I was to deliver to you by my own hand.

Captain McPherson went down with his ship, for the lifeboat in which he would have escaped capsized before he could board her.

I am at this place for an indefinite time. Unless I hear from you to the contrary, I shall take opportunity of calling upon you immediately I reach London. If on the other hand you should be aware of any importance attaching to a message from Captain

McPherson, and can visit me here, I will keep any appointment you care to make.

Yours faithfully,

ROBERT BLENKINSOP.

I put up the letter. "That's it," said I.

"May I see the signature?" Tolefree asked.

"Have the whole thing." I passed it over. Tolefree examined it. "Seen his hand before?"

"Once or twice," said Tolefree, contemplating the paper. "He writes a nice fist. A little distinguished. A man of quality."

"I'm no graphologist, but, yes – it is rather good."

"And are you aware of any importance attaching to a message from McPherson?"

"None – except that he was so particular to see that his messenger delivered it into my hands. It made me curious. That was why I telegraphed Blenkinsop that I would see him this evening."

"Puzzling," said Tolefree, and took a long look over the sea. "No doubt you're dying to know why I'm interested in Blenkinsop?"

"Not exactly on the point of death," I answered. "And if I were it would be useless suffering. Because you're not going to tell me."

"I can't."

"Of course. I'm not going to ask you, my dear fellow. Anyhow, Blenkinsop's nothing to me. Let's talk of cabbages or sealing-wax – the censor bars kings."

The train was very late, pushing its way by stages through crowded junctions. Dusk began to fall as we reached Westport; and darkness was coming on when we arrived after six. A taxi with hooded lamps took us through unlit streets to the Imperial Hotel.

Tolefree drew me aside in the lobby, crowded with men and women in uniform, after we had shown permits, signed the register, and sent up our bags.

"Could you put off asking for Blenkinsop till we've had dinner?"

"Certainly, Tolefree, if you wish. What's the idea?"

"That you ask the head waiter to point him out to you and let me have a good look at him before you introduce yourself."

"Very well. Dinner's at seven, they say. It's now half-past six. Let's find a table in the lounge and have an aperitif."

The lounge was very full, also with people mostly in uniform, and all agog. There had been an occasion in the city: distinguished visitors had come and gone. The talk was of them.

We found one small table unoccupied in a corner, took it and gave our orders.

Not all the uniforms were those of the fighting Services. There were fire brigade officers, ambulance officers, and a tall warden in his dark dress and his brassard. This last one stood by a small unoccupied table in a corner, and, seeing us searching, indicated it. We thanked him and he saluted as he moved away. We called up a perspiring waiter and gave our orders.

People continued to squeeze in. There was much drifting about and eager chatter.

One tall, dark-visaged man in khaki with a captain's three pips on his shoulder-strap passed twice in front of the table and eyed us. Tolefree, seeing him presently with a chair in his hand, looking for space at a table, moved round to my side. The man murmured thanks, planted the chair and sat down with us. He caught the willing eye of a waiter, ordered a drink, took a tobacco pouch and cigarette papers from his pocket and began to roll a cigarette, looking straight over his hands to Tolefree, who sat opposite.

"Bit of a crush, eh?" he said. "All sorts here today. Ah, excuse me. There's a man I know."

He left pouch and papers on the table and wound his way towards the door. A fair, clean-shaven man between forty and fifty stood there surveying the room. They met with a nod and came forward after exchanging a few words. The man in khaki found another chair.

"May we?" he asked, as they sat down.

The fair man in mufti gave us a slight nod in acknowledgment. His blue eyes steadily contemplated Tolefree. The captain resumed his cigarette making. Tolefree produced a case. "If you don't mind, I prefer it this way," said the captain. The blue-eyed man took one of Tolefree's with a "Thanks."

"You were saying," Tolefree reminded him, "all sorts here—"

"Big affair today. Yes – all sorts, aren't there?"

"Say many sorts," replied his companion.

He rejected his first paper and rolled his tobacco in a second. Tolefree gave him a light.

"We saw nothing of the affair," he remarked. "Just got in on the train."

"Ah? You tell them," he said to the man in mufti.

I listened to a description of the ceremonies, and watched the captain smoking the homemade cigarette and idly doodling on the rejected paper.

A gong broke in on the recital. The crowd stirred and moved towards the glass doors of the dining room.

"Well, Farrar – shall we — ? Are you dining?" Tolefree asked the captain.

"No. Going to the mess."

"Then, good evening," said Tolefree, and passed on with me.

The head waiter stood by his little pulpit just inside the room.

"Mr. Blenkinsop, sir?" he said, answering my inquiry. "I don't know him; but I'll inquire. That's a table for two and not reserved," he added, pointing.

I found Tolefree abstracted. He responded smilingly enough to attempt to make talk, but kept nothing going. He looked often to the head waiter's stand. He fiddled with his implements.

This demeanour persisted till a waiter stopped behind his chair and said to me, "You were inquiring for a Mr. Blenkinsop, sir?"

"Ah, yes," said I. "Is he here?"

"No, sir; we have no Mr. Blenkinsop on the books."

I looked blank. Tolefree chimed in, "A pity. But, Farrar, what about Perry? Should we find out whether Mr. Perry's here?"

"I'll go and see, sir," said the obliging waiter. He soon returned. "Sorry, sir. Mr. Perry is dining in his room; he's not too well."

"I understand." I made a sympathetic noise. "What's the number of his room?"

"They'll tell you at the office, sir," the waiter replied reprovingly.

"Of course. Thanks."

"Told off, good and hearty," said Tolefree with a smile. "Would you mind assailing the office at once, Farrar? Better you than me."

I dropped napkin on chair and went out, leaving Tolefree fiddling with various scraps of paper. I was absent not more than two minutes.

"Number 57," I said, taking my seat.

"Well! If that's not a coincidence! I've just been looking at the figure 57."

I turned two sauce bottles, shook my head, and said, "Where?"

Tolefree unfolded a screw of flimsy paper in his hand.

"You know my besetting sin of curiosity. When I see people doodling I always want to know why they doodle and what's the subconscious inspiration of their doodling. Our friend the captain in khaki doodled on a cigarette paper while his friend with the blue eyes was talking to you. Here's what he doodled."

He handed the unfolded paper to me.

"Fifty-seven – you see? – between something like a clock and a mighty asterisk. Characteristic doodling, don't you think?"

I said, "No, I don't. Come off it, Tolefree. Do you take me for a mental defective? Here's something more than doodling. Here's a reference to Blenkinsop – plain as a pikestaff. And it really is a clock face, not something like one. The clock points to eight. How did you get hold of it?"

"Picked it off the table as we got up. So, you don't think it's doodling? What is it, then?"

"A message. With some allusion to Blenkinsop and a time. What else I can't guess."

"If you're right, Farrar, and it's not doodling, that mighty asterisk must mean something too."

"Undoubtedly. And you probably know what it is."

"Then you think it's a message for me?"

"If not he wouldn't have left it in full sight for you to pick up."

Tolefree retrieved the paper. "I assure you I never saw the fellow in my life before this evening. But you may be right. Who can tell? Do you see his friend talking to the head waiter? I have an idea about that."

"That he's trying to discover from the head waiter what your little game is."

"My little game? I like that! You notice that the head waiter treats him with a touch of obsequiousness – or, say, respect."

"Same thing in a head waiter? It occurred to me, too. Why do two people like that make a point of coming to our table and entering into conversation with us? And why does one of them doodle? And the other come in and make inquiries about us?"

"He hasn't looked our way once."

"No, but the head waiter has, several times. We won't look their way too pointedly. Because fifty-seven is the number of Blenkinsop's room. And it's now twenty minutes to eight."

I looked resolutely away from the head waiter's pulpit. A minute later, Tolefree murmured, "Ah – he's gone."

"Well," said I, "shall we go back to the lounge for coffee?

"Could you possibly do without coffee tonight? I'd dearly like to get outside for five minutes and see what the weather's doing."

"Certainly." But I looked curiously at Tolefree. He wasn't usually much concerned about the weather except as it affected his going and coming. He was in a queer mood at the beginning of this queer night.

He went through the lounge to the lobby and got our coats, for the March evenings were chilly. Beyond the swing doors a barrier of echeloned curtains prevented light from the hotel reaching the outer air. And it was here that the queerness began. Between two curtains Tolefree stumbled and exclaimed.

"What's up?" I cried into the darkness.

"Got a torch? Put it on!" said Tolefree's voice. The torch was in my hand as he spoke.

His dark head bent over a figure lying on the ground – a man about thirty, well-dressed, fair, with light hair, high of forehead, features well cut. He seemed to be unconscious. His head bled from an injury to the right temple.

"Gosh! – is he — ?"

"No," said Tolefree, "just knocked out. He'll be round soon. Better get him inside."

"I think not," said another voice startlingly out of the blackness.

I leaped round and swung the torchlight into the face of the man in khaki who stood between the two curtains.

"You? What the devil d'you mean by that?" I burst out.

For all the notice he took I might not have been there.

"I think not," he repeated, leaning down to Tolefree. "Unwise. He'd better go to – well, say to hospital."

Tolefree rose. He came into the beam. I expected him to spout wrath upon the intruder or show the suspicion that I felt. Instead he did a queer thing.

"That's what you think?" said he. "All right. How shall we get him there?"

"In my car. I'll fetch it. Hold on here. Get him back out of the way. Don't show a light. Shan't be two ticks."

The curtains flapped and he was gone.

"Well! – of all the damnable impudence—" I began.

"Yes – wasn't it? But convenient, Farrar. This young gentleman isn't our pidgin, and we don't want to draw attention to ourselves, do we?"

"Why on earth don't we?"

"Sometimes, my dear fellow, you seem deliberately – but here's our friend... You're better than your word, aren't you?" The captain's voice said, "Ready? Hurry! There's not much time. Put your light on a moment, sir."

I pressed the switch. He stooped and took the young man under the shoulders. Tolefree caught up his legs.

"No need for that. Let him walk. Light out, please. Now, quick!"

"Come on, Farrar," said Tolefree.

The next few seconds were a confusion of curtains flapping in my face, stumbling footsteps and low-voiced objurgations from the strange captain. Then I found myself going down the broad steps by the pillars outside the hotel, saw the dim sidelights of a car, into which Tolefree pulled me, and we were moving. I had no time to guess what was happening or why.

The car slid through black streets for not more than three minutes, slowed and stopped, as I supposed at a hospital. The captain got out, opened the door, touched my arm. I stepped on to a pavement. I heard sounds of movement but could see nothing. Then Tolefree spoke in my ear:

"Keep hold of me and follow."

With a hand on his sleeve I stepped into what the hollow sound of shoes on flagstones identified as a paved passage. A door clanged behind us.

"Show a light, will you?" said the captain's voice. My torch shone out. Tolefree was by my side. Ahead was the captain, supporting the young man with the bleeding temple.

"To the right – ten steps down."

We descended. From the foot of the steps stretched a long corridor, with closed doors on either side. The captain pushed open the third door on the right. Our procession entered a large room, vaulted, whitewashed, dazzlingly lit. Presently I made out a set of tables close to the walls, each occupied by a man or a girl wearing telephone headgear. On the end wall a red light glowed. One or two of the operators glanced at us, but for the most part we passed unnoticed.

The captain, still holding up the tottering young man, passed through to a door at the far end, knocked and entered. We followed into a similar room which was bare save for a flat-topped desk, a few chairs and a portable electric fire.

Behind the desk sat the fair man who five minutes before had been talking to the head waiter.

"Hello!" said he. "What's this?"

3

I looked at a clock on the desk. It showed thirteen minutes to eight – seven minutes since we had risen from table at the hotel.

The captain pulled up a chair and pushed his charge into it. "Here he is."

The fair man shook his head. "Where did you get him?"

"Lying in the hotel doorway."

"He's had a nasty crack. I'll see to it!" He pressed a bell-push. "He'd better stay here till it's over."

"Serious this time?" asked the captain.

The fair man nodded. "Hell, I guess." He looked at the clock. "Nearly zero. What are you going to do?"

"Back to the hotel. You don't think this is the bird?"

"I wouldn't say so, though you never know."

He rose and came to the captain's side, looking down on the young man in the chair, who had bent over, elbows on knees, head in his hands.

The door opened and a youth in ambulance uniform entered.

"Take this man away and patch him up. Keep him down here till further orders. See his identity card. Enter his name and number."

The youth saluted.

The wounded man started up, holding to the back of the chair.

"But you can't!" he groaned.

"Can't I? You just see! For your own good. You'll know that in two shakes. Don't be a fool. Get on with him, officer."

"Now, sir, this way."

As he was led away I saw fright in the man's dazed eyes.

"Who the devil is he?" said the captain.

"Don't know. He came in on the train this evening, so he's not the bird."

"You may be wrong, Stevenson. I'd been watching that fellow for a bit. He did a funny thing—"

"Excuse me, won't you? There's no time to talk now." He eyed the clock again. "If you're going, better go. Or you can stay here till it's over if you like."

"No, thanks. Been away from the hotel too long already. My car's outside. See you sometime. Now, Tolefree—"

"Listen!"

We fell silent. A faint wailing sound reached us. The fair man stepped to the table and pushed over a switch. From a microphone somewhere burst a loud shrieking of sirens.

"You may have two minutes,"

In less than that Tolefree and I entered the hotel lobby, leaving the captain to put away his car. Late diners were trooping out of the dining room. Casual guests hurried away. A porter stood directing residents down a corridor, saying "Air-raid shelter first on the left and through the yard." People ran down the broad staircase and joined the stream.

But not all sought shelter. Nonchalant men and women sat about the lounge with cigarettes and drinks. Some stood aside watching the throng with a hint of amusement in their looks. As Tolefree and I stood a few moments waiting for the captain, one of them said to me:

"You'd think there'd never been an alert before!"

"Better safe than sorry," I answered, and he turned away from me with a smile which registered a mild contempt. The captain suddenly appeared beside us. Tolefree raised his eyebrows in a question.

"Nothing yet," he said. "Now, Tolefree – Number fifty-seven I think, eh?"

"Yes," Tolefree replied. "Farrar, will you stay here for a few moments? If there's any rumpus, make for the shelter and I'll join you there."

"No," said I. "If you're going to Number fifty-seven I'm going as well. I have a particular reason for wanting to see Number fifty-seven, as you know."

The captain said, "You — !"

"I'll explain later," Tolefree told him. "Well, come along."

I had a big bone to pick with Tolefree, but this wasn't the time to do it. They started up the stairs two at a time. I followed without another word. Most of the people were already down. We found the staircase and the upper corridors almost empty. No. 57, a wall placard informed us, was on the second floor. We found it in a passage dimly lit by light bulbs painted blue. The door did not open when the captain turned the handle. He knocked sharply. There was no answer. He tried again. He bent to the keyhole.

"No light. Probably went down to the shelter before we came in. But I'll get the key, Tolefree, and make sure."

He ran along the corridor. We waited beside the door.

I began to pick my bone with Tolefree.

"You and your doodling!" I reproached him. "This fellow knows you like a brother. What's it all mean, Tolefree? Why've you dragged me into a conspiracy against Blenkinsop? What's the use of teaming me up with this crowd? What's going to happen to the poor devil we found downstairs? And what—"

"Help! I'll make it all plain later on, Farrar. As for teaming you up, you've been of the greatest help to me – far greater than you suspect. Leave it all till we find out whether Blenkinsop's in his room or not."

But for my curiosity about Blenkinsop I might have thrown in my hand there and then, despite Tolefree's blarney. But there were a hundred things I wanted to know – and in particular the meaning of the so-called doodling on that cigarette paper.

We were, however, to get no further with explanation that night, nor were we to discover whether Blenkinsop was in his room or not.

For, just as Tolefree finished his sentence a terrific uproar shook the whole building. Salvoes of gunfire half-deafened us. Along with that thunderous crashing a muddled overtone – the higher notes of engines running at speed, the shrill cries of people out in the streets, and the noise of rushing vehicles. In the midst of it, the captain's voice shouted from the end of the corridor, and he came panting towards us.

"No go," he said breathlessly. "Everybody gone to shelter and the office closed. No sign of him here? Then he must have gone down. This row would wake a corpse. Now, you two, come down out of it. I'll show you something."

He started back towards the stairs. Before we could reach them a shout of "Help!" "Fire!" came from above. The captain went up instead of down, and we after him. In the corresponding corridor on the third floor two men came running towards us, dragging a short ladder.

"Incendiary – up there!" cried one. "Help with this ladder, guvnor?"

We seized and hoisted it to a manhole in the ceiling, holding it while the fire-watcher went up, carrying a bag of sand.

What followed as we stood at the foot of the ladder was two minutes of infernal confusion. The man's companion went up with more sand, returned immediately and slid down the ladder, saying, "They're all over the place – raining bombs it is. There's two stirrup pumps if one o' you—" He dived to a corner.

"Let me do this," said I; "I'm used to it," – as indeed I had got used to it in London.

With the help of Tolefree and the captain, we got both the stirrup pumps, with their buckets, up through the manhole. There, it was clear in two seconds that instead of stirrup pumps we should need a thousand gallon tank. Half a dozen fires had started and seized hold of the old wood of roof beams and battens. In another ten seconds the place would be an inferno.

The two plucky fire-watchers gave it up, driven back by smoke and heat.

Tolefree and the captain had come up to take a look.

"Hopeless!" shouted the captain. "Everyone down!"

We got down not a moment too soon. Fire-bombs had penetrated even to the second floor. The corridor to No. 57 was impassable. The building burned like a flambeau, and the roar of its flames added to the din of shooting, the shrieking and the racking concussion of bombs outside.

Clearing the staircases in less time than it takes to write the words, we reached the lobby. As we crossed it all the lights went out.

"Your torch!" the captain yelled. I put it on. "I'll take it. This way."

Following his gleam we ran down the passage to the yard, bits of plaster and masonry falling about us. The shelter for hotel residents was a wine-cellar deep in the basement of the opposite wing. It was full. People had crowded in from the street – all sorts and conditions of people. The captain gouging a way for us with little ceremony, we stood just inside the door. The crowd was silent, listening to the pandemonium without, quite orderly, apparently confident in the protection of the enormous walls and the vaulting strengthened by steel girders. I daresay many of them realised that if a big bomb came down on the building overhead the protection would avail them nothing; but by that time people had accustomed themselves to the possibility of sudden extermination. If, as they said, a bomb had their name on it, Kismet – they were for it, and that was that.

Speculations of this kind did not interest the captain, I imagined, watching him. He was intent on his quarry. A tall man, he could probably see the face of every person in the cellar. At any rate, he scrutinised each one in turn. A hundred people may have been there. Not one seemed to miss his steady inspection. When it was finished, Tolefree gave him a questioning look. He shook his head.

"Come on," said he.

"At least," he added, as we filed up the cellar steps, "I suppose you fellows don't want to stop there? If you do—"

"I should dislike it very much," said Tolefree.

"And you, Farrar?" It was the first time he had used my name. I told him I preferred to take a chance.

"Well, I don't know that I really prefer chances," said he. "Not on a night like this. Wait till you get outside. But I've an idea." He paused at the top of the steps. "I'm still curious about that bird, Tolefree."

"And I – very," Tolefree answered.

"If my car's still intact, I thought we'd collect him and make for a place I know of. What about it?"

"So far as I'm concerned, you decide. Farrar — ?"

"I go with you," said I.

We stepped into the yard. A blast of heat and smoke and a lurid light met our eyes and a terrifying concert of sounds assailed our ears. The hotel, on the side we had left, was a fiery furnace. Through the smoke drifting overhead we saw an eerie light. Every moment fire-bombs crashed and at short intervals their noise was drowned by the whistling and crumping of exploding bombs and the dull roar of falling masonry as buildings crumbled.

"A dirty night," said the captain. "Follow me. Keep close to the wall. Lie down flat if you hear one coming. If the car's not burnt we'll soon be out of it."

With no more than a crack or two from falling scraps of building, we came into a narrow lane behind the hotel. The car stood there intact. A man keeping guard on it touched his hat.

"Hope you'll dodge 'em all right, sir."

"Thanks."

"Main streets are full of fire engines, sir. I should go round by—" He mentioned a number of streets. How far away it was I could not guess, but a whistle rising to a scream seemed to be coming right at us. We threw ourselves flat. The bomb shook the earth and burst with a ripping, tearing noise; somewhere near a building crashed to ruin. A rain of small debris fell in the road.

"The Huns mean it all right this time," said the sentry, picking himself up. "Good night, sir. Good luck."

Now every detail of every building in sight was illuminated by the strangest light I had ever seen. Burning houses strove to assert their scarlet flames against the intense glare from the sky. The breeze, momentarily blowing aside the rolling smoke-clouds, revealed the source of this illumination. Flares like arc lights floated above us.

"Get in," shouted the captain. "We'll chance it."

Indeed, one place was as good as another that night. They had a saying in London: If you hear the bomb burst you're safe. This was like any other blitz but undoubtedly a bad one, and it seemed likely to go on indefinitely.

Tolefree and I tacitly left everything to the captain. He was a hard-boiled egg. Whatever his idea might be, he went straight at it. We had reached the entrance to the place where we left the wounded man quicker than before, though by devious ways. The flares in the sky and the flames from the ground lit the scene like day. I then saw that this was one of a group of stately buildings, of which the roofs were on fire. All round it fire engines poured streams of water into the air, which appeared to turn into steam before they fell. The captain's car was stopped once or twice, but at a word he got permission to pass. In the underground corridor the telephonists were streaming away. The captain held up one of them.

"Orders to quit," said he, and rushed on.

The captain told us to get back to the steps and wait. He himself went forward.

Presently he reappeared dragging with him the young man, whose head had been bandaged.

"Help him up," said the captain. We caught his arms and pulled him with us. He seemed to have lost the power of lo-comotion. He was paralysed with fright. Somehow we got him into the car. The captain took the wheel. In ten minutes, dodg-ing craters, bumping over fire hoses, winding through narrow streets, passing a great church with flames tearing through its painted windows, splashing cataracts of water in front of us, half stifled by smoke and hot fumes, marvelling at the daring of firemen perched on dizzy ladder towers, we passed out of the worst of it. In another twenty minutes we were on the outskirts of the town, where the air was clearer. But here, on a main road, many other people had evidently been smitten with the captain's idea. We joined a thin stream of cars going eastward; another line of traffic passed us, roaring towards the town – fire engines, ambulances.

In three miles we turned off the road into a narrow lane steeply ascending and, passing a darkened village, went on to the summit. Through many twists and turns the captain brought us to a farm gateway and into a yard between dark buildings, their gables cutting silhouettes against the reddened, angry sky. He left the car, banged on a door. No light was shown, but we heard a rumble of voices between the bursts of nearby gunfire.

He came back, got us out of the car, and led us into the house. In a large kitchen an aged man and woman stood looking at us as we entered.

"These are the three, Rawlings," said the captain. "I'm leaving them with you till the morning. Tolefree, I shall go back – you understand?" Tolefree nodded. "You'd be useless: you don't know the place. Look after this bird. I'll be out here, with luck, by daylight. O.K.?"

"If we can do nothing—" said Tolefree.

"Nothing. Better get him to bed pretty quick. Have a look at his head. Stay put, will you?"

He was gone without another word.

"Rather the cap'n than me," said the old man. He spoke with broad accents. He had white hair and a grizzled beard. He was thin, with stooping shoulders, farmer written all over him. "Now, gentlemen – you'd like something 'ot? Mary—"

"Of course they would." The old woman turned to a dresser for cups and saucers. Her kitchen range was built into a vast chimney place, which had for keystone a block carved with some heraldic device. She rattled up the fire in the stove and soon had the kettle singing.

These good people, living in an ancient house long abandoned by its owners and turned into a farm place, were hospitality itself; but they have little to do with the events which developed out of this night of terror in Westport. They were friends of "the cap'n" and prepared to take us on trust.

Our hours of waiting on the fringe of the tragedy contained only one or two incidents with a bearing on what followed. We drank tea. We persuaded the wounded man to take a cup. He was almost comatose, sitting with his head in hands on a chair in the corner of the chimney-place. We followed the captain's instruction to get him to bed. Mrs. Rawlings lighted us with a candle up a broad staircase to a finely panelled room, barely furnished, with two beds, and left us there.

Our charge had not spoken a word in our hearing since that agonised groan, "But you can't!" Now, when Tolefree suggested that he should undress partly, he took off coat and waistcoat and sat on one of the beds. Tolefree examined his injury, gently replaced the bandage, and shook up the pillow. He sank back and closed his eyes. Tolefree pulled a blanket and coverlet over him and told him to go to sleep.

We sat on the other bed, watching him. His troubled face gradually cleared. It was not a badly-shaped face in repose. Something in the expression of his eyes I did not like, a nervous furtiveness; but that might have been a reflection of whatever mishap had befallen him. We had no clue to his character. We had stumbled into him not much more than an hour before with no anticipation that we should count for anything in his life.

Now he slept.

He slept through the storm of the guns roaring far and near, the screams of diving bombers and the crump of bombs. He slept when heavy footsteps on the stairs and a knock on the door came to our ears. Rawlings entered the room with a candle in his hand. Tolefree put a finger to his lips. The old man spoke in a whisper:

"There's the most terrible sight you ever seen down there," said he. "Would you have a look? You can see everything from the tower."

"You go, Farrar," said Tolefree. "I'll stay and watch him."

I stole out with the farmer to the end of a passage, where he opened a low door giving onto a stairway.

"I'll go 'fore," he said; "but I'll have to dowse the glim up there."

"All right; I have a torch," I told him.

The stairway wound up perhaps thirty feet in a sort of turret. At the top we stepped into a small room with a narrow window in each of its four sides. Through the west window came a glare of light from the sky, reddening floor and walls. I looked out to behold a picture out of Dante's hell.

We were on the summit of a high, steep hill, with woods and the village below us, roofs gleaming in the lurid light. Beyond them in a broad river valley, the glare reflected on the water from the turbid, burning heavens picked out the course of the stream till it vanished in a fury of smoke and flame.

The town was blazing from end to end. There were miles of fire. Volcanoes of flame shot up hundreds of feet minute after minute as bombs roared down into the smoking ruins. But the greater terror was above the pall of smoke and the billowing fire. Strings of flares shining like suns hung in the blackness, slowly descending. Over our heads shrieked bomber after bomber, diving miles from the east to discharge its load of death and havoc. In a great circle round us gun flashes flickered like lightning; in the sky shell bursts pockmarked the clouds and murk; tracer bullets cut red lines across the scene. Shells hit flares; they disintegrated. But more flares followed them down. More and more bombs crashed to the ground.

I stood in that window like a spectator looking at the stage from the gallery. Woods surrounded the house except on this side. It was a secluded spot. And the strange captain was down there under that livid avalanche of fury...

The raid continued all night well into the small hours. Half an hour's watching, with a sense of helpless futility, depressed me sufficiently. I turned away. The old man, whose presence I had forgotten, still stood behind me. I said:

"It's very dreadful, Mr. Rawlings. I think I've had enough."

The old man bowed his head. He said harshly,

"Enough! Yes." He shook his fist at the sky. "I've got a boy in there: he's in the fire brigade. Yes, sir. We'll go down. I ought to be with the ol' dummon. 'Er's brave, but 'er feels it underneath."

I found Tolefree in the bedroom sitting at the small dressing table looking through some papers. Here the hellish cacophony outside was not quite so loud. No gleam of the mephitic light entered the room. The patient lay as I had left him. He seemed asleep.

"Gone off soundly," said Tolefree, speaking low, in answer to my unspoken question. "And not very bad. That crack on his head was nothing."

"Nothing! It laid him out, anyhow."

"So it seemed," said Tolefree. "Well – this is a bad business. I've been trying to count the H.E.'s, and I lost count. Our friend the captain's gone into a hot spot."

I said I'd been thinking of that and feeling rather small. "Of course," he agreed. "But this was my business, Farrar, and I couldn't leave it. And you – what could you have done? Just nothing. You've had enough in London."

"This is as bad as anything I saw in London – and more concentrated. But I suppose you're right."

I looked at the table. A wallet lay there with its contents strewn about. Tolefree said,

"Mrs. Rawlings was up here just now. She showed me another bedroom across the way and put a candle there. Let's go over."

He picked up the papers and the wallet, changed the key to the outside of the door, and locked it as we left. I found the opposite door with my torch; Tolefree lit the candle. We were in a room much like the first, a farmhouse bedroom; but it had panelling on ceiling as well as walls.

"Must have been a fine house in its time," said I.

"Yes – I heard about it from Mrs. Rawlings. But the family which had lived here hundreds of years didn't think it fine enough some time in the eighteenth century and they built an immense place in the valley. Some happier day we might have a look over it. Tonight – about our friend across the passage."

He dragged up a small table to the side of the one bed in the room and spread on it the papers in his hand.

"I can't quite fathom the young man," he said. "Look at these. He's not Blenkinsop—"

"You never thought he was, did you?"

"Until I examined his head I thought he might be."

"His head?"

"I mean his injury. It's not bad enough for him to be Blenkinsop."

"What the deuce d'you mean, Tolefree?"

"If anybody had wanted to knock out Blenkinsop you can bet he wouldn't have hit him a glancing blow which just took off a bit of skin. Anyway, he's not Blenkinsop. Here's his identity card. Identity cards aren't encyclopædias, are they? Just tell you the man's name and number – not even his address, or anything about him."

"Why should they? This is a card for him to use not you," said I, taking it.

The name was "Fonthill, William Hasty," and he had signed in a small neat handwriting, "W. H. Fonthill."

"Can't guess why you're interested in Mr. Fonthill, Tolefree," I said, passing back the card.

"Why shouldn't I be?"

"Why do we pick up this unfortunate youth in the hotel lobby and spirit him off to that place – what is it? – the Report Centre?" He said it was. "And keep him there against his will, and then Shanghai him out here? He's probably some quite unoffending visitor who's met with a mishap."

"Probably's too strong," declared Tolefree. "Possibly. But in that supposition, why was the captain so insistent upon taking him along, and afterwards on rescuing him from the raid and bringing him out here with us for his guard?"

"I might answer if I knew something about your captain," said I. "And there are a few other things I'd like to be told. Evidently you knew about Blenkinsop before you telephoned me, you old fraud. How did you find out that Blenkinsop had got in touch with me? Is the captain one of your Whitehall gang? Why did you prevent me from hunting up Blenkinsop as soon as we got to the hotel? Read me the riddle of that cigarette paper—"

"Kamerad!" Tolefree exclaimed. "All in good time. I can't tell you anything of the captain without his permission, except that he's a rare good fellow and as brave as a lion. I expect you've guessed how I knew of your interest in Blenkinsop. We'd read letters of his, including the one he wrote to you. I wanted to see Blenkinsop before you saw him, so as to be able to identify him in any circumstances – even if for any reason I had to lose sight of you. The cigarette paper—"

"Ah, yes! – with the zero hour of eight and the mysterious asterisk. What about that?"

"The captain's way of giving me some information privately. We knew already that Blenkinsop was in number fifty-seven, but we didn't know the conditions in which we'd be looking for him. The captain did. Eight on the doodled clock for zero hour, and a doodled asterisk for the first bomb."

"Well! How did he know—"

"I think he'd only just learned when he came in. I judge that by the company he was keeping. Now do you realise why I asked you to go without your coffee? But we'd better get back and see how Mr. Fonthill progresses. Mr. Fonthill, if you ask me, is in a deadly funk."

"Can you wonder?" I asked. "That is if this happens to be his first blitz?"

Making out the light we returned to the patient's room. It was in darkness. I switched on my torch, and immediately put it out. The shutters were pulled back; the window was open.

I banged the shutters into place and shone a light over the room.

Mr. Fonthill was not there.

2

1

This was a staggerer. We had been away from the room not more than fifteen minutes. When we left it Fonthill was apparently sound asleep and in a state of exhaustion. But he had done something at which a man fully awake and in rude health might have boggled. He had climbed out of a first floor window and dropped at least fourteen feet to the ground.

Tolefree, as he lit the candle, said, "He's done it! A clever bit of foxing, indeed! Farrar, he was in a blue funk, and it wasn't about the blitz, because he's gone right out in it, your inoffensive innocent. But he can't have gone far. Down we go—" and he was out of the room.

The farmer and his wife, sitting by the fire, looked up startled as we burst into the kitchen. Tolefree told them what had happened.

"Mercy on us!" exclaimed Mrs. Rawlings. "On a night like this, too."

Old Rawlings got up. "Come along," said he, leading the way. Out of the house there was no need for torch-light; a red twilight speckled with flashes, pervaded the sky. We ran through the yard to a gate giving onto a garden and went round the wall to the spot below the bedroom window. I half expected to find Fonthill lying smashed on the ground. But we saw instantly how he had escaped. Masses of ancient ivy clothed the wall. Descending from that window had been as simple as walking down a ladder.

"Which way would he go?" Tolefree asked. "Would he have to pass through the yard?"

"No, sir. This path leads to the old drive you came up by. He'd get out in the road in half a minute."

"And then?"

"Woods both sides of him. Looking for him now you'd be looking for a needle in a bundle of hay."

That was evident. Nevertheless, we hurried along to the road – the lane by which we had come. The trees of thick woods overhung it on both sides.

"Useless," said Tolefree. "Let's get back – unless there are any other houses near, Mr. Rawlings?"

There were no houses nearer than the main road. Rawlings had a telephone, but it was dead when we tried it. Telephones did not stand up well to their treatment that night.

Ten minutes later we sat in the panelled bedroom again. The roar of the inferno outside rose and fell as waves of bombers were met by salvoes of gunfire. We talked spasmodically between the bursts.

Tolefree seemed not much worried by the disappearance of our charge. He put the wallet on the table. "That'll cook Mr. Fonthill's goose," said he. "We've got his papers, his identity card, and all his money except the coins he may have in his trousers pocket. He can't get far. There's nothing to do but wait for morning."

There was no chance of sleep till the raid ended. The time was now half-past ten. We sat in that room till two o'clock, listening to the noises of the siege, speculating about the fate of the luckless town, wondering at times whether we should ever see the captain again. Beside this colossal upheaval, as the night grew, any interest in the adventure of Mr. Fonthill faded away from my consciousness. But Tolefree did not forget him.

He had spent some time on the things in the wallet. Finally, he packed them all back except one, which he passed to me.

It was a rather good photograph of a girl, printed in postcard size. She had a pleasant, expressive look, on the verge of a smile. Her hair was abundant and dark; her eyes dark, too, I judged, and they were wide and frank. She might have been any age between twenty and five-and-twenty. A New York photographer's name appeared on the card. I turned it over and read the legend, "From Vi to B.," with a date, "September 4, 1937," and the words, "Many happies."

"A nice exhibit," said Tolefree.

"Very nice indeed," said I. "Bill Fonthill's in luck – or he was."

"If B Stands for Bill and his other name's Fonthill – yes."

"No doubt about it, is there?"

"Circumstantial evidence all in favour of the theory," said Tolefree with a little smile.

At two in the morning, or thereabouts, the noise of the bombardment suddenly declined and in a few minutes had stopped. An uncanny silence took its place. Before we lay down I suggested a visit to the room in the tower. There were no flares in the sky. The enemy had departed. But Westport still burned before our eyes. It was a distressing scene. We stood for a few minutes without speaking, and then, by common consent, turned away to shut out the tragic vision.

I slept fitfully till daylight, and had snatches up to seven. Finding a primitive bathroom at the end of the passage, I washed, dressed and sought out Tolefree. He was not in his room. Downstairs, Rawlings told me he had gone out half an hour ago. He returned as the old lady was putting breakfast on the table.

The two old people seemed stunned. Their son was safe, but the messenger who brought the news had told them a fearful story of the night – hundreds of killed, far more hundreds injured, the centre of the town wiped out, thousands of homeless people setting off along the roads into the country to look for roofs for the next night.

It was unheard of. It seemed to them impossible that such things could happen there. They had heard of Warsaw. But Warsaw was a long way off; it hardly entered their consciousness. The old man, it appeared, had been a volunteer soldier in South Africa forty years ago. He knew something of war from the soldier's standpoint; but this — !

Tolefree at this point said nothing of his morning constitutional. When we were alone waiting for the captain's arrival, he told me he had looked for traces of Fonthill but found none save possibly a few freshly made footprints on the loose earth of a bank – where somebody had certainly scrambled up into the woods. Beyond the point where they ceased among the dead leaves it was useless to look. But he had walked down to the village, discovered the police sergeant and enlisted his help.

"What reason could you give him for putting the police on to Fonthill?" I asked.

"Quite a good one. I told him the man was wandering about without an identity card, and that I wanted to see him. You're quite a champion of that young man, aren't you, Farrar?"

I shrugged. It was no business of mine, but it did strike me that Fonthill was being treated off-handedly.

"Perhaps you'll cool off when we've heard what the captain has to say."

Time passed. The captain did not come. The telephone remained dead. We began to fear. At ten o'clock there was a diversion. We suddenly heard many voices in the yard and from the window saw a little crowd of women and children with a man or two, and Rawlings in the midst of them.

"Advance guard of the refugees," said Tolefree.

A few had bundles. Most had got away with the clothes they wore and nothing else. Rawlings listened to their stories and their pleas. Somehow in half an hour he disposed of them – women with babies in rooms of the old house, families with older children in the great barn across the yard. They were all uncomplaining, cheerful and grateful.

"That sort of thing must be going on all over the country-side," I said; and Tolefree answered, "Let's hope everybody's going to be as good as Farmer Rawlings."

In the midst of it a car was driven into the yard.

"Ah – the captain!" cried Tolefree.

He got out of the car looking much more the refugee than any of the others. He limped between them as they made way for him. He was haggard, his uniform wet and soiled, his face unshaven, his boots caked with mud.

We met him on the stairs. It was then that I heard the captain's name for the first time. Tolefree greeted him,

"My dear Barrett! – you're injured!"

"Nothing, Tolefree. Fell over a hose or something. You heard Stevenson say it would be Hell – and Hell it was. Hardly a building left standing in the middle of the town. But you'll see. I want a bath and a feed. Then we'll go in. How's the bird getting on?"

Tolefree told him how the bird had flown, and what he had done about it. He blamed himself for having left him alone even for those few minutes.

Barrett made light of it. He said the police would be sure to pick the man up, though in the present confusion it might take a few days. The escape confirmed his own impression that the bird was a bird, notwithstanding what Stevenson said. "But I'm more concerned about Blenkinsop," he added. "Tell you after I've cleaned up."

Mrs. Rawlings came with clean towels and Barrett followed her along to the bathroom.

"Well, Tolefree," I said, when we were alone in the bedroom, "two cats have jumped out of the bag of their own accord."

"Which ones?"

"You've endowed the anonymous captain with a name, and the captain's given a name to his friend. You don't seem to understand how annoying it is not to be able to put names to people."

"My dear fellow! – I couldn't mention Barrett's name to you without his consent. It just slipped out in an excited moment. As to Stevenson, there was never any mystery about him. He's a superintendent of the Westport police. I know him well. You heard what Barrett said? Stevenson's generally right, but he may fall down on his infallibility here."

An hour afterwards Barrett was closeted with us. His bath and his breakfast, Mrs. Rawling's attention to his clothes and the old man's to his boots, had made a vast difference in his spirits and appearance.

"Now, Tolefree," said he, "let's have a look at that wallet. Your petty larceny may be useful."

He scrutinised everything in it.

"Fonthill?" he mused. "Never heard the name. Can't place the bird."

"Why did you think he was a bird?" Tolefree asked. "That's what's worrying my friend Farrar."

"Ah? Well, let's have Farrar's name and number first."

"That's his real name. He hasn't got a number. But he's a good friend of mine, and we've been together in many a scrape since we met in the last war." And Tolefree explained our association.

"Well, that's all right," said Barrett. "Farrar's on the square. Then – the reason why I thought Fonthill a bird to be watched was this. Sometime after I left you last evening to go to your dinner, I saw the fellow come into the hotel in a big hurry, worm his way through the lobby and go up the stairs two at a time. There was something in his manner – I can hardly give it a name—"

"A furtive manner?" said I.

"You've got it, Farrar. Moreover, it was strange for a human bird to go flying up that long staircase when he might have gone up in the lift. So I followed him. But I wasn't quick enough. In the maze of staircases and corridors I lost him. I knew he'd gone up two floors, but couldn't tell whether he'd gone higher. I went up, hung about a minute or so. No sign of him. Then, as I was coming down from the top, the bird flew out of the second floor corridor before my eyes, and down the stairs—"

"The right-hand corridor, where we found Number fifty-seven?" Tolefree asked.

"That's it."

"And he wasn't to be seen in it when you passed up?"

"I could swear he wasn't. The light was none too good, but I could have seen anybody who was there."

"Therefore he'd gone into a room on that corridor?" said Tolefree. "I see. Go on."

"I went after him down the stairs. He turned and saw me following. Then he made for the entrance and disappeared. I pushed right through to the street. Pitch black outside. I couldn't have been two yards behind him when he passed the swing door, but there was no sign of him. I asked the porter on the steps whether anyone had come out within the last two seconds. He said nobody had passed him for several minutes. Then the idea of the curtains occurred to me, and I was fumbling about among them when you got there and had the luck to fall over him."

"Highly interesting," said Tolefree. "Whatever else Mr. Fonthill is, he's a fox. That crack on his head wasn't really a crack, but a graze which bled. He wasn't knocked out. We wasted our sympathy on him. He foxed in the porch, he foxed at the Report Centre, he foxed in this bedroom – and the last was the best bit of foxing of all. He must have been aware that I took his wallet and knew everything it could tell me. The only important thing it told me was his name. Therefore Mr. Fonthill would have some reason for fear if his name became known."

"Yes, plain enough. But he can wait. We'll get him sooner or later. At present, I've graver news. About Blenkinsop. He's missing, too."

2

"On the morrow of such a night, Barrett, anybody might be missing," said Tolefree.

Barrett nodded grimly. A gruff voice half hid the emotion with which he said, "Plenty missing down there."

"Then," said Tolefree, "you spoke with some special intention – about Blenkinsop?"

"Call it a special suspicion. I have a suspicion, Tolefree, that Blenkinsop was in his room last evening when we knocked at his door—"

Barrett swallowed hard. I had a painful sensation watching the Adam's apple moving and the pulse beating in the neck of this hard-boiled man.

"That he was in the room," he continued, "and that he never came out of it."

He glanced away from my stare of horror and half closed his eyes.

"Number fifty-seven," he said, "doesn't exist. It's a heap of rubble in a steaming, smouldering pit – or empty space in mid-air between blackened walls – just as you like. There's no hotel any more, only a shell that the first gale of wind will blow down."

His words and manner added a fresh touch of tragedy to what we had seen last night. We gazed at him for a moment or two, tongue-bound. Then Tolefree said,

"Yes. It's ghastly. Doesn't bear thinking about. Blenkinsop gone! – that's a blow. But what's the evidence that he was in that room?"

"Plenty," said Barrett, shaking off his mood of gloom. "I've been into all of it. First, Blenkinsop was ill. You didn't know that? I didn't. He was in no condition to move."

"But – he'd locked his door!"

"He hadn't. Impossible: he couldn't get out of bed. He'd been in bed ever since the day after he reached the hotel. The key was on the outside of the door at seven when the waiter took up some food and a fresh bottle of medicine to him. Blenkinsop was then in bed – worse, and exceedingly weak. I've talked to the medico the hotel called in. He says Blenkinsop was in high fever. By the way, he knew him as Perry. He saw him each day. Yesterday morning he was running a high temperature – bad bout of malaria. Told the doctor he got it abroad: hadn't been able to shake it off. It took him every now and then. He usually doctored himself with quinine. This time he felt very bad, weak as a rat. The doctor saw him at six in the evening. Told him to stay in bed. Fed him quinine. He says the fellow couldn't have moved across the room. And if he could have – why should he lock himself in?"

"Yet, when we were there at a minute or two before eight," said Tolefree, "the door was locked, and we made enough noise to wake the Seven Sleepers of Ephesus."

"He'd be deaf with quinine. They give it to you in doses like H.E. bombs for malaria. Ever had it?"

Tolefree hadn't; but I knew. I nodded. "He wouldn't care a damn who knocked on his door even if he heard," said I.

Tolefree pondered the story for a moment. He said slowly to Barrett, "So this is it? – somebody locked the door and took the key?"

"Couldn't be any other way, could it? And I can think of only one person."

"Of course."

"And when I saw that bird—"

"I quite understand. But somehow Fonthill didn't seem to me that species of bird."

"I know your ideas, Tolefree. You may be right. You're not often wrong, I admit. But I distrust appearances if there's evidence. And there is evidence. I saw him in the corridor myself."

"You did. But it's a tremendous assumption – tremendous!" Tolefree got up and walked to the window. He turned to look down on Barrett. "Let's see what you have to assume. That Fonthill knew what you knew when you doodled on the cigarette paper. That he locked the door just before twenty minutes to eight, assured that in all probability what has actually happened to Blenkinsop would happen."

"My God!" I exclaimed.

"And why not?" Barrett asked. "If he's the man I'm thinking of – why not?"

Tolefree fell back on his formula. "Fonthill had a secret – no doubt of that. He dreaded to have it known. But that sort of secret?"

They were talking in the air and leaving me on the ground. "I wouldn't want to force anyone's confidence," said I. "But I'm interested in Blenkinsop too."

"You!" cried Barrett. "How could you—"

Tolefree explained.

"Well," said Barrett, "you'll get no message from Captain McPherson. That's a certainty, Farrar. But I guess it was only a personal one."

"I expect you're right. He and I were old friends."

Barrett looked at me appraisingly. Suddenly he turned to Tolefree. "If you like to tell him about Blenkinsop I don't mind."

"All right," said Tolefree. "I would like. We don't have many secrets from each other and Farrar's a good man in a tight corner. So here goes. I'll make it short."

Blenkinsop, he said, had been much in the mind of an office in Whitehall for more than a month past. He had become its pet mystery. No one knew anything about him. He was no more than a name; but above that name were written extraordinary things.

"We had a letter by air mail from the United States five weeks ago. It brought information of a fantastic little plot – sort of

Fifth Column affair – which was to be carried out in England by a man he named."

"Was it Black or Perry?" I asked.

"Neither. It was a man rejoicing in the intensely English name of Smith with the appropriate front name of John. If Smith really was his name I imagine it ought to have been spelt Schmidt, prefaced by Johann. Don't take too much notice of names. Perry was the name of the man who wrote to us – or rather to the authority which handed over the letter to us. The two men saved from the ship were the only passengers she carried. That's an important point. They were in their pyjamas; everything else they possessed went down when the ship foundered."

"I see," said I. "And they were in the happy position of being able to take any names they pleased."

"You've got the idea," Tolefree replied. "Smith or Schmidt may have turned his name into Black. Probably he did. The other man wrote to us as Perry. But he turns up in a letter to you as Blenkinsop. And we'd seen a letter from Blenkinsop before. All incoming letters from foreign countries are examined."

"But how the deuce did you know about mine, Tolefree?" I inquired, puzzled and, incomprehensibly even to myself, annoyed. "That wasn't from a foreign country."

"You mustn't pry into the mysteries," he said, with a smile. "Or can he, Barrett? I think so – a little way, Farrar, your correspondent used an envelope that we happen to know fairly well. We get curious about the contents of such envelopes when they are posted in England. Do you follow me?"

"I suppose you mean that some nosey-parker in the Post Office smells a rat, wonders whether it came from Lisbon, and gives the tip to the Censor?"

"All correct except the bit about nosey-parker," Tolefree answered.

"Well – that was only a manner of speaking. Of course I understand," I assured him.

"Well – the rest follows. We know that Perry is Blenkinsop conclusively by his handwriting. Inferentially – well, you'll see. His letter giving the outline of the plot mentioned that John Smith was sailing on the same boat from New York as himself, the steamer *Bridgend*, bound for Lisbon, and that Smith was under the delusion that in Perry he had an accomplice. Perry, as an Englishman coming home to enlist thought he could do the best for his country by fostering the delusion and passing the voyage in squeezing all he could out of Mr. Smith about his plans and his associates. He proposed to report to us as soon as he reached home. Now you can guess why we were keen on seeing Perry, and if possible still keener to lay hands on Mr. Smith."

"That's plain enough. But – well, never mind. Go on, Tolefree."

"The *Bridgend* was sunk off the Portuguese coast. The boats, launched in a hurry, capsized as she went down. All the crew lost their lives. These two men happened to be good swimmers. Unhampered by clothes they kept themselves afloat for an hour, were rescued and taken into Lisbon. After they'd been questioned and given the names of Perry and Black they were put to bed in an hotel. From that moment Messrs. Perry and Black vanished as completely as if they'd never existed."

"How the deuce—" I began.

"Seems extraordinary? But not if you know Lisbon in wartime. I should wager that Mr. Smith had contacts in Lisbon which would provide him with anything he liked in the way of a hidey-hole, false passports and cash. I should wager that he well knew underground ways of getting about. Of course we had people at Lisbon on the lookout for the *Bridgend* and Mr. Perry. They watched the hotel. But these two must have obtained clothes and made a perfect getaway. Imagine our surprise when we learn that Perry (as we knew him) is in Westport and has written a letter to you!"

"I can imagine it. How was it done?"

"Mr. Smith, with his apparatus of false passports and credentials, of course. And the luck of the very devil. Everybody who had seen him and Perry on this side of the Atlantic was drowned. They hadn't got to produce photographs except those taken of them at Lisbon. It was as easy as pie. They didn't reach Westport in a certain ship, as you thought. But as soon as we knew Perry is here in Westport the hunt's up. Superintendent Stevenson and Barrett are advised. They locate Blenkinsop = Perry at the Imperial. That was yesterday. They keep an eye on the place till I can arrive. The most plausible way for me to get into it and give Blenkinsop the once over without causing suspicion is to travel with you. Does that give us a background?"

"Why, yes," said I. "Anyway, it's open confession of your wiles, Tolefree."

"Then we'll let Barrett get on with what happened last night. But first I want to tell him something. It bears on this chopping of names. Perrys are legion: Blenkinsops are rare. In the last two days we've traced every Blenkinsop family in the country. There isn't one with a son or brother in America."

"Well – Perry or Blenkinsop, we've seen the last of him, unfortunately," the captain sighed.

"Without ever seeing him at all," Tolefree added. That wasn't the least curious fact about Blenkinsop: none of the people who were so anxious to meet him had the least notion of his age, appearance or condition. Tolefree knew only that, judging by his handwriting, he was a person of some education.

"But," said Barrett, "the doctor was useful. The hotel people were no good – too busy to take particular notice of anybody. To them he was just a man who'd signed his name in the register and gone sick. But he interested the medico. He was a very sick man. Looked as if he'd spent years in the tropics and they'd taken it out of him. Dried up with the sun. Full of fever. Thin as a lath. About thirty years old, he thought. And a gentleman."

"Ah? Well, that's my impression," Tolefree remarked. "But, Barrett, why in Westport? He couldn't get here by sea. He must have come in by rail or road. Therefore he landed at some other port. Why come to Westport instead of to us in London?"

"It makes you think," Barrett agreed.

"There's a possibility. He'd want to keep tabs on Smith. And Smith might have been coming to Westport. What's more likely? Blenkinsop comes with him. Or Blenkinsop follows him. Immediately he gets here he goes down with fever."

"If that's so," said the captain, "Smith's in the town now! That is, alive or dead. If he's alive, we'll get him. But, Tolefree – the bird! If he's Smith—"

"If he is, we'll wring his neck," said Tolefree.

3

By noon we were on the road to Westport. It was a strange and melancholy experience.

We drove into a haze of smoke which thickened every hundred yards. The acrid reek half choked us. Along the way, as on the night before, two lines of traffic ran. But now the main stream set towards the town. People then driven out by the flames were now returning.

Motorists had picked up passengers from among the droves of walking men and women: they hung all over the cars and lorries. Barrett pulled up for a moment and beckoned with a finger. Instantly three joined us in the back of the car and one stood on each running board.

Thus laden Barrett drove through the suburbs.

All eyes were on the grisly tokens of a night's terror. They grew in a great crescendo as we crawled by.

First single houses were down in masses of rubble, more than one with a crater in the road beside it and a gang of men shovelling the pathetic rubbish into the hole. Then whole terraces were missing. The privacy of a villa had been raped: some missile tore away its walls and left beds and fireplaces poised in the air, with here and there a picture awry on a remnant of wall, but still fantastically hanging. A hospital for the blind stood as a mere shell, with a whole section of it shifted off the foundations and drunkenly askew. A man beside me shook his fist.

"God, damn them!" he muttered.

His curse was the only sentence uttered in the car in all that ride.

In the town the destroyers had done their work so thoroughly that no detail seized the mind. Where there had been streets were ruins. We bumped over innumerable hosepipes. The road-ways ran with water in torrents. Our ears were deafened by the clangour of engines. Clouds of smoke and steam obscured the scene as hundreds of firemen shot their jets into the smoulder-ing mess, or crawled on twisted girders, axes in hand, to batter away masonry which threatened danger, or with pick and shovel dug into the debris searching for buried people.

Within this space, which, twenty-four hours before had con-tained all the big stores, the great historic church and the civic centre, any but essential traffic was forbidden. Barrett's car, as though by magic, passed all barriers. At the first he shed his passengers. He drove by the roofless and battered old church and the skeleton of the guildhall, and came in the end to the hotel.

One of its classic porticos stood, and windowless walls be-hind it; but of the interior nothing remained save a pile of broken masonry under the sky. Here, too, were firemen playing on smoking embers and digging in the rubbish.

Stevenson, now in uniform, standing on the steps, saw the car arrive and came forward.

"Anything?" Barrett asked.

The superintendent shook his head. "I've had a roll-call. Ac-counted for everybody except Perry – and one other."

"Ah?" Barrett raised his eyebrows. "Who's that?"

"Man thought to be called Black."

"Good God!" Barrett exclaimed.

"Well – that is, Black as far as they can remember. Of course they've lost all their books and papers, and they're not too sure. But I've kept everyone, Barrett. I can't keep 'em long, you know—"

Barrett nodded. "Where?"

"Out at the north end. Commandeered a house. Want to see them now?"

"Right away. You can come yourself? Good. Jump in, Stevenson. How long will they take about that job?" He pointed to the pick and shovel men.

"No saying. It may be hours – or days."

Guided by the superintendent, Barrett drove two miles through the devastation and up the hill to the north, turned in at the gateway of a short drive, and pulled up before a large suburban house. Stevenson entered, passing a crowd of forlorn and anxious people in the hall. They stared curiously at us as we waited by the car.

"That's strange news, Tolefree," said Barrett.

"Very strange."

"Looks like two birds with one barrel, eh? – and our job at an end."

"Maybe," said Tolefree; "but to judge by Stevenson nobody seems certain. Better suspend judgment, don't you think? It would be unlike my conception of Herr Smith that he should allow himself to be caught in the fire. Blenkinsop – yes; he was a predestined victim. Queer that Smith, or Black, should risk the same hotel. Hardly in character?"

"Well, we'll soon know. Here's Stevenson."

He signalled to us from the porch and led the way to a room at the back where a worried man waited.

"Mr. Forrester, the hotel manager," Stevenson said by way of introduction. "These are the gentlemen, Mr. Forrester. Give them any information you can."

We pulled chairs up to a table. Barrett began:

"Terrible day for you, Mr. Forrester. We'll make our little job as easy as we can. About a Mr. Perry, who was in the hotel, and another man named Black. As to Perry – no hope for him?"

"Not a spark, I'm afraid," said Forrester. "He couldn't have got away if, as Stevenson says, the door was locked."

"Well, it was. See anything of Perry yourself?"

"No. I learned he was ill and arranged for a doctor. If you like you can talk to the reception clerk, the chambermaid, and the waiter who attended him."

"Presently. Then, about Black. Did you see him?"

"No. He came in yesterday afternoon. Nobody noticed him but the porter and the clerk, and they can't remember much about him. He was one of several who arrived, it was supposed, by the afternoon train."

"Whereabouts was his room?"

"Number fifty-five, on the same corridor as Perry – next door."

Barrett took a long look at Tolefree.

"This man Black's missing, Mr. Forrester. But is there any reason why he should be missing any more than anybody else in the place?"

"No special reason? Certainly not. But we've rounded up everybody else except one, and we can't find a trace of Black."

"Who's the other?" asked Tolefree.

"A young man – the clerk can't recall his name. But you think you know who he was, Mr. Barrett, I believe? And you think he got away?"

"I think so," said Barrett. "But about Black – a chance that he might have gone somewhere else, or left the town last night?"

"Of course. I hope so. But he's not been seen since he went to his room immediately after he came in. Didn't order anything – wasn't at dinner so far as we know, and wasn't seen in the shelter. Just disappeared."

There was a pause, then Stevenson said,

"Mr. Forrester, we've got to face the unpleasant possibility of finding two bodies down there."

The manager shuddered. "Horrible! Rotten luck – when we thought everybody in the house should have been safe."

"Cheer up," said Barrett. "You're not responsible anyhow. But, Stevenson, your possibility's a certainty for Perry, I guess. The other fellow – well, we'll have to wait and see."

The manager shuddered again. He leaned over the table, face on hands. Tolefree looked curiously at him. He said, "You have something on your mind, Mr. Forrester. What is it? Get it off."

"Yes, I have," Forrester looked up miserably. "It's this. A man who was in a room on that corridor told me something."

"What? When?" asked Stevenson, shortly.

"Not ten minutes ago. I've had no chance of passing it on. It was this. He went up to his room when he arrived. He was writing there till the Alert went. Some time before he heard the siren he was startled by a loud noise. Said it seemed to come from the corridor—"

"What sort of noise?"

"A bang. He listened a moment, guessed it was a door slammed. You know, everybody's nerves just now—"

"Yes, I know," said Stevenson impatiently. "You didn't have a slammed door on your mind, though. What is it?"

"He went on with his writing. Then he heard a second and louder noise – and it wasn't like a door banging—"

"Like a shot, I suppose?"

"He said so. Went out and listened. Not another soul about and not a sound. He called himself a nervous fool and went back into his room. Soon after the siren sounded and he packed up and went down to the shelter. Forgot all about the bang in the excitement, and it never came back to him till he heard about a man who'd been in a locked room on that floor."

"His name!" said Stevenson, sharply.

"It's Jackson."

"Is he here?"

"Yes. Shall I fetch him?"

"No." Barrett intervened. "Take Mr. Stevenson to him. Send the reception clerk in to me, Stevenson, while you're seeing Jackson I'll have the hotel servants."

For a while after Stevenson and the manager had departed there was silence. Barrett and Tolefree looked gravely at each other. I had an intolerable vision of that locked door and a horrible imagination of what was behind it while we knocked and waited. Tolefree at last said quietly,

"Two bangs make you think."

"Furiously."

And upon that came a knock at the door and the reception clerk said, "You want me?"

He was a middle-aged man, slightly diffident in manner. Barrett signed him to a chair.

"You're the reception clerk, Mr.—"

"Vigurs, sir."

"Well, Mr. Vigurs, just a point or two about the guests who were in the hotel yesterday. Particularly those on the second floor main corridor. A Mr. Perry had been there three or four days, I think, and ill all the time."

"I only heard that. All I know of him was that he booked a room and I gave him fifty-seven. The maid would know more about him."

"Naturally. Then there was a Mr. Black in number fifty-five. I believe he came in yesterday afternoon."

"I just remember the name and that's all. Several people came in about then and I had a job fitting them up with rooms. I found three vacant on that corridor, and I gave one to Mr. Black, one to Mr. Jackson, and one to a young man with a queer name I can't recollect."

"What sort of man was Mr. Black?"

"Couldn't say for the life of me. I remember Jackson, but only because I've seen him since."

"Then there couldn't have been anything remarkable about Mr. Black – voice, accent, appearance?"

"I should say not, sir. But you know what it is with a crowd buzzing round and everyone in a hurry."

"Couldn't say whether he was dark or fair?"

"I have the impression of a fair man with a small moustache, but it's not reliable. I couldn't take an oath on it."

"I'm not surprised. And I don't want you to worry. You've all had the devil of a time. Thanks. Now, if you'll ask them to send in the porter—"

The perquisition of the servants went on without success. The porter remembered Perry because he'd taken in his bags for him and put them in the lift. He noticed how ill Mr. Perry looked, and wasn't astonished when the hotel called in a doctor. As to Black, he knew nothing. Whatever baggage he had he must have carried in his hand. Nor did he recognise Mr. Jackson, who seemed to have arrived with a small suitcase and humped it himself. We gathered that the porter didn't approve of people who humped their own baggage, for he went on to remark that Mr. Perry was a real gentleman.

Nor did the chambermaid on the second floor add anything to our knowledge. She could tell of Mr. Perry, but as to Number fifty-five, or fifty-six, or fifty-four, she had not even seen them before the raid, though Mr. Jackson had been pointed out to her this morning. She had heard no unusual noises last evening, but then her own room was in the other wing.

From the waiter Barrett had already obtained all he could tell.

Not till the superintendent came back with Jackson in tow did any light fall on what happened on the second floor. Jackson was an intelligent-looking man of between forty and fifty, fair-haired and clean-shaven. He looked at us with a bright curiosity. Before he entered Barrett had said to Tolefree,

"Shall I carry on?"

Tolefree had answered, "Yes. I prefer to sit back. This is your ground."

Barrett therefore took the lead by asking Stevenson, "Is this Mr. Jackson? Yes? Howdydo, Mr Jackson? I'm told you've something to say about what you noticed last night. Will you sit? Congratulations on your escape."

Jackson sat down at the table. "I've told the superintendent all I know," he said. "But—"

"You won't mind giving it to us at first hand, will you? I believe you came in yesterday afternoon on the train. From London?"

"No. Bristol. I'm in business. Made a call there yesterday and came on to Westport. But business here today—"

He shrugged his shoulders.

"Yes. A sad affair," said Barrett. "Well, you were putting up at the Imperial, and you got there – what time?"

"About six or after. The train ran late."

"You asked for a room and they gave you fifty-four on the second floor, I understand. There was another man who booked a room just then on the same floor, Number fifty-six. Did you happen to notice him?"

"Afraid not. Bit of a crowd round the office window, you know. Everybody eager to get in."

"So the clerk says. It may be important to know something about Number fifty-six, but if you can't recall him, you can't. Now, I believe you had only small baggage?"

"One little suitcase. I travel light these days. Porters are scarce."

"You're wise. You took your own bag upstairs. You didn't come down to dinner?"

"No. I'd lunched late on the train. I was busy – lots of letters to write. So I stayed in my room and wrote them."

"And then you were disturbed by an unusual noise. What time would that be?"

"Can't say exactly. I should guess some time after seven."

"Ah," said Barrett. "One moment." He looked at Tolefree who was frowning as a man might in doing a calculation.

"Yes, Mr. Jackson," Barrett pursued. "After seven. And what sort of noise?"

"A bang – sharp. I'd call it a report. It was sort of muffled, but I thought it was a report, I listened a moment. All quiet. Nobody else seemed to have heard it, and I suppose I was mistaken. Probably a door banged. I went on with my letters. Three or four minutes after there was another bang – same sort of noise but sharper and louder. This time I opened the door. Nothing doing in the corridor. Thought I heard running footsteps, but they didn't come near. I started work again. There weren't any more noises till the siren went."

"None at all?"

"Oh, yes, there were. But not that sort of noise. Somebody knocking on a door, making a devil of a row. But that was not long before the siren and the explosion, and to tell you the honest truth I forgot about any other noises. I've had some of that in London, so I just scooted for the air-raid shelter."

That was all Jackson could tell us. But it was quite a lot – more, I supposed, than he could guess. For he timed everything with fair exactitude – the noises that startled him at about the time when we knew Fonthill to have been in the corridor, our own attempt to stir Blenkinsop out, the beginning of the blitz.

But the noises. If they really were shots —

Barrett was thanking Jackson for his help. Jackson was asking whether he would be wanted again and being told that he might and he might not. But would he stay in Westport for a few hours and see Barrett at six?

"All right," said he. "There's nothing for me here now, unfortunately. If I could catch the night train?"

"Probably," Barrett told him. "Give us an address."

"I shall be going to London tonight. I lived in Surrey, but I've given up my house for the duration and I'm staying in Pitt Street, Bloomsbury. Here's a card."

He took a business card from his wallet and passed it over.

"Well, thanks again, Mr. Jackson. Be here at six this evening, will you?"

"Right. But excuse me for asking – is there anything funny about this?"

"I shouldn't call it funny," said Barrett. "Let's say something peculiar."

"Ah," said Jackson. "I rather thought there might be."

Stevenson opened the door for him.

3

1

If those noises were shots...? For the next hour that possibility and its inferences occupied Tolefree, Barrett and the Superintendent.

Few restaurants were at work in Westport that day. Stevenson took us to lunch at a canteen in a schoolroom, improvised for police and firemen, crowded with tired, sweating, bedraggled men, served by girls and women of all degrees who had flocked in as volunteers. Sparse fare, taken in strange conditions of confusion and excitement.

No conference could have been more private. No one paid attention to us. It occurred to me that, had we called for silence and shouted our problem at the top of our voices, not a person in that packed room would have thought it of the least importance. They were actors in a vast tragedy beside which any individual treachery or crime counted less than nothing. The laws were silent amid arms.

But for a C.I.D. Superintendent, a Barrett or a Tolefree, Cicero's doctrine did not hold. They were on the track of a criminal. If the world burned they would still try to get him.

Was he Fonthill?

As Tolefree had said before we heard of Mr. Jackson, the circumstantial evidence made Fonthill a man to be suspected;

but he did not seem to me to be cast for the rôle of Smith, or Black, to give him the last name he had assumed. And how had Fonthill got his injury? Stevenson said little while Tolefree and the captain chewed over the few facts they had. But before we rose he asked Tolefree, "Do you really think Fonthill may be your bird?"

"Keeping an open mind," said Tolefree.

"Just badly scared, I'd say. Ever heard of shell-shock?"

"That won't do, Stevenson," said Barrett. "He was a badly scared man before ever a bomb dropped. Why! He was with you when the bombing began, and safe as houses."

"Yes, but frightened out of his wits. He'd had a bump on the head and didn't know much about anything when you brought him in. When he came to hell was bursting all round."

Barrett hesitated. Then he said, "What if the crack on his head was a fake?"

"Eh? Fake! Well – was it?"

"Tolefree says so. Tell him about last night, Tolefree."

"He was unquestionably foxing all the evening," said Tolefree, and went on to describe his examination of the wound and its sequel. "What I'm interested in, Stevenson, is Mr. Fonthill's chance of a clean getaway."

"Oh, we'll pick him up some time. But you'll find more evidence down there than Fonthill's likely to give you. There's an idea in my mind that doesn't seem to have smitten either of you."

"What's that?" Barrett asked.

"Tell you after. Shall we go along?"

Barrett's car took us back through the littered streets to the hotel. Stevenson led us into what had been the lobby. We climbed over the ruins to a spot where we looked down upon the moiling gang of men digging into the mountain of broken masonry and charred timber. Thousands of gallons of water had turned it into a pasty, steaming mess. We observed that they excavated deeply in one spot.

"Why is that?" Barrett asked a ganger who stood directing them. The man noticed Stevenson and saluted.

"They say there's two bodies – or may be, sir. They reckon the rooms they come from was over that spot."

The news had spread. Other men stood by watching every movement of the diggers, every spadeful of rubbish, every scrap of timber they threw out of the hole. Pitiful things came to light – scraps of clothing, wreckage of furniture, a broken trunk, a woman's handbag almost intact.

"They're getting down towards the basement," said Stevenson. "If there's anything we'll soon know."

But it was long before we did know. The gang enlarged the pit while they deepened it. They were making a roughly rectangular excavation.

"About the size of two rooms?" I suggested to Tolefree.

"Looks like it."

"Steady on, there!" the ganger suddenly shouted, and scrambled down into the pit while the workmen stared up at him. He reached the side of a man whose pick was levering out the iron framework of a mattress. He called two or three others to help. With hands and gentle strokes of the spade they uncovered the bed and lifted it. They closed in and from beneath it, out of a mass of black and sodden material, they raised a body.

I turned away, qualmish.

This was the body of Blenkinsop, as we were to learn. At that moment it might have been the remains of any poor devil trapped in a fire and battered out of human semblance by the collapse of a building.

Conjured from somewhere, a couple of men in the St. John uniform appeared with a stretcher. Handling the job expertly, they got the body away. It was decently covered with a dark blanket as they passed us.

Stevenson had disappeared from our group. Now he came back. Tolefree raised his eyebrows in a question. Stevenson nodded.

"Yes, Blenkinsop, no doubt. Hardly a shred of clothes on him, but there's the collar of a pyjama coat around his neck. Burnt in his bed, poor chap. If there's another he'll be nearby. D'you want to wait?"

Barrett looked inquiringly at Tolefree, who said, "No. Stevenson will let us know. This is a depressing place. Where can we go, Barrett?"

"I snaffled a room for myself this morning. Come along there. You'll send a message at once, Stevenson, if anything turns up? I'm at Horridge's place."

"All right, Captain. If we get anything before half-past five I'll let you know. You remember you're seeing Jackson at six?"

Not till then did we learn that Barrett's rooms had been burnt out and he had lost everything but the clothes he wore.

"A friend of mine did the Good Samaritan – gave me a room in his flat. I hope you'll like him, Tolefree. He should be a man after your heart."

He led us a few hundred yards towards the waterside quarter, whose narrow streets and gabled houses three centuries old had escaped the worst of the night's fury. Under an archway and through a courtyard we came upon a quadrangle of houses obviously rebuilt and pretending to be Tudor, but not unattractive. Children played in the square, women stood in doorways talking in a gleam of afternoon sunshine. The horror outside seemed banished and remote. This was a group of workers' dwellings and at first blush a queer place of residence for a friend of Barrett's. When we had climbed to the top of a house in one corner to Horridge's flat, we found that queerer still, and Horridge queerest of all in these surroundings. On the narrow landing Barrett called out,

"Here we are, Horridge. Coming in, old man."

He pushed open a door, and a burst of sunlight through a long, low window lit an unexpected scene. We were in a room on the outer corner of the quadrangle, with windows in two walls, and through the sunlit one we looked across rooftops between wooded hills above brown cliffs. But neither the room nor the scene it commanded had our first attention.

A man rose with difficulty from a chair by the fire, put down a book and limped towards us. His lameness needed an iron boot. Otherwise he was a fine figure – tall, dark, with a mass of brown hair, and fine features and glowing eyes.

"Horridge," said the captain, "these are the blokes I told you about this morning – Tolefree and Farrar."

He held out a hand to each of us in turn.

"Tolefree I know about," said he. "Farrar — ?"

"Tolefree's faithful Achates," said Barrett; "outside the ring, but in the know."

We stowed ourselves in leather chairs and the host handed cigarettes.

"I suppose I've got to explain you, Horridge," Barrett remarked. "He's one of us, Tolefree – or he was before he lost a foot at Dunkirk—"

"I'm not quite ignorant of Horridge," Tolefree put in. "You had bad luck."

"Think so? Well – I might have been dead. A good many are. This" – he held up his iron – "put paid to my job. But I have this room and my memories, and a few books, and a few friends. On a complete reckoning I've not done so ill."

"Likes to pretend he's a philosopher," said Barrett, "but grieved to be out of the game."

"I really did grieve last night. As bad as Dunkirk, Tolefree. I sat in that window and saw the town burn. Barrett was luckier. He was out in it – came in this morning looking like a chimney-sweep. Had the time of his life. But you're dying to tell me something, Barrett – eh? Have you got anywhere? What became of the bird you were after?"

"Tolefree can tell you that," said the captain.

"A melancholy tale," Tolefree responded, and told it.

"Not your bird, Barrett," was Horridge's verdict. "I'm of Farrar's opinion – and Stevenson's. He may be some other sort of bird – probably is. But the police will get him. I shouldn't worry. Now – what did they find at the hotel?"

"Blenkinsop's corpse," said Barrett.

"Of course. A pity, but predestined. He was bound to be a corpse from the moment when he decided to come to Westport instead of going straight to Scotland Yard. But how did he become a corpse? Your theory of the locked door and the other fellow's foreknowledge of the raid – well, it's a bit hard to swallow."

"Needn't strain your throat, Horridge," said Barrett. "There's a better theory. What if it wasn't Blenkinsop who was locked into the room but Blenkinsop's corpse?"

"So soon dead? Well, it's a more likely theory than the other. Any facts?"

"Presumptions. I'd better tell you what Mr. Jackson, in a room on the same corridor, heard."

"Tolefree," said Horridge, when he had heard it, "that's strange. If there were two shots, I mean."

"So strange," said Tolefree, "that Jackson may be mistaken about the first sound he heard. He said the second was louder, and, as I gathered, more unmistakably a shot."

"Nobody thought of looking into Black's room, or knocking him up when you were trying to wake Blenkinsop? But I'm forgetting. You didn't know then that Black was on the premises."

"We didn't," Tolefree answered. "And clearly we can't arrive at anything till the doctors have decided, if they can, how Blenkinsop died, and the police discover whether Black is – well, still on the premises."

"You can't. But I shall wager that Black hasn't been on the premises since the raid began. I'm wondering about your bird, Barrett. How did he get his crack on the head? Could he have disturbed Black at his dirty job and dodged a bullet that missed killing him by an inch and a half?"

"That's an idea!" Barrett stared. "Possible, Tolefree?"

"Of course it's possible. But it didn't look that sort of crack. And if that happened, why didn't Fonthill make a fuss about it? And why did he take French leave from Mr. Rawlings's hospitable house?"

"Shell-shock, as Stevenson said?"

Tolefree compressed his lips and shook his head. "I should judge Fonthill's trouble psychological, not physical. He may have had a shock. He was terribly afraid – of something. But it wasn't the raid. He was in the bottomless pit of fear before the raid happened. Touch of mystery about him. Don't forget he had in his wallet a photograph taken in New York."

"Anybody might have a photograph taken in New York," Barrett objected.

"Doubtless. But I don't much believe in coincidences. Can we do any profitable guessing till we know what happened to Black?"

All agreed that we could not. By common consent the talk turned elsewhere, to adventures in many parts of the world to scenes of war in Europe, and finally to Horridge's queer choice of a dwelling.

Horridge, who then seemed so casual an acquaintance, was by chance to have his part in what followed. As Barrett had foreshadowed, he proved to be a man after Tolefree's heart – a bachelor, a bit of a philosopher, and kicking against the pricks of his disability only in a half humorous fashion. He appeared to have been a student of sociology from the practical side in earlier days, one of the Toynbee Hall type, and a friend of the underdog. That accounted for his rooms in Hawkins Square, with whose inhabitants he was great pals.

He took us into his bedroom to look down from its window on the quadrangle where children played in the wan sunshine of the March afternoon. Their game was English v. Germans – not realistic, for the English were on top all the time by reason of superior numbers. The rôle of the Germans was not popular.

A favourite game, said Horridge: the little beggars showed our statesmen what they ought to have learned some years ago – that Providence was always on the side of the big battalions.

"A lot of their sort were killed last night," he sighed. "You know, Barrett, your nasty little case looks pretty trivial today."

"But, by Heaven, it isn't!" Barrett avowed. "We're after one of the brutes who made their killing possible!"

"All right – all right! You win. Go and get him, alive or dead."

"You bet we will. May he be alive when we get him! I want to see him hang!"

A knock came on the door. Stevenson put in his head.

"Ah, I hoped I might catch you here. Good afternoon, Mr. Horridge," said he. "I've just come from the mortuary."

2

It was in Horridge's sunny room that we heard the grisly story Stevenson had to tell.

While Blenkinsop's body was on its way to the mortuary, the rescue gang went on digging. In less than ten minutes they came upon another corpse – just as badly burned, but remnants of clothes showed that the dead man had been fully dressed. They found him not three yards away from the spot where they unearthed Blenkinsop.

He went to the mortuary in his turn, and Stevenson followed. He said the scenes in the streets near by were extraordinary. The news that the searchers had found bodies seemed to have spread with the wind. Outside the barriers crowds gathered and many people moved along with bared heads in a mourning procession.

"Didn't know whom they mourned," said Barrett. "If they knew, they'd have stoned the corpse instead."

Stevenson said perhaps so. But nobody could know who the corpse had been by any evidence from the remains. It had no features. Clothes were mere cinders. All the corpse told was that it had been a man of about five foot six.

"Well, Stevenson," said Tolefree, "what killed Blenkinsop? Not fire?"

"No. A bullet in the head killed him – the doctor found it. A heavy bullet from a large calibre gun."

I shuddered. Tolefree said,

"We needn't pity him – he was saved the horror of being cremated alive."

No wonder we could not wake Blenkinsop by knocking on his door.

"So," Tolefree went on, "Jackson was right. If you reflect, Barrett, the assumption that somebody locked Blenkinsop in his room knowing what was going to happen and intending him to be burned to death wasn't tenable. Even a man in the last extremity of fever would have managed to get out somehow, or attract attention. His window looked out on the courtyard where people were going to shelter—"

"By the time the fire broke out," said Barrett, "they were all in shelter. Still—"

"But after the rush to the shelter we were there trying to rouse him."

"Your trick, Tolefree," Barrett nodded.

Stevenson had not finished. He said, "Jackson was right twice. There were two shots, not one."

"Eh? How do we know that?"

"Because the other fellow was shot through the head too. The bullet went right through him, and we'll never find it. But no doubt about how he was killed."

We gaped silently at the superintendent, trying to make sense of this astonishing supplement.

"Gosh!" Barrett broke the silence. "What's that mean?"

Stevenson shook his head. Too soon to say. It might mean, for instance, two suicides. Or it might mean a murder and a suicide." He startled us again by adding, "But there's no doubt this was the man you knew as Black."

Barrett exclaimed, "No doubt? You said just now the remains couldn't be recognised by anybody."

"They can't. But we had a queer find – or rather two finds – in the wreckage. One was a big suitcase, badly burnt – just a heavy lump of charcoal. In the middle of it, though, was a small iron box."

He paused. A look passed between Tolefree and Barrett.

"The thing was locked," said Stevenson, "but we easily broke it open. Must have been red hot in the fire. Charred papers, which fell to bits – all but one thing, and that was a passport. I've got it here. Wants careful handling. Better let me do it."

He took a package from his pocket. We stood round the table, eagerly gazing as he unwrapped it.

"Paper ash, all of it, except this. The cover of the passport protected it a bit – enough for the purpose." He opened the little book gingerly. "The bottom half didn't stand up to the heat. You see the photograph – a black mess. But here's the name—"

We bent to inspect the browned and blackened page, and saw " – ack, Charles."

"Black, of course," said Stevenson, "and part of his description. See?"

We deciphered, " – xion – Fair"; " – es – Blue."

"Charles Black, a fair complexioned man with blue eyes. The rest is burnt. But that's the fellow you want. Here's all the evidence – in the visa pages. Only one visa to be read, the last entry, at Lisbon, 11th March. Will that do?"

It seemed conclusive. As Stevenson gently turned the pages, charred bits fell away. Rougher treatment would have destroyed everything.

Barrett said, "So he won't hang – curse him!"

Stevenson re-made his parcel. We turned away.

"That's one discovery. What's the other?"

"This!" Stevenson pulled from his pocket a heavy pistol and laid it on the table. The ugly weapon was clogged with damp ashes, but otherwise apparently unharmed, save that the clip was torn to pieces.

"Mauser," Barrett pronounced.

"All the shots in the magazine went off in the fire," said Stevenson. "But I guess that's the thing that killed 'em both."

It seemed certain that Stevenson was right: we knew now that the two men for whom Tolefree had come to search in Westport were dead, powerless to do good or evil any more.

We knew, too, that the unhappy Blenkinsop had not endured the terror and torture of fire while he lay helpless on his bed.

What we did not know was why the mysterious companion whom he was about to deliver over to justice accompanied him on his last journey. Not that it mattered much now. Black – or Smith, or Schmidt, or whoever he might be – was removed beyond all possibility of going on with his horrible plot.

I said something of this sort after Stevenson had gone. Barrett said (and seemed to mean it),

"He escaped roasting alive. But I hope he's now roasting in hell."

"But," said Tolefree, "Farrar's point is important. If this body is Black's, why did he die that way? Did he kill himself? Or did somebody shoot him?"

"He must have killed himself," said Horridge.

"Or Blenkinsop killed him and then committed suicide," I suggested.

"But think, Farrar! That gets them both into Blenkinsop's room behind a door locked from the outside," Tolefree objected.

"Possible, isn't it? Remember Fonthill. Before we knew there'd been any shooting Barrett had the idea that Fonthill locked the door."

"A guess. Barrett didn't actually know that the door was then locked," Tolefree reminded me.

I still thought it possible, however unlikely. But the subject was not pursued. Stevenson, when he left, appeared to be relieved by the way in which Tolefree and Barrett took the revelation. Their attitude, at any rate on the surface, indicated that for them the Blenkinsop-Black affair was finished. The police could do the rest. Stevenson agreed, but evidently thought the police had more urgent things on hand.

"You know," he said, "this worked out exactly according to the idea I told you about. When it was clear that Jackson had heard two shots, I thought to myself, 'Blenkinsop and Black?' And this is what I thought too, though nobody's mentioned it: Black shot Blenkinsop and locked the door on him. Then he went to his own room and shot himself. That's a better possibility than Mr. Farrar's."

Tolefree cogitated on this.

"Say as good, Stevenson," he suggested. "I didn't think murder was in the make-up of Fonthill, but every man's a possible murderer. Scoundrels like Black are generally pretty careful of their own skins, but they do occasionally commit suicide – to avoid worse things. The question is, what happened to make Black prefer dying to living? I can't conceive of anything."

"Yet, Mr. Tolefree, you won't have the only man who looks like a possible murderer. You don't want him dead do you?"

"No," said Tolefree, "not that way. I'd much rather he escaped. He ought to escape."

"You mean there's a chance that he did escape?"

"I think there is."

"Then whose body is it?"

"If we knew that we shouldn't be talking about it," said Tolefree. "Mistakes have been made about dead bodies. Not that the probabilities aren't all in your favour."

Stevenson went off, looking a little discontented because a doubt had come into his picture. Barrett shortly followed him to keep his appointment with the witness Jackson.

Tolefree and I stayed with Horridge to await the captain's return.

"We shall dine at eight," said Horridge. "Too late for a cup of tea?"

For Tolefree and me it was never too late for a cup of tea. Horridge rang. An elderly woman came in smiling, "Tea, sir? I thought you was never going to ring."

"Three cups, Betsy, a good potful, and a few biscuits... My daily housekeeper," he explained. "And a neighbour. Mother of three of the British Army out in the courtyard, and one of the best. She does for me as she might for a son. There's a mort of good in my neighbours, Tolefree."

"Of course. And you're more than a neighbour, I perceive. A fellow-countryman with your 'mort of good'."

Horridge grinned. "I tend to get back to the vernacular when I'm here. I daresay Farrar will sympathise. If you heard him at home in Scotland, I bet he'd be unintelligible."

"I've been only once with Farrar on his native heath," said Tolefree. "But, like you, Horridge, he tends to reflect the old surroundings."

"Well, this is my native heath. I was born in this very town. I'm fond of it. I hate the ruffians who've knocked it about: it's almost as though they'd assaulted my mother. I like living here among people who lead the same sort of life – and some of 'em in the very same houses – as the Sea Dogs three or four hundred years ago. I keep a couple of rooms in London still; but I don't go there very much. Curiously I seem to feel more definitely on the shelf in London than I do here."

"I can understand it," said Tolefree. "Where in London?"

"In a slum in the West End. Where are you now, Tolefree? Your slum's disappeared, hasn't it?" Tolefree's face darkened a little. "Destroyed long ago. I've been living anywhere and any-how – the way you know all about. The ruffians burned all my books and small belongings."

"Well, why can't you make use of my rooms when you're in London? I'll give you a key."

That was characteristic of Horridge, as we were to learn. Though he was a little dogmatic and apt to jump at conclusions, he had a nice mind; and he couldn't do enough for his friends. Tolefree demurred and the point was left in the air. But it had a bearing on one of the sequels to the shooting in the Imperial Hotel. Tolefree wandered to the bookshelf which covered the back wall of the room, picked a volume here and there and looked into it, remarking on the great number of books on sociology and the complete absence of criminology.

"With this, you know," said Horridge, pointing to his iron boot, "to linger on the old subject would for me be crying over spilt milk. I threw it all out. I thought I'd done with it for good and all till this morning, when Barrett came along with his story. Now I feel like the old war horse sniffing the battle. This is a queer business, Tolefree. I suppose you're satisfied up there that Blenkinsop's the man who wrote to you as Perry, and that he's jonnick – or was, I should say?"

"I think so. One or two strange things, though. If I weren't quite satisfied that his letter to the Special Department was genuine, I could build up a splendid intrigue, in which Perry would disappear from the ship and somebody else take his place – even Black or Smith, or whatever the agent was called, with a feud at the end between two rival scoundrels, ending in the death of both."

"It might be," said Horridge. "I remember one case where that happened, though not at sea."

"But my mind doesn't go that way. The evidence of Blenkinsop's genuineness, despite his change of name—"

"But why a change of name?"

"There might be many reasons. The most likely is that he gave a false name to the agent and stuck to it while he was trying to circumvent him. But when he was in England and wanted to get in touch with Farrar he used his own name. I don't think you can hold that a crook would have invited Farrar to come and see him at the hotel. It's occurred to me that a man playing a dangerous game for honest causes might have been quite likely to take the skipper of the boat into his confidence, in case of accident, and that may account for the fact that he was the bearer of Captain McPherson's last message to his friend in London. All speculation, of course. The complete disappearance of everybody on the ship except these two makes almost anything possible. One thing I'm quite sure of, Horridge, and that is that the same man wrote the letter to the Special Branch and to Farrar."

"Yes. That's well argued," Horridge admitted. "But what happened here in Westport doesn't fit in. There's Fonthill. Could he have been a contact of the agent on this side? Otherwise, why is he in Westport at the critical moment?"

"There's another possibility," I ventured.

"What, Farrar?"

"That Fonthill was not in it at all – a casual visitor who's got tangled up in this affair in our imaginations. There's no precise evidence, is there? Barrett's slight glimpse of him isn't conclusive."

"I'm afraid," said Tolefree, "you must take all the circumstantial evidence together. Fonthill was foxing all the time for some urgent reason. He behaved just as a guilty man would have behaved even when we had no suspicion of guilt to hang on him. He was on the spot. He was terrified when he found himself in the hands of the police."

"But," I persisted, "you could account for all that without bringing him into contact with the Blenkinsop affair."

"But you couldn't account for his conduct when he knew that I had been through his wallet and discovered his name and seen the photograph taken in New York. Then all the strings come together. It's merely a matter of curiosity. There will probably be no need, but if I were set to try to get to the bottom of the Blenkinsop affair, I should certainly track down Mr. Fonthill, and expect to find him in it."

"Well," said Horridge, "I agree with you, Tolefree. Fonthill's a loose end."

But there was no chance of pursuing the loose end further then. Barrett came back about half-past seven with a report on his second meeting with the witness Jackson, and we dined at eight, very simply. Probably any dinner eaten in Westport that night was a simple one.

Jackson had kept his appointment. He had been told nothing of the manner in which his two neighbours on the second floor had come by their deaths. Stevenson wished to keep that quiet until the inquest was held. But Barrett went through his evidence closely, confirming times as nearly as possible.

There appeared to be no question that he had heard both the shots that killed the two men. They had been killed while we were at dinner. They were both dead when we knocked at Blenkinsop's door.

Jackson had given full particulars of himself. He was an agent in two or three lines of soft goods, and his card showed that he was living at a boarding-house in Bloomsbury and at present conducting his business from that address. He undertook to return to Westport on being informed of the date of the inquest, if necessary.

"It will be very necessary," Stevenson had said.

"Then I suppose there was some dirty work on that corridor before the blitz?" he had asked.

"Something," Stevenson had told him, "needs explaining, and your evidence may help to explain it."

He was going back to London on the midnight train. Tolefree and I took the same train. There was no point, either for him or for me, in hanging about at Westport. We spent the evening with Horridge, and Barrett drove us to the station.

4

1

To all appearance, when the inquest at Westport had been opened and adjourned, the Blenkinsop affair was over for Tolefree, however much it might mean to the police.

His correspondent was dead and so they assumed, was the man Barratt had hoped to hang. There were other fish for Tolefree to fry. He went back to them.

My job as a fire-watcher and a Home Guard left me time enough for speculation not so much on Tolefree's end of the business as on the astonishing difference war-time made to the common proportions of events.

At a time when the unfortunate Coroner at Westport was holding mass inquests, and its clergy were conducting mass funerals of victims of the raid in communal graves, the deaths of two men unknown to Westport could be nothing but a trifling incident. For up to the adjournment *sine die* the police had not revealed the full medical evidence about their fate. So far as the public knew, these two were chance guests of the hotel who had perished in the fire. Even their names were unmentioned. The remains could not be identified; the hotel registers had been destroyed.

Jackson had told his story exactly as he told it to us, except that he soft-pedalled on the theme of the shots, no doubt under instructions. The noises he heard, he admitted, might have been banging doors. You could even read into the observations of Coroner and police the hint that this witness was a bit of a sensationalist.

The fact was, I imagined, that the authorities had resolved to keep secret the story of Black (or Smith's) mission and Blenkinsop's part in it, and I could understand why.

At any rate, Captain Barrett was neither called nor mentioned. If the business ended in the way that looked likely, the less the public knew about it either at home or abroad the better.

In this frame of mind, I was surprised to get a call from Tolefree five days after we had returned to London.

"Farrar," said he, "our holiday on Westport was a flop. I've still a week's leave left. What about a day or two in the Cotswolds?"

"I could get away," I answered.

"Good! Then, look here—"

"Half a tick, Tolefree. It might be good. But I haven't a car. You can't see much of the Cotswolds from the train, and it means a lot of walking. You're not notoriously fond of foot-slogging."

"I can do my five miles with the best of hikers," he returned. "But what I have in mind is an inn in one of those grey Cotswold villages, near one of those trouty streams that run down to the Avon – all stone houses built centuries ago, a church with a stumpy tower, and a manor house or two up the valley – all like you see in the novels."

"What's it called?"

"Stowford. Know it?"

"I've driven through Stowford. A nice little place enough, Tolefree. But not a place for you in the middle of a war. There's a catch somewhere."

"Suspicious mind you've got, Doubting Thomas! Of course there's a catch – in the river. The trout season's been open more than a fortnight. What about it?"

I fell. Then Tolefree said he'd taken advantage of Horridge's offer of his flat in Half Moon Street, and Horridge had come to London for a few days. He asked me to join them at dinner that evening.

I found them in a tiny sitting room where a fire burned in a tiny grate – and walked into a surprise: the table was laid for four people. The fourth arrived within two minutes of me. He was Mr. Jackson, the essential witness of Westport.

"I knew there was a catch in it!" I whispered to Tolefree, as Horridge took his guest away to put up his hat and coat.

"Don't get a catch-complex," he said with a grin. "No such thing. A point occurred to Horridge and he blew round to see Jackson. As he was out on business, Horridge left an invitation to him to have a bite with us this evening. That's all the milk in the coconut, Farrar."

Whereupon Horridge and Jackson came back to the room, and presently we were talking round the dinner table, waited upon by an elderly man from the service department of the flats.

Jackson turned out to be a more entertaining fellow than he seemed when Barrett catechised him at Westport. He had travelled a good deal. I gathered that as an agent in the soft goods business, he had a fairly wide connection. He knew several European countries, or at any rate their chief cities, and he had been over in America. He could chop observations of many places with Horridge, and it was some time before our host got round to the point he wanted to raise.

"I suppose you thought it strange to get an invitation out of the blue to dine with a man you'd never heard of?" he said.

"A little. But I'm used to surprises in my line of business," Jackson answered. "You mentioned your interest in the Westport affair. That made me curious."

Horridge explained that he and Barrett were friends, and that they'd discussed the case together.

"You see, Mr. Jackson, I'm a Westport man. I feel strongly about this. You've no doubt the noises you heard were really shots fired inside the hotel?"

Jackson said that after what happened at the inquest he hadn't the least doubt.

"After the inquest—"

"Why, yes. You weren't there? Well – if you had been you'd have seen at once that nobody wanted any shots to have been fired. The idea was thoroughly unpopular."

Tolefree smiled at this. "You're sensitive to an atmosphere," said he.

"Atmosphere? It was a shout! Didn't need any special sensitiveness to feel that whatever happened in the Imperial Hotel was going to be hush-hushed. They kept me completely in the dark, and there I am now. Perhaps you could tell me – those two men were shot, weren't they?"

Horridge hesitated. "I wouldn't know," said he. "Tolefree, you could probably tell Mr. Jackson more about it."

Tolefree said, "Well – Mr. Jackson will see the need to be – let's say discreet – while the police are still inquiring. But yes, they were shot. The difficulty is to discover when, how, why and by whom. Mr. Jackson has more or less fixed the when for one of them. It was the moment when he heard a shot fired."

"I heard two," said Jackson.

"Yes, but you were only dead certain about the second one, weren't you? The first sound seemed more distant, and might have been a banging door. At least, that's how I understood your evidence."

"It was a more muffled sound, a thud. But the banging door was only a casual thought which came when nothing happened and nobody else seemed alarmed. Afterwards—" He shrugged his shoulders.

"Well, you may be right. But, whether one or two, you settle the time. The question is – who pulled the trigger?"

Jackson shrugged again. "I can't help you there."

"I wonder," said Horridge.

Jackson looked surprised.

"I wonder," Horridge repeated, "whether you mayn't be able to help, even though you don't see how. That was why I asked you to come along tonight."

Jackson looked thoroughly puzzled.

"Ah?" said he. "Well, you tell me."

"I'll try. The shots you heard, or the noises, whatever they were, came almost together?"

"No, that's not quite right. I listened a bit after the first and then went on writing. It was two or three minutes, perhaps more, before I heard the second. I can't be exact."

"One hardly knows how the time goes when he's writing," said Tolefree.

Horridge nodded. "My point is that somebody must have gone along the corridor before the shot and entered the room. Mr. Jackson heard no footsteps till after – then they were footsteps hurrying away."

"Nothing strange in that, is there?" said Jackson. "If a man's going to murder somebody he doesn't draw attention to himself by making a noise beforehand, I imagine. Afterwards he's in a hurry to get away."

Horridge leaned back in his chair. He scrutinised his guest through half-closed eyes.

"Ninety-nine times out of a hundred that would be true," said he. "This is the hundredth time."

"Then," said Jackson slowly, with eyebrows up, "you've got some evidence?"

"We think so. A person hurried along that corridor – pounded along is the phrase used. Not many minutes after he rushed back again. Apparently you heard his footsteps the second time but not the first."

"That's easily explained, Horridge," said Tolefree. "The first time Jackson was behind a closed door, writing. Nothing had happened to distract his attention from what he was doing. The second time he'd been disturbed, and he had the door open when he heard the footsteps."

"I thought," Jackson said, frowning a little, "I was reckoned to be the only man on the corridor at the time except the two who died? I got that idea from the police superintendent."

"They thought all the rest were out or down at dinner. But a man was seen and heard, as I've said. The curious thing is that the shot or shots weren't heard," said Horridge, "by anybody but you."

"And your point is that I ought to have heard the fellow running in the corridor?"

"Ought? Oh, no. But if you had heard him it would have been an important piece of evidence."

"How's that?"

"It would have settled the question whether he went into the corridor before the first noise you heard or between the two."

"Well, I didn't hear him, and that's that," declared Jackson. "Are you thinking he's the—"

"Not thinking at all in that sense. Just speculating and trying to put two and two together."

Horridge rang. The elderly waiter brought coffee and pushed the table back against the wall. We sat round the fire talking and smoking for half an hour before Jackson went.

The affair of the corridor was quickly dismissed. Jackson remarked that we had certainly got something to speculate about. "Looks to me," he said, "like one of Scotland Yard's first-class headaches. This fellow that pounded along the corridor so's I couldn't hear him – can you lay your hands on him? Must you have him?"

Tolefree looked surprised. "I think so," he said, looking curiously at Jackson. "Why d'you ask? Got another idea?"

"Not to call it an idea. Say just a speculation. Seems to me you might be satisfied with two suicides or a murder and a suicide. Then there'd be no necessity for me to hear the fellow pounding along the corridor."

Tolefree smiled at this whimsical repetition of Barrett's phrase. "I see you're not a worshipper of the law of averages," he remarked.

"How's that?"

"I wonder what are the mathematical chances that two men who happen to be given rooms close to each other on an hotel corridor will shoot themselves almost simultaneously?"

"Hundreds of millions to one, of course," said Jackson. "But when you're dealing with two mysterious persons nobody knows anything about – or nobody will let on that he does know anything – and they do actually die by shooting within two or three minutes of each other, the law of averages goes overboard. Especially as they may very likely not have been two casual persons stuck into those rooms by accident. If I could deduce anything from what I heard and from what the police discovered, I'd say those two weren't strangers. Then what you're up against would become a plain case of murder and suicide. One man shoots the other. Then he shoots himself. That would just about measure up to the interval between the two shots, and it seems the common sense of the affair."

We all stared at him for a few seconds after the end of this oration. Tolefree broke the silence.

"On the facts you have, Mr. Jackson, that's a good argument. If the question of the third person in the corridor hadn't cropped up it would have been both logic and common sense: nothing else would explain the fact. But we have the third person and we can't eliminate him."

"The bombs may have done it for you, eh?"

"There's reason to believe he wasn't in the hotel when the bombs fell," said Tolefree. "However—"

Horridge, looking round from pouring more coffee, said that, though Jackson couldn't help us to place the entry of the intruder, it was very good of him to come along to see us. Tolefree agreed, and the talk went in other directions till Jackson took his leave. While Horridge was seeing him off the premises, Tolefree asked me what I made of Jackson on a closer acquaintance. He seemed to me a reasonably intelligent man. What he called his deduction was rather good.

"He's a Yorkshireman by his accents," said I. "And now tell me why you and Horridge stalled him off on so many points. You treated him as if he were a hostile witness, as they say in the Courts."

Tolefree laughed. "Hardly that. Still, he showed a certain hostility towards the theory of a third person in the corridor, didn't he?"

"Yes. I fancy he felt you were badgering him. If he didn't hear Fonthill pounding through the corridor, he didn't, and as he said that's that."

Horridge returned. Tolefree greeted him with, "Here's Farrar, says we've been badgering Jackson."

"Oh? Did we give you that impression? I thought we'd done it rather neatly and pleasantly. But, as a matter of fact, we were badgering him. That's what I invited him here for. I've not been able to make up my mind about our Mr. Jackson."

"Why? He seems to me a perfectly straightforward chap," I protested.

"You may be right. But why won't he have a third person in the corridor at any price? He says because he heard nobody. It isn't possible. Barrett, who was there, declares that it wasn't possible. Stevenson, who knows the building well, agrees with him."

"If that was so," said I, "by inference Jackson is a crook. I don't believe he's a crook. I think he's a plain, middleclass Englishman, and I'll bet you he's doing his bit on something or other – fire-guard or warden, something like that."

"You win," said Horridge. "He is a fire-guard. We know all that there is to be known about him. Ask Tolefree."

Tolefree said, "I've come to no conclusion about Jackson. But there are gaps in his story, Farrar, and before we left Westport I asked Horridge if he'd like to take a hand by keeping tab on our witness. He did like – very much indeed. Now, there's precious little he doesn't know about Jackson – that is, if this man really is Jackson."

"If he is—" I stammered. "Good heavens! What are you suggesting, Tolefree?"

"Only speculating. And they're Horridge's speculations, not mine. But they're certainly interesting. They go this way: Nobody in the hotel saw Jackson after he checked in that afternoon until he turned up in the air-raid shelter, and then naturally nobody noticed him particularly. He was in the hotel for three or four hours, in which time he could have done anything on that corridor unknown to a soul now alive. Suppose the man we know as Jackson isn't Jackson at all, but Jackson is the man who shared the fate of Blenkinsop? Think that over."

The suggestion almost paralysed me with astonishment. For a few seconds I could only gibber, "But – but—" When speech came I poured out a flood of objections.

It was absurd – unthinkable! Horridge's idea – I turned on him – was it that this patently decent Englishman was in fact Black, or Smith, or Schmidt, or whatever the name of the conspirator might be, that he'd killed Jackson as well as Blenkinsop and assumed his identity?

"Not an idea," Horridge insisted. "Merely a speculation. But I've known stranger metamorphoses."

"But think how impossible," I cried. "What about the hotel servants – the porter, the reception clerk? They accepted Jackson as Jackson."

"You forget the state of things in the lobby that evening after the train had come in. The reception clerk couldn't really identify anybody. He was rushed off his feet. He just handed out numbers. He said himself he took no special notice of the guests who came in at that time. He made them sign the book and pass on. Jackson and the conspirator both seem to have had fair hair and blue eyes. Both were clean-shaven. No satisfactory identification there, Farrar."

I began to waver on the question of impossibility. But I had several other objections to raise. I pointed out that if the real Jackson was the man who went to his death with Blenkinsop he must have been either in Blenkinsop's room or Black's. "How do you get him there?" I asked.

"No trouble about that," said Horridge. "Here's a reconstruction that fits in with the facts and with my speculation. When the waiter last saw the door of Blenkinsop's room it was not locked, as we know, and the key was on the outside so Black simply walks in. He'd have no difficulty in doing it unobserved. Shortly after seven the dinner-bell clears the corridor of all its inhabitants except Blenkinsop, Black and Jackson – and Black was not aware of Jackson. He goes in, he shoots Blenkinsop. He takes from Blenkinsop's baggage anything that interests him – papers, letters. He's sure to do that because no doubt Blenkinsop has things about him relating to their plans. It takes a little time. Meanwhile the shot has disturbed Jackson and he goes out into the corridor to see what's up—"

"But that was after the second shot!" said I.

"According to the pseudo-Jackson. But the real Jackson went out into the corridor and tried the doors in his neighbourhood, for he hadn't a doubt that what he heard was a shot. The only one with a key on the outside was Blenkinsop's.

"He opens the door: he sees Blenkinsop lying dead on the bed and Black busy overhauling the baggage. Instantly Black drags him into the room and shoots him—"

"All imagination! Fantastic!" said I.

Horridge took no notice. He went on: "Black is a perfectly callous man in a perilous position. Before the shot, if heard, can bring anybody else to the corridor he has locked the door, taken the key and dashed into his own room. After an interval he comes out to examine the corridor. If he's seen he'll be on his way down to dinner. But he's not seen. He discovers an open bedroom door with a light on inside. He looks in: no occupant, letters written and half-written on a table, a suitcase at the foot of the bed. Clearly the occupant was the man who heard the shot and is now dead in consequence."

"You're inventing it as you go!" I cried, impatiently.

"No," said Horridge. "It's all necessary to my speculation and in harmony with the facts."

"But you might have a dozen different theories in harmony with the same facts."

"No doubt, Farrar. But this is mine. While he's in Jackson's room, a change of identities strikes Black as a better bet than a complete disappearance from the hotel in a town with which he's not familiar. He might find himself in danger if by any chance the murder were discovered within the next hour. So he becomes Jackson. He takes a risk, banking on the probability that nobody knows Jackson well. But he will know how to handle the situation, claiming the identity only when he feels that it is quite safe. Jackson's papers tell him all he wants to know about him – his business, his address, the fact that he's unmarried. He returns to his room and shifts everything compromising to Jackson's—"

"Absurd, Horridge! How can you possibly construct that from the material you have?"

"It's necessary to explain his conduct. He waits in Jackson's room, spends his time in absorbing the Jackson atmosphere till the sirens blow. Then he still waits until the hotel is on fire and he knows that everything on that corridor will be destroyed. He may even have been in the room when you two and Barrett were doing a bit of fire brigade work upstairs. Then he makes tracks for the air-raid shelter. He is now Jackson."

That ended the farrago. "Horridge," I exclaimed, "you fellows have your minds so cluttered up with plots and wiles that you can't believe anything simple. I'll bust this speculation like a bubble. What about the people in London who know the real Jackson – the people in his rooms or his hotel and his business? Are they deluded?"

"Jackson took a room in the Bloomsbury boarding-house last autumn. After the first fortnight he was hardly ever there. Until last week he'd not been there for months, though he kept the tenancy of the room. They know nothing of any previous residence. We can't get at Jackson himself on this point without awakening suspicion in him. His business is a purely personal affair, he has no associates and he works from whatever place he's inhabiting. At any rate, that's what he tells people."

This certainly looked queer.

"What d'you think of it, Tolefree?" I asked him.

"It's good theoretical stuff. It could have happened that way, Farrar."

Horridge broke in: "Farrar, you won't have Fonthill a murderer. There's only one alternative, and that's mine."

"Do you think that, Tolefree?"

"It's a large assumption. No – not quite. But let's drop the subject, shall we? You and I are going to have a few days peace and quiet in the Cotswolds, and catch a fish or two, while Horridge stays in London and keeps an eye on Jackson – with ample assistance, of course."

"If Horridge's theory is sound, Jackson will want watching twenty-four hours a day," said I.

"Don't worry about that," said Horridge.

2

Having made arrangements to be away for a week, I met Tolefree at Paddington Station next morning. Both of us were armed with fishing rods.

All the way to Stow, where we dropped off the train, Tolefree talked of fishing holidays. He declined absolutely to discuss the dinner party at Horridge's. If there was anything in his hunch Horridge would work it out. As for himself he kept an open mind.

I could see that he was not much in love with the theory of a transmigration of bodies between Jackson and Black. The person who interested him most was Fonthill. As I seemed to resent any imputations against that youth, Tolefree would not pursue that at present.

There was no taxi to be had for the six miles to Stowford. We routed out an ancient driver with a horsed cab. This inspired Tolefree to discourse on the petrol restrictions, the consequent peace and quietness of the roads, and the superior travel joys of our grandfathers, who were content to bowl along them at eight miles an hour and thought ten a dangerous pace.

Stowford is rather a show place in the summer. But the visitors are birds of passage. No one can stay more than a few hours unless he gets a room at the Stowford Arms, whose accommodation is limited. Stowford has not a single bungalow or lodging to let. Tolefree did not exaggerate when he said the houses were all centuries old. One of those villages owned by lords of the manor, who permit no new building on their land, Stowford makes but a single concession to modernity: it allows the old lady who keeps the Post Office to sell picture postcards.

Our horse ambled up the slope past the classical gates which Inigo Jones or somebody had built in the seventeenth century for the owner of Stowford Manor, through the village clustered round the gates, breaking into a slow trot along the road running through a thick wood beyond. The larches were beginning to show a misty green in the pale sunshine. There were birds galore. It was a pleasant English scene through which we clip-clopped in the authentic B.B.C. manner. We might have been a thousand years and a thousand miles from the war. I had the sense of being a supernumerary in a stage play.

The Stowford Arms when we reached it did nothing to dispel the illusion. Placed at a discreet half-mile from the village, it stood back from the road in a rectangular clearing of the wood. Aloof from Stowford, it was of a piece with it – an oblong house of grey stone, the roof heavily tiled, the windows mullioned. A signpost square to the road was gorgeous with the heraldry of Stowford in gold and scarlet.

"What d'you think of my inn?" Tolefree asked, as the cab swung into the clearing and pulled up at the porch.

I duly admired Tolefree's taste in inns.

"Not two hundred yards away towards the river is one of the innumerable trees King Charles slept in after the Battle of Worcester," he informed me while the ancient cabby was taking our bags off the roof and putting them down in the porch.

"A pity," said I. "You always have to pay extra for King Charles."

Tolefree's copious fund of local information re-aroused my suspicions that there was a catch somewhere. He knew far too much about Stowford. And the suspicion justified itself...

A polite and highly superior person with her hair dressed in the latest fashion and her tongue attuned to Oxford served us with tea. I guessed we should have to make a contribution to the hairdresser's fee and pay interest on Oxford. She informed us that the bags would be taken up to our rooms, which were numbers One and Two on the first floor.

"So," I said, as Tolefree poured tea, "you've fixed it all up – rooms, etcetera."

"Everything. Naturally."

"It doesn't seem quite natural to me. Where's the catch? You're not down here for trout fishing."

"Guilty, m'lud. You always see through me, Farrar. But I if I'd asked you to come on what may be a wild-goose chase instead of on a fishing trip, would you, now? The rod is camouflage. I'm fishing on dry land with other implements."

"But why me? I haven't had a letter from anybody at Stowford."

"Quite unlikely. But you had one from Blenkinsop. That's the reason."

"So? The same old game! You'd better confess everything," said I.

"Open confession is good for the soul, as my grandmother used to tell me about other fishing expeditions. I will. We've come to Stowford to see Mrs. Wollaston."

"Have we, indeed? She's a new one on me. What has she to do with Blenkinsop?"

"I don't know. But perhaps more than anyone else had to do with him. We shall have to find out. Mrs. Wollaston is a widow-lady who lives at Stowgate, about a mile further along the road. We're going to dine with her at seven o'clock. I accepted on your behalf, so you can't get out of it."

This confession, I declared, left much to be desired. "Fill it in, Tolefree," I commanded.

"Mrs. Wollaston has been twice married and twice widowed. Her first married name was Blenkinsop."

"Oh? His mother, then?"

"Maybe. It's a guess. No, a little more than that."

"How did you discover her?"

Tolefree disclaimed any credit for the discovery. The Stowford policeman discovered her, but not till the inquiry had been out a few days. Soon after he got back to London, Tolefree received a document issued from the Gloucester County Police Headquarters. He turned the sheet out of his pocket, and passed it to me:

Reference your inquiry re Blenkinsop. The only person in this county who might be of use to you in your inquiry is Mrs. Wollaston, of Stowgate, Stowford, Glos. She married the late Mr. George Wollaston of that address, after the death of her former husband, who was named Blenkinsop. Further inquiries can be made if necessary.

"It sounds rather remote," I suggested.

"But the further inquiries seem to bring it a bit nearer. We shall see. In a sense, Farrar, I hope it will stay remote. If not we shall have some bad news for Mrs. Wollaston. In another sense, though, I hope it won't. For we may get some light on Blenkinsop's mystery."

"So you're still interested in his mystery? I thought that from your point of view it was all over. You'd lost Blenkinsop, but you'd also got rid of the other fellow. It was just the same as if they'd both gone down with the ship."

"If that's true," said Tolefree, "there are others. Few lone hands in this sort of wickedness. Did you see a report of the inquest?"

"A few lines. All hush-hush. You fellows—"

"I'm not going to discuss our fellows, Farrar. Quite plainly we'd prefer any of those others not to know what had happened to Blenkinsop and his companion. We want to get the ends all nicely tied first, and we think they ought to tie in a certain way. When I say 'we' I mean the Department."

"And what do you mean when you say 'I'?"

"Generally as little as possible." He grinned. "On this point nothing at all – except that I don't think it possible to tie the ends as we want 'em. To my mind they'll make an utterly different sort of knot."

"Tolefree," said I, "you're running to figures of speech, and vague ones at that. Put some sense into it."

"I don't believe in the official view of the case of Blenkinsop v. Black, Fonthill intervening."

"Fonthill intervening! So that's the way of it?"

"Not my way. Tell you more about it when we've seen Fonthill."

I said, perhaps petulantly, "Another problem postponed till after the war! You've no news of Fonthill, have you?"

"Hardly a sound. You're fiercely ironical, aren't you? But I'll wager that before long we do get news of Fonthill. The police picked up his tracks and lost them. The longer he's loose the harder for them to catch. They're looking for the man. I'm going to look for people who know him."

"Where on earth?"

"If I had to make a guess it would be somewhere round here where no one would think of looking for a fugitive. But it all depends on Mrs. Wollaston. If she's a connection of our Blenkinsop she probably knows our Fonthill, or knows of him. Then—"

Tolefree certainly had an edge on that young man. He denied it. "But," he said, "I've a terrible itch for five minutes conversation with Mr. Fonthill. If he has no link with Blenkinsop or Black, he must produce some other reason for his eccentric conduct. Foxing! Jumping out of a window! My dear Farrar – and you talk about no link!"

A pleasant walk on the road through the woods that evening brought us to Stowgate – an unpretentious good house, kind of rural villa, built, I judged, some fifty years ago. Reaching it in the last of the dusk, we could see little of its surroundings, save that to the south and west a clearing of the trees must have let in a great deal of magnificent sunshine.

The moment a maid admitted us it became plain that Tolefree had arranged his plans and salted the ground. She said, "Mr. Tolefree and Mr. Farrar?" with a note of expectation in her voice, laid our coats and hats on the hall table, and took us directly to a drawing room where Mrs. Wollaston sat beside a cheerful fire.

In that flickering light she looked a very young woman to have been twice widowed – slim, dark-headed, graceful. She rose to greet us, sorting us out. When the maid switched on the light, however, Mrs. Wollaston's face and eyes revealed a woman between fifty and sixty, and the possibility that she might have a son of Blenkinsop's age came at once into the perspective.

She held out a hand: "Mr. Tolefree?" Tolefree took it. "Mr. Farrar?" My turn came. She smiled pleasantly.

"That was a rather mysterious note Colonel Franklin sent me, Mr. Tolefree," she said. "But he was most positive you had something important to say."

"The Chief Constable's been helpful," Tolefree answered. "I suppose he gave me some credentials?"

She indicated chairs. "He said you were on a confidential mission. His word's enough. I wondered what I could have to do with a confidential mission – but, shall we dine first? War-time fare, you know."

Mrs. Wollaston was wary and self-possessed. I felt some doubt about her complete ignorance of our mission. But before an hour had passed it seemed to be baseless doubt. We dined simply, attended by two elderly maids. Until they had withdrawn the talk was all of Gloucestershire scenery and history; of the London children sent there for safety from bombs, the war news. The mission was not touched.

"Will you stay and drink port, or shall we go into the other room for coffee now?" she asked, rising.

"Coffee and now," said Tolefree, "eh, Farrar? We want to get down to cases, especially the reason why we've invaded you. Very good of you to receive us."

By the time this speech had faded away we were crossing the hall. The fire in her drawing room had been made up afresh and she signed us to chairs around it. Mine was opposite hers at the corner of the hearth. Tolefree sat between, looking into the fire. She found cigarettes, invited us to smoke, took one herself, served coffee from a low table at her side.

For all his anxiety to get down to cases, Tolefree sat silent for a minute or two, sipping coffee, gazing from the fire to the shelf above it with its two or three photographs in silver frames, and from the shelf back to the fire.

"Well, Mr. Tolefree?" said our hostess at last.

"Yes... It's difficult," said Tolefree. "Colonel Franklin gave you no hint?"

"None at all. Only that the business was important and I was to give you, I think he said, any information you wanted. Though what information I can give—"

"It was a personal matter," Tolefree told her. "But the chief part of it I know now – since I came into this room."

"Good gracious!" she exclaimed.

"The worst of it is, Mrs. Wollaston, that I now have to give you some information, and I wish to heaven it was somebody else's job. You had a son—"

"I have a son," she said, stiffening in her chair. "What of it?"

"He went to America, I believe – how long ago?"

"Nearly five years. But... is all this necessary to your mission, whatever it may be?"

"I assure you," said Tolefree gently. "It is the mission. This isn't idle curiosity. Information about him is the essence of it. But please say nothing you don't want to. We are entirely your debtors. Merely we shall be grateful for help. He went to America five years ago. Have you heard much from him?"

"Regularly for the first year or two. After that he went exploring in a distant part of South America. They call the country the matto grosso. You know of it?"

"Yes," said Tolefree; "in the back country of Brazil. By Jove! – that accounts for much."

"Does it? You leave me in the dark."

"I'll make it clear directly. Since then — ?"

Her face grew grave. "I heard nothing for years. I feared everything. I'd really given him up for lost. Then – well, I had a letter from him. It was a great shock – and a great happiness."

"When was that?" Tolefree asked.

"A month – no, five weeks ago."

"From New York, telling you he was on his way to England?"

"Yes. How did you know?"

"I thought it possible. Did he give you the name of his ship?"

"No. He was looking for a ship. He said it was hard to get a passage, but he'd try to let me know before he sailed."

"And did he?"

"I'm still waiting," said Mrs. Wollaston. "In these times, sea voyages—" She shivered.

Tolefree's job became more difficult every moment, and his unease more apparent.

"These times," he said, "are terrible; every ship runs great risks. And mails – extremely uncertain. I wonder whether I might see his letter? Or perhaps you could tell me parts of it – if they throw any light on his last few weeks over there?"

Mrs. Wollaston had gone pale. Her hands trembled. But she pulled herself together.

"He's my only child. We have a very special relation. There are things in the letter – but, yes, I'll read to you what you want to know. Excuse me. I'll fetch it."

Tolefree turned to me as the door closed behind her. "Phew! – It couldn't be worse, Farrar. A hateful job. Look at that!" He pointed to a large photograph on the middle of the mantle-shelf. I rose to look.

A picture of a bride and bridegroom – he in full morning rig, she in white dress with veil and coronet.

The bridegroom made a fine figure of a man – tall, robust, his fair hair shining in the sun outside a church porch, his features well moulded, his eyes creased into a smile. She was a dark girl, wide-eyed, smiling too, as she leant on his arm.

She was the girl who had written the legend "Vi to B," on the postcard likeness in New York. Tolefree took the card from his wallet.

"Now, Farrar, how did your friend Fonthill get hold of that?"

Tolefree put back the card. Before I could answer we heard the door. As Mrs. Wollaston came in I was moving my coffee-cup on the table and Tolefree was in his seat facing the fire. She had an envelope in her hand.

"You want to know about his recent doings on the other side?" She took her chair. "There's not much. Mr. Tolefree – I must tell you that my son had a sad experience – tragic. He was a mining engineer. Five years ago he had an appointment in California. Before he went he married a splendid girl, a neighbour of ours here. They began their honeymoon with the voyage. Every letter for two years after that showed that they were as happy as a man and woman could be. Then – she had a baby and died of it. And the child too. Bob's life crashed. He threw everything over and went off travelling and prospecting. All those three years with never a word from him—"

Tolefree murmured his understanding. Blenkinsop had disappeared into jungle and forest whence many a man never returned, his mother sat at home fearing.

"But," she said, "you don't want to listen to an old woman's worries. I've had a letter from him at last, and at any rate he's alive. That's something, isn't it?"

I was horrified. Tolefree said nothing but gave her a look of sympathy.

"Here's what he says from New York," she went on:

"I reached here two days ago, and I'm looking for a ship to Europe. I want to get into the war. It's not easy to find a berth, though. All sorts of restrictions and complications.

"Would you believe it? – until two months ago, just before I got down to Pernambuco, I never knew there was a war on. I've been back of beyond, trying to forget things. Plenty of adventures. I'll tell them to you over the fire at Stowgate. Can't begin to write them.

"I picked up a queer chap at Pernambuco and travelled here with him. Seems likely to be useful in the search for a ship.

"I sent two letters for you down the river, but there's no guarantee they ever reached you. You'll get this one anyhow..."

"And then," said Mrs. Wollaston, "he goes on to private matters. And I'm afraid I can't tell you anything more. He should be home soon."

It was a frightful experience. I felt hot all over, wondering how Tolefree would deal with it. He said, kindly,

"I told you just now I had to give you some information—"

"I wondered what it could be."

"And that I wished somebody else had the job. Well, Mrs. Wollaston, I'm not going to beat about the bush. You're a brave woman, I think. You spoke of 'Bob'. Your son was named Robert?"

The brave woman flinched. "You're going to tell me he is—" She faltered. She put her hands up to press her temples.

"I have to tell you he sailed from New York in a steamer called the *Bridgend*, bound to Naples."

"Oh... oh!"

Her face drained of colour. Her eyes closed. "That boat – it was torpedoed and sunk. Two men were saved – no more. Wasn't that it? I saw it in the paper."

"Two men," said Tolefree, "were all the survivors. Two men named Perry and Black."

Mrs. Wollaston rose, stretched out her arms, blindly, tottered, and would have crashed to the hearthrug at my feet if we had not both caught her. I lowered her to the floor. Tolefree seized a cushion for her head.

"Water! – in the dining room," he said.

I rushed out. A maid was in that room, clearing up.

"I'm afraid Mrs. Wollaston isn't very well," I told her. "Will you—" But before I could say another word she was running across the hall. I grabbed a carafe and followed. She gave a little scream as she caught sight of the figure on the floor. Tolefree had his finger on the bell-push and immediately another maid came running. Both of them looked daggers at us.

"What have you done to her?" cried one in a rage.

"Keep your head," said Tolefree, sharply. "Mrs. Wollaston has fainted. Look after her while we wait in the other room."

We waited ten minutes. Tolefree, wiping his forehead, said, "A deuce of a job! Poor, poor woman... we've knocked the bottom out of her world."

"And she doesn't know the worst horror yet," I reminded him. "She doesn't know what really happened to Blenkinsop."

"Why should she? Now, I mean? Later on, perhaps. But it's enough agony for her to know him dead. Let her think he was drowned. I shall go no further."

I thought the truth must come out in the end, but agreed with him that it would be inhuman to add to her grief by telling the true tale of Westport. Tolefree declared that he would tell her only one thing more at present – the reason why he and not some other person had been obliged to inflict this pain on her.

"Why say anything at all?" I asked.

"Only because what she may be able to tell us is vital to the case. We're bound to let her know that we don't put her through a catechism out of idle curiosity."

We fell silent till one of the maids came to say that Mrs Wollaston was better and wanted to see us.

Back in her chair when we returned, she had composed herself, though she looked pale and ill.

"Foolish of me to faint," said she.

"You had a bad shock, Mrs. Wollaston. I fear I broke the news clumsily," Tolefree apologised.

But, she said, however it was broken it would have been a shock. "I've had doubts and some fears for – oh, for many days, when no news came. There was something – but I won't speak of that. In fact, Mr. Tolefree, if he had to die I'm glad it was by drowning."

Tolefree shuddered and was silent.

"Now," she went on, "why did you come to tell me this news, and why did you want to know anything about Bob? And what did you mean when you said you knew most of it as soon as you came into this room?"

"I knew his identity, the most important point for me, when I caught sight of the photograph on the mantelpiece," said Tolefree.

"Then – you knew him!" she exclaimed.

Tolefree shook his head. "No, I never saw him. I wasn't even aware of his existence till a few days ago. But the photograph—"

"Then, you knew his wife?"

"No. But I'd seen a photograph of her – saw it in remarkable circumstances. They don't matter now. The true reason why I'm here at all is that queer chap your son picked up in Pernambuco. My Department's interested in him. It thinks he's a little more than queer. It wants to know everything it can discover about him. It understands that he too sailed on the *Bridgend* – but after that it loses sight of him. So it's looking for any information that might lead back to his tracks."

Mrs. Wollaston, leaning back in her chair, looked at Tolefree with a puzzled expression in her eyes.

"But," Tolefree pursued, "it would be terrible to ask you to go on discussing our little affair now. We'd better leave you, and perhaps tomorrow, if you feel well enough—"

"That's kind of you. I'm all to pieces. But if you want information about that man – well, when I read you bits of the letter just now I left out something because Bob asked me to say nothing of it to anyone. I feel sure he'd have agreed that I ought to tell you now. Take it, and read as far as you think you ought to."

She pointed to the letter lying on the coffee table. Tolefree picked it up and turned over the sheets. He settled down to read at one point, turned back and read again. Then he passed it to me, indicating a place. I read, in the handwriting now familiar to me:

I picked up a queer chap at Pernambuco and travelled here with him. Seems likely to be useful in the search for a ship. But there are other things.

I'd better not say much, but in case anything should happen I'd like you to know enough to explain it. Don't mention it to a soul, will you?

This fellow looks and speaks like an Englishman, but I have my doubts. If English he's a traitor. If not he's a spy. I'm going to keep an eye on him and put a spoke in his wheel if he's up to any tricks.

He seems to think me a grouchy bloke not too well off and possible to be used. I let him think.

Mother, I believe I've not been quite sane since Vi died. Anyhow, I've had the luck of a lunatic. I ought to be dead ten times over, but there's nothing wrong with me except that I'm chockful of malaria. That'll work out.

By the way, I've not been too free in all these adventures with the name of Blenkinsop. Whatever scrape I got into I didn't want it to reflect on our name. So I've had different ones in different circumstances, and as to this chap (he calls himself Smith) he knows me by a common name which wouldn't give anything away.

When I heard coming down the river that this war had been on for a year and a half I came to my senses. I ought to have been in it from the start. I know something about Nazis on this side of the water. Now I'm just in a fever to be home and see you and then to get busy.

My darling mother...

I read no further. Tolefree replaced the letter on the table

"Does it tell you anything?" Mrs. Wollaston asked.

"It confirms an impression," said Tolefree. "It gives me an admirable picture of your son. Yes – it tells me the name of the hotel where they were staying, which may be useful. And now, I insist that we shall bother you no more tonight. We'll ring up in the morning and if you feel well enough then, we may walk up again. I should be grateful if you'd let me discuss two other points with you."

We'd been through a harrowing experience and given a nice woman a horrible one. And we didn't seem to be much nearer Tolefree's goal.

When I said this as we walked back to the Stowford Arms, Tolefree retorted: "We've made the acquaintance of Blenkinsop's mother and cleared the ground for the real thing. That's enough for one evening old man. I'll get on the phone and pass on the name of the hotel. Then we'll go to bed early if you don't mind. There's going to be a busy day tomorrow. Don't you find it interesting – this building up of a character? Blenkinsop's dead, poor fellow; but he's coming to life before our eyes."

I said it was interesting enough, but it didn't bring us a step closer to Fonthill and the real mystery of that tragic hour in the hotel at Westport.

"Fonthill's for tomorrow, or I miss my bet," said Tolefree.

3

We saw Stowgate next morning in the full sunshine of a bright April day.

The impression of a late Victorian villa was stronger in the morning light than in the dusk of evening; but its setting took on a rare beauty of woodland as background to gardens full of spring flowers.

"Blenkinsop must have often thought of this," said I, as we walked up the short drive, "or dreamed of it in his fevers out in the matto grosso."

"And perhaps in the last hours he spent in that bedroom," said Tolefree. "It's going to be difficult to explain ourselves to his mother without desolating her with the real facts of his death."

And so it proved.

She received us more kindly than the bearers of our news had any right to expect. She had endured a sleepless night. Too exhausted to rise from bed, she insisted that we should come to her room. We saw a woman looking years older for the night she had passed, but composed, with a certain sternness in her pale face.

"You wanted to talk about two things," she said. "What are they? How do they affect my dead son?"

Tolefree was landed in the midst of his difficulty.

He told her the first thing was her son himself. He said the country had cause to be grateful to Blenkinsop. But for him it might have known nothing of the queer chap mentioned in his letter.

"He had suspicions more definite than he said even to you. He wrote to us to put us on our guard. We were hoping to have a visit from him and to thank him. But it could not be. If it isn't too painful for you, we should be grateful to you for a little information. You remember I said that photograph of his wife came to us in peculiar circumstances. You might clear them up if you would tell us something about her. Will you look at the picture?"

He handed it to her.

"You notice," Tolefree went on, "that it was taken in New York – I suppose shortly after the marriage?"

"It must have been. They were off to California within a few months."

"And it's inscribed, 'From Vi to B.' That would be from Vi to Bob, no doubt. Could you tell us exactly who Vi was?"

She looked at him very straight. "You're surely not suspecting—"

"Mrs. Wollaston! – I assure you we have no thoughts at all about the poor young woman, except regrets that her life was cut short so tragically. But merely to know the elementary things about her – name and family – might solve the puzzle which put it into my pocket."

Mrs. Wollaston reflected. "I don't understand it in the least. But I can tell you those things. Everybody here knows them. She was Viola Arscott, the daughter of Mr. William Arscott – he's dead now – who had a small place on the other side of Stowford, about a mile and a half away. She was a lovely girl, what in the old days would have been called the toast of the neighbourhood. Bob won her against the competition of all the young men within miles. They were a perfect couple."

"I can well believe it," Tolefree said. "Thank you. There's only one thing more. Your son was a mining engineer. Had he been much abroad before he went to America?"

"Hardly at all. A few excursions on the Continent."

"Never worked abroad?"

"No. He was with my husband, Mr. Wollaston who had biggish mining connections – he was an engineer himself. Bob's father died when he was an infant. His stepfather was everything to him, educated him, brought him up to his own profession. Bob had lived here all his youth. Stowgate was Mr. Wollaston's property. Then he went to London in his stepfather's office and spent his holidays with me. We're not rich. It was the appointment in California that made it possible for him to marry Vi Arscott."

Tolefree seemed to have got everything from Mrs. Wollaston that he wanted, though I could not see that it put him any further on his road. I said so when we had taken leave of her and turned back towards Stowford.

"Well, the mystery of the photograph is still a mystery, and we aren't a yard nearer Fonthill," I remarked.

"I don't agree about the photograph," he replied, "and as for Fonthill every step you're taking now leads you a yard nearer Fonthill."

"How's that?"

"We're on the way to Stowford Manor. I have a letter of introduction to the Lord of the Manor. I got your name put into it, Farrar."

"And who may the Lord of the Manor of Stowford be?" I asked.

"Mr. Henry William Fonthill," said Tolefree.

I stared. He had brought out this startling announcement without turning a hair. He forestalled my reproaches.

"Surprise is the spice of life, you know," he said, smiling.

"To the surpriser," I retorted.

"Couldn't resist the temptation of keeping this one up my sleeve, Farrar. No bones broken, eh?"

I ought, of course, to have put two-and-two together from his allusions to Fonthill the day before. So I said, merely,

"Another parent?"

"Father, if I'm not mistaken. In fact, I'm sure. That identity card—"

"But you yourself said identity cards don't convey anything but the owners' names."

"And numbers. Don't forget the numbers. In the hands of skilful and diligent persons, those cryptic letters and figures can be made to say quite a bit. In this instance they said that William Hasty Fonthill was registered in 1939 as living at the Manor House, Stowford, Gloucestershire."

"You do hold all the cards, don't you?" said I, shortly.

Within twenty minutes we passed through the classic gateway which was so strange an introduction to an Elizabethan manor house. Five minutes later we were ushered into the presence of Mr. William Henry Fonthill.

5

1

Our encounter with the Lord of the Manor of Stowford opened a new phase of the Blenkinsop mystery.

Tolefree's instinct had been right. Stowford looked like the key of the enigma. It set up the definite connection between Fonthill and Blenkinsop which at Westport had seemed so questionable

We were shown into a small study where a fire burned bright and sunshine poured through the windows. A tall, silver-haired man rose from his chair by the fireside and laid The Times on the table. He looked every inch a lord of the manor.

Mr. Fonthill, it appeared, had, like Mrs. Wollaston, expected us. His keen grey eyes looked from one to the other as we entered.

"Mr. Tolefree?" he said, holding out his hand. "And — ?"

"Farrar," said Tolefree.

"Howdydo?" ... He installed us in chairs near the fire. He presented a cigarette case. "My friend Franklin thinks I can be useful to you. Only too happy. What's it all about?"

Whereas Mr. Fonthill had dived into the middle of the pond without delay, Tolefree took an unusually long time to tap and start his cigarette. Then he looked straight into the grey eyes before he said,

"It's rather a long story; but perhaps I'd better assume that you know nothing of it and begin at the beginning?"

Mr. Fonthill inclined his head.

"You'll have to forgive me for bringing in personal matters," said Tolefree. "But first I'll give you their background. Of course you know young Blenkinsop – a neighbour of yours, the son of Mrs. Wollaston?"

Mr. Fonthill knew him quite well. "But I haven't seen him for some years. He's been abroad. There was a tragedy in his life—"

"A sudden widowing, I believe?" said Tolefree.

"Yes. He married a girl of these parts, Viola Arscott, and she died giving birth to her child out in California. That knock sent Blenkinsop off wandering about South America, and his mother's heard little of him since. It also killed her father. But – what of Blenkinsop?"

"This," said Tolefree. "I've just had the painful job of breaking to his mother the news of his death."

"Blenkinsop? – dead!" Mr. Fonthill spoke without excessive emphasis. Somehow the news shocked him less than one might have expected – though, true, everyone was getting used to sudden death. But he went on, after an appropriate pause, "Bless my soul! – that's dreadful for her. And – how?"

"He died a violent and a very terrible death," Tolefree answered. "So terrible that I've not told his mother of it. She's under the impression that he was drowned at sea. I let her think so. But I must tell you the truth – and, for the present anyhow – confidentially."

"Certainly," said Fonthill. He passed fingers through his silver hair. He looked grave but puzzled. "I shall see why as you go on, I expect."

"Colonel Franklin has probably given you a hint about the Department concerned in this affair—"

"Yes. I think I understand that."

"Well – our attention was drawn to Blenkinsop by Blenkinsop himself, and that's important. We'd not have known anything in the ordinary way about a mining prospector who'd been lost to view in the matto grosso or thereabouts for two or three years. Two facts about Blenkinsop were greatly to his credit, Mr. Fonthill. He'd heard nothing at all about the war till three months or so ago he drifted down to Pernambuco. Then his first impulse was to sail back home at once and get into it as fast as he could. Next, while he waited for a ship, he tumbled across evidence of a plot. He sent us a warning and kept on the track of the plotters. That bit of work for his country was unhappily the proximate if not the direct cause of his death."

Mr. Fonthill's gaze on Tolefree was intent. "A spy conspiracy?" he exclaimed.

"Not much doubt about it. But remember, I said it was possibly only the proximate reason why this poor fellow died so horribly. That's the mystery we're trying to riddle out. Now let me tell you what happened after Blenkinsop sailed from Pernambuco on the steamer *Bridgend*."

Mr. Fonthill sat upright in his chair, hands clasped on knees while Tolefree related the story of the voyage, the letters to the Department and to me, the loss of the ship, the disappearance of the two survivors, the discovery of Blenkinsop's body and the thing that had happened to him.

Mr. Fonthill did not interrupt, nor did he shift his gaze from Tolefree's face.

"That," Tolefree ended, "is the puzzle set for us, Mr. Fonthill: Why was Blenkinsop killed, and who killed him?"

"Yes," said Mr. Fonthill. "Poor young fellow! It's hard to imagine that villainous thing happening to him. But on the face of it I should have thought there wasn't any real doubt who killed him and why?"

"Eh? You've seen more than we have!" Tolefree exclaimed.

"Surely not? The newspapers reported two men found dead in the ruins. What of the second man? Blenkinsop's a patriotic young man who seems to have made the mistake of thinking he could tackle a conspiracy single-handed. The man he's watching is not deluded. He seeks him out and kills him. Then, either he kills himself or he's caught in the fire."

Tolefree stared at him for a moment.

"That's a theory!" he said. "But unfortunately there's no evidence. The second man was quite unidentifiable. If he was the conspirator, why would he kill himself? If he shot Blenkinsop, his victim was dead, his danger removed. The evidence of his crime was about to be destroyed. He could have escaped. Why didn't he?"

"I can only imagine he was trapped in the fire."

Tolefree said that would have been possible but for one thing: Jackson, writing in a room near by, heard the shot. It was fired before the raid began. Jackson had plenty of time to escape; the other man could therefore have got away.

Mr. Fonthill pondered it. "Yes – I suppose that's true. But if it happened the other way round and Blenkinsop shot this man first? Poor Blenkinsop was in no condition to escape?"

Tolefree shook his head. "No – not that way, Mr. Fonthill; certainly not that way. For even a man in a fever, threatened with fire, will get away somehow. You've overlooked the master fact."

Tolefree regarded the lord of the manor curiously as he searched for the meaning of this, frowning hard. He raised his hand suddenly.

"Ah, yes! – the locked door, of course. He couldn't get away. What does that imply?"

"One of several things. Which of them depends on the question whether the door was locked before the shooting or after. Blenkinsop was shot in his own room. His body was found tangled up in his bed, and he had only the shreds of night-clothes on him. Therefore, if the other man killed him, it must have been in Blenkinsop's room. If we could discover who locked the door—"

"But that's long odds against, isn't it?"

"You never know. Some little thing may put us on the track. For instance, I mentioned a young man Barrett saw in the hotel – in the very corridor where Blenkinsop's room was."

"But – he disappeared, I thought?"

"He did. The police have been busy looking for him, but he seems to have gone to ground most successfully. However, if we should come across any traces of him, that might make a difference."

Mr. Fonthill's eyes narrowed. "I suppose so," said he. "Is it your theory that this young fellow locked the door on the two miserable men?"

Tolefree measured his answer. "No – it's not my theory. I should be particularly sorry to have to believe it, Mr. Fonthill."

"Why sorry? – I mean particularly sorry?"

"Because I know his name," said Tolefree.

"Good God!" exclaimed Mr. Fonthill, starting up. He sat down again. "I mean – what an extraordinary reason. If you don't think he locked the door, what difference could it make whether you discovered him or not?"

"This, Mr. Fonthill. That he must have been in the corridor about the time when the shots were fired, and that his conduct afterwards was so strange. I don't doubt that, if he would, he could give us valuable information. But he eludes us."

Mr. Fonthill shrugged his shoulders. "Ah, well," said he, "you know your own business. What help can I give you?"

"You can tell us where to find this young man," said Tolefree, deliberately.

I gasped. Tolefree's quiet words took the man like a blow between the eyes. He shrank back in his chair and I thought he would collapse. But in three seconds he had recovered.

"That's an astonishing statement," he declared. "How can I—"

"Mr. Fonthill," Tolefree interposed, "I want to spare you the needless trouble of vain inventions. The young man is your son. You don't want me to tell you what that means. The chief facts are that he was well acquainted with Blenkinsop, that he sprang from nowhere into Westport while Blenkinsop was there, and that he was within a few yards of Blenkinsop about the time when he died—"

"But — !"

"Don't misunderstand me," Tolefree pursued. "I'm making no charge against him – even in my mind. I've been blunt because it's better than beating about the bush. Evidently your son has been in touch with you—"

"How, sir—"

"Don't deny it, Mr. Fonthill. It's so obvious. I want you to persuade him that he'd better come out in the open and tell us all he knows."

"But, Mr. Tolefree – it's absurd to suppose that Bill's concealing anything important. Bill and Blenkinsop were close friends."

Mr. Fonthill had got back his aplomb. He was no longer the frightened parent, but the silver-haired lord of the manor in command of the situation.

Tolefree said, "I suggest merely that he should come out in the open – tell us why he was at Westport, whether he saw Blenkinsop, and why he had in his pocket after Blenkinsop's death a photograph of Blenkinsop's wife given by her to her husband."

For an instant Mr. Fonthill blanched. Then he answered, "I can continue the discussion only on one condition – that you accept from me the statement that I know nothing of Bill's whereabouts."

"If you say so, I accept it. Of course," said Tolefree.

"Very well. Then I think I'll tell you something about my son. He was head over heels in love with Viola before she married Blenkinsop. All the young men were. Bill's was a particularly bad case. But I believe he was a loyal friend. He never forgot her. He bore Blenkinsop no malice. Her death upset him badly. Since that time, though, whatever griefs he had he nursed in private. I can't imagine how he got hold of the photograph – unless Blenkinsop sent it to him."

"Ah – that's possible in the circumstances. Did they write to each other?"

"So far as I know Blenkinsop sent only one letter, about the time his wife died. He may have put in the picture. Not likely, though. There may have been other letters. I can't say. Bill's been living in London for two years."

"Where?" said Tolefree.

"Why would you want to know?"

"Because don't you see? London's the best concealment a man can have. No one has thought of London in connection with your son. He may even now be in his rooms, unconscious of any hunt for him."

Tolefree had certainly laid that on thick. The last we knew of Fonthill was as a fugitive who escaped from Mrs. Rawling's window and must be well aware that there would be a hue and cry after him. But Mr. Fonthill appeared to detect no guile.

"Perhaps you're right," he said, "you can discover. His address is 57, Half Moon Street."

That startled me. Tolefree gave no sign.

"Thanks," he said. "You mentioned that he's been in London two years. Before that? – here with you?"

"Yes. Since he came down from the University, Bill's had a disappointing life, Mr. Tolefree. A cardiac trouble prevented him from playing the games he liked. He just scraped through with a poor degree. Then there was Viola. And now the war – the army doctors won't look at him."

"Well, that's a tale of woe! Too bad, Mr. Fonthill. You'll be interested to know that Farrar here championed your son from the first – refused to have a single suspicion."

Mr. Fonthill looked at me with a lift of the eyebrows and his first hint of a smile.

I said, "I thought the young man wasn't the type to be mixed up in a plot. He'd been under stress of some sort, and he'd had a knock on the head. I thought the two together might account for a certain eccentricity – that's all."

"It sounds like common sense to me," said Fonthill's father. "Bill's not eccentric by nature – only too anxious to be perfectly correct and conventional. He certainly wouldn't be mixed up in a plot. 'Twould horrify him."

"Climbing down the ivy in the dark from a window high above the ground," said Tolefree, "couldn't have been particularly good for his cardiac trouble."

Mr. Fonthill flushed a deep red. I thought he was going to explode. But he got control of himself immediately and said, quietly, "You're right. It couldn't."

"I came in the hope that you might have had some communication with your son since he left Westport," Tolefree told him; "a visit, a letter, a hint of any sort—"

"None whatever," came the curt answer. He was disliking the inquisition more and more.

"A pity. Of course you'd help us if you could." Tolefree said this in the tone of a challenge. The old gentleman's eyes sparked under the dark eyebrows. It was too much for him.

"I'm not sure I should," he declared. "If my son's the person you're searching for I feel certain you're searching for the wrong person. I don't know that I should do anything to put him in jeopardy – or even in the unpleasantness of any association, however remote, with a foul crime."

Whereupon Tolefree cooed like any sucking dove. He said he understood perfectly how Mr. Fonthill felt. "I should probably feel just like that in the same position. But you misinterpret me. What we want from your son is information about what he saw or heard in the corridor of the hotel and an explanation of his sudden, and, if I may say so, unconventional leave-taking."

Mr. Fonthill winced at that.

"I regret that I cannot help you," he said, and his voice had a kind of doxology ring in it. He wanted us to go. But Tolefree hadn't yet got what he needed. He made, as he confessed afterwards, a shot in the dark.

"I wonder whether Mrs. Fonthill has had any communication with him, but of course, you'd know of that."

"I certainly should, and you may take it from me that Mrs. Fonthill hasn't. She is—" He hesitated, and I had a moment's ghastly fear that he was going to say she was dead. But no. "Mrs. Fonthill is away from Stowford."

"Ah, well," said Tolefree, "we're much indebted to Colonel Franklin for his introduction. And thanks to you for receiving us so kindly, Mr. Fonthill."

Tolefree spoke without any intimation of irony, but I could swear that the lord of the manor was on the verge of losing his temper. However, he held himself in admirably. He inclined his head at Tolefree and rang the bell. A maid came to show us out. We made our exit in state, passing through the portals of Stowford to enter them no more.

"Nice old boy – and plucky," said Tolefree as we set off down the drive. "But lying thirteen to the dozen. Astonishing what even churchwardens will do to defend their offspring. If our job were not so desperately serious, Farrar I could find it in me to run behind the lord of the manor's chariot and cheer. As it is, though, how do we circumvent him?"

"Well, do we? In what?"

"In getting hold of the offspring before the parent has time to shift him from wherever he is."

Tolefree had evidently made up his mind that Mr. Fonthill was completely in the secrets of his son. I asked how he'd reached that point.

"Obvious when we got into the room. He was prepared for our business, had his part rehearsed to a syllable. He resents us. But he holds his horses tight. He's not giving away a point. His line is that he's heard nothing of Bill all this time. But the surprises we sprung on him were no surprises at all. He did a neat bit of character-acting in the rôle of the Spartan father.

But it was acting. I wager that he knows where Bill is now, and as soon as he can get the wires buzzing Bill will know exactly how far we've reached in our chase. But we've still a card up our sleeves – the queen. Did you notice the bit of comedy that followed my mention of Mrs. Fonthill? How he baulked just as he seemed on the point of telling us where to find her?"

I nodded.

"And finally informed us that she was 'away'? If she was innocent of any knowledge of Bill's goings-on, and of his hiding-place, he'd have made no mystery of it. It takes a fast one to get past the lord of the manor, but we've got to swing him down a snorter."

I didn't quite see how we were to get in this lightning delivery, but Tolefree said there were more ways of finding out what a woman was up to than asking her husband.

And so it proved when, at the Stowford Arms, before we sat down to lunch he made a telephone call to Mrs Wollaston at Stowgate. He came back triumphant.

"Mrs. Fonthill is in Wales, Farrar. She's a Welshwoman. Her people were Celtic chieftains in the old days and owned a considerable bit of mountain. Some of it remains to their descendants. Mrs. Fonthill has gone to Bwlch-y-Groes. If I get the name right. She departed four days ago. You will remember that Mr. William Hasty Fonthill hurriedly left the hospitable farm of Mr. Rawlings two days before that. Now, put it together and tell me what we're going to do next."

I said, "I suppose we're off to the Welsh mountains by the next train?"

"Wizard!" laughed Tolefree. "You hole out in one."

But he was the wizard. He did what I could never have done. He called petrol from the vasty deep and it did come – in a large and powerful car. Colonel Franklin, of course. When we had finished lunch a car stood at the door with a policeman beside it, and the man-of-all work of the hotel had put our bags in the back. Tolefree, who had been at the telephone, came out.

"Mr. Tolefree?" said the constable, and, being satisfied, saluted and stood back.

"You're driving, Farrar," said Tolefree softly, "and don't forget to step on it. Shrewsbury the first stop."

So expeditiously and simply began the last lap of the hunt for Fonthill. I had given up being surprised at anything Tolefree did. In a mizmaze, and with a feeling of sharp excitement, I took the driver's seat of the big, fast car. Five minutes after we had left the table I let in the clutch and started on what was my first long drive for more than a year.

There was a thrill in being on the road again in something that could move. Tolefree unfolded a map and studied it.

"Shrewsbury is between ninety and a hundred miles. We should be there by what time, Farrar?"

Pretty clear roads. A vehicle with sixty horses in its innards. No stinting of the juice: "Oh, five o'clock, I daresay."

"And this place with the unpronounceable name is about sixty miles beyond. What time there?"

I abandoned the fleeting idea of protesting against being rushed further into the mystery of Robert Blenkinsop; but I reminded myself that I was on a holiday, and I gently mentioned the fact to Tolefree.

"I don't propose to go haring through the country at sixty," said I. "At any rate indefinitely, without pause for rest and refreshment. Tea at Shrewsbury is indicated. Say twenty minutes. Beyond that the roads get hillier and hillier and rougher and rougher. Say half-past seven."

"Splendid," said Tolefree. "Take half an hour for tea if you like."

I settled down to a steady fifty.

2

Keeping to the A roads for speed we had to pass through several towns in crossing from the vale of Avon to the Severn valley by Evesham and Worcester, and then went on to the ancient border town of Ludlow, and, by way of Church Stretton in its lovely vale, to Shrewsbury. I pulled up at a teashop in the main street at five exactly. We had tea and moved on at a quarter past.

So far, in our own experience, no incident had marked the journey. But something had happened outside our knowledge.

From Shrewsbury to Oswestry is between sixteen and seventeen miles of good road. Some five miles out I overtook a large, ancient Daimler driven by a chauffeur at a sedate forty in the middle of the road. I hooted it into the side, and passed.

"Gosh!" said Tolefree. "Did you see?"

"What?"

"Why, the lord of the manor, Farrar, complete with Daimler and chauffeur! Quick work, eh?"

"Sure?"

"No mistake. It was Fonthill."

"Did he see us?"

"I'm certain he didn't. He was looking out at the near window. What a determined old boy! Not content with a wire. He must have heard that we'd gone off in a police car and shot after us."

"I think not, Tolefree," said I. "If he'd waited till he heard that, he'd have had to push the old 'bus along at sixty to get here in the time. I doubt it. Started before us, and I bet we passed him in Worcester without knowing it."

"I bow to your superior judgment. At that gait, how long will he take to get there?"

"He won't be able to keep that gait all the way. Two hours and a half at least – may be three."

"Well, then, imagine you're on Brooklands in peacetime and get there in an hour. We've got to catch Barrett's bird before his cockalorum can get at him." Tolefree had the map on his knee. "Here! – we can by-pass Oswestry, can't we?"

I knew the road as far as Bala. I could keep a high speed to Llangollen, and even to Bala, but after that the way was into a tangle of mountains with roads that looked impossible at more than ten miles an hour.

"Same for him," said Tolefree. "Drive like the devil as far as you can."

Tolefree manifested an excitement unusual for him. He seemed to have forgotten or put aside all thought of Horridge's theories. It was as though he knew without doubt that Fonthill had the key of the Blenkinsop puzzle. I put the engine flat out on every favourable stretch of road.

"I don't care for driving like this," I told him. "You're dreadfully keen on Fonthill, aren't you?"

"Yes. Fonthill has the secret. Fonthill is the secret. Everything shows it – most of all the lord of the manor's unblushing taradiddles – and his sudden journey. You can't miss it."

"You may be right," said I.

We rolled westward behind our smooth-purring engine at a great pace to Llangollen and Corwen, where we pulled up to fill the tank. Tolefree had conjured petrol coupons from somewhere. We reached the town of Bala at a quarter after six, and that was fifty miles in the hour. I had no doubt we'd left the Daimler far in the rear.

Down the neat main street, out along the north shore of the lake, five miles more in as many minutes, with hardly a glance at the scenery growing wilder and grander in every mile.

Tolefree stopped me at a crossroads by the western end of the lake to look at the map.

Bwlch-y-Groes lay almost due south. A mere track was marked. But the road to the south, though narrow, looked practicable for the car. We could try it, I said. We wound for two or three miles into a deep valley with rocky heights towering two thousand feet over us on the east and more on the west, where the twin peaks of Aran Benllyn and Aran Fawddwy rose. I had often seen them from the estuary at Dolgellau, but never thus close. Black against the evening light they looked harsh and forbidding.

Our road, which worsened at every half-mile, dipped into the bottom of the valley and began to climb the eastern side. Its surface disappeared. It became a mere cutting from the naked rock. It narrowed till it was a mere shelf covered with loose shingle. Rounding a corner where I could see it reaching in a serpentine towards the sky, I said to Tolefree,

"Doesn't look too good to me."

"But here's the name on the map, and the road to it marked," he protested. "If the lord of the manor can do it, why not we?"

"I shouldn't think a vehicle had passed this way in years," said I. "Anyhow, there's no going back. I couldn't turn, and I certainly wouldn't drive down in reverse. Let's go on."

But I warned him that if it got much worse we'd have to abandon Colonel Franklin's car and leave him to get it out as best he could. Tolefree said,

"This is just your famous pessimism flowering like edelweiss in the mountains, Farrar. Get on. I bet you do it. Think of the lord of the manor's Daimler!"

"There's one thing I can assure you, Tolefree," I retorted. "The lord of the manor never did and never will come up here in his Daimler. If he comes at all there must be some other road."

I let in the clutch and crawled in bottom gear like a big fly up a wall. It was all very well for Tolefree. He sat next to the wall; I was driving within half a yard of a sheer precipice a thousand feet deep.

There came, indeed, within five minutes of that halt, a place where I refused to drive farther. The shelf narrowed at a bend and sloped outwards. I could not see what was beyond. I was not going to risk taking Tolefree, the car and myself over the edge.

"Finish," said I.

He had to admit that it didn't look healthy. He spread the map on his knees and studied it. Then he took the glass from his suitcase and through it scanned the gorge that lay between us and Aran Benllyn. He passed the glass to me.

"Look at the map first, Farrar. Here's Bwlch-y-Groes. Bwlch means a pass, I believe. It must be the divide between the Dee and the Dovey, see? Never a house up that way. But over there, the other side of the valley – look through the glass. A green patch below the neck between the two mountains – a wood. Got it?"

I had got it and in front of it, facing us, a grey stone house so much the colour of the mountain that the naked eye did not pick it out.

"A house," said Tolefree, "means that there must be a way of getting to it."

That was easy. Through the glass I could see a narrow way between low stone walls following the course of a little torrent coming down the mountain side. I traced it to the bottom of the valley where it crossed the larger stream by a ford, and curled up our side till it was lost behind a projection of the hill. I pointed it out to Tolefree.

"It must join this track farther up," I suggested.

"Good enough," said he. "*Nous-y-sommes!*"

We weren't quite; but it was worth a trial. "Then – we leave the car here?"

"We certainly do. We go to look for that track. And it's positively impossible for the lord of the manor to get there before us. Leave the bags in the car, lock up, take out whatever part of the machinery the regulations demand—"

"The rotor arm—"

"What a vocabulary it is! Take out the rotor-arm and put it in your pocket. Then if the lord of the manor turns up he can't get by," Tolefree chortled – quite unjustifiably as it proved.

The car stood so close to the edge of the cliff that I couldn't get out to lock the door. I did it from the inside, and squeezed with Tolefree between the near side and the rock wall.

On foot the shelf was quite adequate and safe. It would have been all right even for a horse. Immediately we rounded the bend in front the secret of the track to the house under the wood

stood revealed. Instead of on a right-angled precipice we moved
upon the side of a slope where the mountain receded from the
valley as though a great wedge had been gouged out of it. Our
road went round in an arc and a mile farther up, in the middle
of the arc the track from the house below Aran Benllyn ran into
it.

Everything was now plain sailing. We walked on.

The great defile seemed to be empty of any life but ours. Not
a sheep or a goat could find a living on those naked rocks even if
they could keep a footing. But somewhere on the other side in a
spot now hidden from us by a trick of the land were people who
would resent intrusion. I had given a thought more than once
to the sort of reception Tolefree expected to get when he did run
Fonthill down in the bosom of his own tribe. Such extravagant
terms came to mind in so wild a region. As we walked on,
glancing down now and then for a sight of the track to the
house, some such idea must have shot into Tolefree's head.

"His mother was a Miss Lloyd," he said suddenly. "The
Lloyds – great fighting race, aren't they?"

I could have told him about Camerons or Macdonalds, but
I knew nothing of Lloyds. I said, "All mothers are great fighters
when their children are in danger. But you aren't going to fight
her, are you? You're going to display your famous powers of
spell-binding and have her eating out of your hand in two ticks."

Tolefree pulled up for a breather. This ascent was steep as we
neared the top of the pass.

"Thank you for those few kind words," said he. And then,
"Hello – look there."

We were approaching the middle of the arc. Tolefree had
turned to look back over the trail. From this point, which itself
had been invisible to us, hidden in the protective clothing of the
hills, the bonnet of our car was in sight.

Someone was there... Two people were there, clambering
round it, peering into it... Tolefree took the glass from his pocket
and focused on the car.

"Well, well! If it isn't our lord of the manor and his chauffeur! So the Daimler did get up after all."

He handed the glass to me. I still didn't believe the Daimler could have navigated that road. If by some miracle it had got up, it certainly couldn't come any further, and I doubted whether it could go back. Through the glass Mr. Fonthill's figure and his silver hair were quite distinct. With the chauffeur he stood pointing through the windscreen to the interior of the car. Suddenly they turned. Tolefree went down against the rock face and dragged me with him.

"Let's leave them guessing," he said, "whether we're here if they don't know, or our whereabouts if they do."

I supposed it was not the first time a car had stuck on that road. There was nothing about either of our suitcases to show who we were. The car itself was registered in Gloucester. Mr. Fonthill would have no reason to suspect that we were concerned.

"Except," said Tolefree, when I suggested this, "that he's an uncommonly knowing old gentleman. You can see now why he bolted off on a chase of a hundred and fifty miles instead of having his leisurely lunch topped off with a Corona as usual. He could be here in his Daimler before ever a telegram would have reached the place, even if it got delivered today at all."

"Telephone?" said I.

"No telephone. I looked for wires through the glass. There aren't any. The lord of the manor certainly suspects that we may be somewhere in the offing. But" – Tolefree had raised himself and applied the glass to his eyes again, and was peering down the track – "but he's gone back, Farrar. He'll find some other way. Up to us to get to the house before him. *En avant!*"

We resumed our walk up the side of the still and empty valley. It was now after seven o'clock. It had taken us nearly an hour to cover the few miles from Bala. Thanks to the ingenuity of the late Mr. Willett we had yet more than an hour of light in front of us, though the high mountains to the west cut off the setting sun and left the whole scene in shadow. We reached in three or four hundred yards the point where the track from the other side of the ravine debouched, and began the descent. It was a mere cart-track, impracticable for motors, and giddily steep. It wound by a sinuous route to the stream a thousand feet below. About half way down we found ourselves on a projecting escarpment which gave a view not only of the scoop in the mountain-side where the grey house stood, but of the valley up which we had come.

And we were no longer in an empty scene.

Tolefree, exclaiming, pointed to the house. In front of its bleak plain façade a little terrace had been cut or built and clothed with turf. On it stood a figure. Above the figure a white handkerchief waved.

"Take cover," said Tolefree.

Prone on the ground, peeping over the edge of the cliff, we watched. I had a momentary thought that the signal might be for us. Tolefree, looking through the glass, said no. The man was gazing down the valley as he waved. Tolefree's binoculars moved slowly round.

"Ah!" he muttered, and handed the glass to me. "You'll see the problem nearly at the bottom, on the road we came up."

What I saw was a pair of horsemen. Their mounts seemed to be glued to the side of the cliff. Actually they were standing on the rock-shelf. One of the men waved a handkerchief. As I looked the signalling ceased. The riders went on down the road, the horses picking their way carefully over the shale. They disappeared round a bend.

"So you were right about the Daimler," said Tolefree. "The lord of the manor knows his onions. He must have left the Daimler in Bala, got horses, and then found himself blocked by our car. Is he well and truly stymied? Or can he get round another way?"

I felt certain there must be a track of sorts on the northern side of the valley, Tolefree nodded.

"Well, we get a little grace. Let's make the most of it. The fellow over there has gone in. We might creep near the place without being seen."

Creep! What was the need for stealing up to the house unobserved? "Tolefree," said I, "you're enjoying this – like a boy playing I-spy."

He laughed. "It's a good game. You don't forget that young Fonthill's a slippery customer? If he knew we were within ten miles of him he'd shift his quarters on the instant. Don't want to miss him this time. If we can get down to the stream unseen, I guess there'll be cover enough for the climb up the other side."

It seemed likely.

"That wasn't Fonthill waving, was it?" I asked.

"No. An elderly man, stocky little chap with a beard. A Lloyd, I expect. I have a notion that the Lloyds are tough guys, Tolefree. Also wily guys. It's going to be interesting."

In the event, our visit to the ancestral abode of the Lloyds certainly didn't lack interest. Before we reached the stream the house had disappeared from sight. The crossing was a ford at a point where the torrent broadened and shallowed. On the upper side of it, stepping stones allowed us to get across dry-shod. The track then followed the stream downwards for a hundred yards or so before turning up into the combe which fed it with a tiny tributary. Here the greenery began. Both sides of the brook were clothed with ash and thorn and sycamore, which even thus early in the spring, gave us cover as we climbed. We saw no one, and believed ourselves unseen, before we came to the gate which ended the track and opened upon a yard at the side of the grey house. It looked like a farm place though there were no signs and no possibility of cultivation. Long sheds bordered the yard on one side and at a right angle to them stood a range of stables. There was a smell of horses.

"A strange place," Tolefree murmured.

"Sheep farm," I suggested.

But we had no time for speculation. If nobody had seen us we must have been heard. For, as we stood at the gate, a man came across the yard – clearly the stocky man who had waved from the terrace. He might have been sixty years of age. He was dark, his beard and hair almost black with a peppering of grey, his eyes an intense and shining brown, his forehead broad, his nose long and straight.

"Good evening," he said. "Have you lost your way? Will you come in, now?"

His voice was a soft baritone. He spoke in a cultured way, but with a marked Welsh accent which was quite pleasant.

"In a sense," said Tolefree, "we have lost our way. Thank you," as the gate was opened and we stepped through. "We had the misfortune to take a very bad road over the hill opposite and went on till the car could go no farther. This was the only house we saw, so we struggled down to it."

"I thought as much. You're not the first, indeed. The Bwlch-y-Groes is deceptive. Only fit for young harum-scarums with motor bicycles or sports cars. You must be tired. Come in."

He led the way through a wicket-gate to the front of the house and a path behind the patch of lawn edged with cupressus where we had seen him standing. Both Tolefree and I gasped at the view from this eyrie. We stood stock-still to look.

"What a place!" said Tolefree.

"The builders of this knew where to put their house," said I.

The old gentleman looked as pleased as Punch.

"It is a view much admired," said he. "But you should really see it in the morning light. Will you come in now and take a little refreshment?"

Tolefree thanked him for the courtesy; but, said he, we came for information, and as night was coming on we had better discover where our destination lay and get there as soon as possible.

The host insisted. We could have something to eat and drink before we went on. "And can I help you to locate your destination?" said he. I thought he smiled over the formality.

"Why, yes, no doubt," Tolefree said, "we are looking for the house of a Mr. Lloyd – Mr. John Lloyd – which, we are told, is near the Bwlch-y-Groes."

"It is indeed. So you are looking for Mr. John Lloyd? You need look no farther. He is now speaking to you."

3

Tolefree's acting as he expressed astonishment at his good fortune was superb. I played up to him as best I could. If the worthy Mr. Lloyd was not deceived that was certainly not our fault.

For the present he seemed as pleased as we pretended to be. He declared that, whatever business we had to do with him, nothing must be done till our physical man had been seen to.

He shepherded us into the house. That was another surprise. It seemed a dull, gloomy, flat-fronted place from the outside, as harsh as the mountains around it. It had a fitness in that respect, for, built of the stone dug on the spot it looked as though it had grown out of the hillside on a little terrace.

But the interior was beautiful. We entered from the canopied stone porch a small hall, a square apartment with naked stone walls, but furnished with fine things in black oak and gay rugs and cushions. A great log burned in the chimney place. A staircase ascended on the left-hand and turned into a gallery running across the back of the room. Below it, each side of the hearth, were two deep chesterfields, the only concession to modern comfort in the place. No one was there.

He led us through the hall and a passage behind it to a washroom where he left us with the astonishing remark,

"Dinner's ready to be served. We don't dress for dinner since the war began. I'll see you in the hall. My brother-in-law, Mr. Fonthill, will be here in an hour or two, but we shall not wait dinner for him."

I stared at Tolefree as the door closed.

"A plunge right into the middle of things," he said, with a grin. "Beginning to be interesting already, don't you think?"

It made me speechless.

"What's the betting he'll produce young Fonthill at dinner, Farrar? That would be a glorious climax to our misadventure."

I muttered something about having stumbled into a devil of a hole. Suppose Fonthill was not there? How could we explain our business to Mr. Lloyd?

"I imagine Mr. Lloyd knows all about it already," he answered. "He has a glint in the eye. He's amused. Anything may happen in a place like this, Farrar. We're going to be vastly entertained."

Tolefree's guess was better than mine.

The old gentleman waited for us in the hall and took us to a drawing room where several people stood about – and among them, sure enough, William Hasty Fonthill. A maid held a tray of cocktails.

Lloyd made a sign and a lady, slimmer, than he, but just as dark, came forward.

"Gwyneth," he said, "these are the two gentlemen who lost themselves in the pass. Mr. — ?"

Tolefree gave his name and mine.

"Mr. Tolefree and Mr. Farrar – Mrs. Lloyd." He made the introductions. "And Mrs. Fonthill," of the second lady. "And Mr. James Lloyd, my brother," of a man much like himself but younger. "And Mr. Bill Fonthill. Now you all know each other."

We bowed and nodded. Tolefree said,

"I've had the pleasure of meeting Mr. Fonthill before," and held out his hand. Fonthill took it. "A much less pleasant occasion, though. In the midst of a frightful calamity. But no doubt he's told you—"

"The escape from the blitz? Really!" said his mother. "Horrible! Bill doesn't like talking about it."

"I'm sure he doesn't," Tolefree put a world of sympathy into that.

But the others did like talking about it. They showered questions on us. Tolefree gave them a little picture of it, said we had taken Mr. Fonthill away from the danger zone for the night, and hoped that he'd quite recovered from the shock.

Fonthill, who behaved calmly, said, "Quite." He was a very different person here from the cowering, shivering young man we had seen at Westport and the fugitive who had climbed out of Mrs. Rawlings's window. He had the air of being at home, secure, confident among these people. The simile of the tribe came forcibly to me now. This really was a tribe. They were all Lloyds but Fonthill, and he was half a Lloyd. They had a strong family likeness. There was a sort of secret understanding between them. If we seriously challenged the tribe I felt certain it would fight.

The cocktails disappeared. A sign passed between the maid and Mrs. Lloyd. Lloyd said, "We shall go in now. Mr. Tolefree, will you take my wife? Mr. Farrar, will you take Mrs. Fonthill?"

Thus we made procession across the hall to the dining room. A table laid for eight was lit by shaded electric lamps. A log fire murmured on a big open hearth. Mrs. Lloyd placed us. Tolefree was on her right, next to Fonthill at one end of the table. I was on her left, opposite Mrs. Fonthill, Lloyd himself sat fronting his wife, with James Lloyd between him and Fonthill. A vacant seat at the end of the table next to me was reserved for the lord of the manor when he should appear.

The host briefly apologised for a scanty menu which he put down to the war (and entirely approved), and for the fact that the cook and one maid were the only two servants he had left (also a perfectly proper arrangement in war-time).

But a good dinner was well served. Tolefree deliberately set himself to keep the talk on Wales and its mountains, and away from the business which had brought us there. He was completely successful, for he contrived to get the Lloyd men launched on the topic of their ancestral history, and this astonishing house in the wilds. It had been an ancient place, though

not much of the present building was more than two hundred
years old. A Lloyd house stood there "when Harlech Castle
was built." Lloyds had been in this fastness before that and
ever since. In the days when everybody rode horseback it was
not a particularly inaccessible place. Now that everybody rode
in motor cars, it was. But that did not matter to the Lloyds.
They still rode horseback. It was still possible to bring the things
they needed up the pass and across to the house by cart. They
had farms in the lower part of the valley. They ran sheep on
the mountains. They were perfectly self-centred and perfectly
happy.

I listened to all this with an irritating feeling of its unreality.
Tolefree was out of my line of sight and Mrs. Lloyd kept him
pretty busy answering questions. But there were two people at
the table who in that moment failed to be interested either in
Lloyd history or in Lloyd activity in the war drive for farm pro-
duction. They were Mrs. Fonthill who faced me, and Fonthill
himself, neighbouring Tolefree and disliking the neighbourhood very much.

The vision of a terrible corpse being dug out of the smouldering ruin at Westport was in the background of my thoughts
while I made some sort of answer to the remarks Mrs. Fonthill
threw across the table to me. Tolefree had cleverly made a point
of that scene in the talk before dinner. It became the central
feature of the blitz – entirely out of proportion but vividly
effective. I had not the slightest doubt that Fonthill knew why
that was done. I thought his mother knew also. Maybe all the
Lloyds knew.

An extreme uneasiness came upon me. I felt that we were
alien to these people and that they were hostile to us. If, as I
imagined, Fonthill after escaping from the house of Rawlings
had made his way immediately to his home, told the story to
his people and asked his father's advice, then it was plain that
the family had thought he would be secure from pursuit if he
disappeared into the Bwlch-y-Groes and his mother came here

with him. What could be safer than such a fastness, in the heart of the tribe, and no doubt with henchmen handy who would obey orders to the last gasp?

Perhaps we had done better, when Lloyd pressed his hospitality upon us, to fear the Greeks bringing gifts. Within a few hours I came to that conclusion: there was no perhaps about it. But for the present, if they were all aware of us and knew why we had come, they gave no sign. Once during dinner the serving-maid entered to whisper something in Lloyd's ear. He excused himself to us and went out. He was back in three minutes and took up the talk where he had left it. But only momentarily, for Tolefree, thrusting into a brief silence, said across the table,

"Oh, Mrs. Fonthill, I believe you knew a young man in whom I take great interest – Robert Blenkinsop. A neighbour of yours, wasn't he?" The effect of this question was remarkable. The name of Blenkinsop dropped on the table like a bomb. Everyone was startled. Mrs. Fonthill faltered, "Ye-s, I knew Mr. Blenkinsop some years ago."

No one else spoke. Lloyd sat back in his chair, regarding Tolefree with a sombre deliberation. Tolefree seemed to leave the subject. But it was only to drop another bomb.

"Fonthill," he said, "was that your father arrived just now? I heard horses."

Before Fonthill could answer, Lloyd said, "No – that was a messenger from one of the farms. I went out to speak to him. You needn't expect Henry till the morning, my dear," he addressed his sister. "He won't ride up in the dark."

Tolefree flung a third bomb. "If he's not here now, I shan't be surprised, Mrs. Fonthill, if he doesn't ride up at all."

"I really don't know what you mean," she said.

"You see, he came only because he expected to get here before we did. As we happened to arrive first there would be little point in finishing the journey."

An outrageous infraction of the decencies of the occasion. Tolefree admitted it afterwards. But it produced the effect he wanted. Lloyd said without temper,

"Well, Mr. Tolefree, doesn't that bring us naturally to your reason for wishing to see me?"

"What makes you think that, sir?"

"I answer the question with another. How do you know anything of Mr. Fonthill's motive – or intention in paying me a visit?"

"It's a deduction from facts. Farrar and I called upon Mr. Fonthill this morning and communicated to him some information, most of which he had already—"

"You called on him!" Lloyd was taken aback.

"We asked him for some information in return," Tolefree continued, not heeding the exclamation, "which he said he hadn't got. So we had to go elsewhere for it. When we obtained it we set out on our journey to see you. But we discovered that, even before we started for Bwlch-y-Groes, Mr. Fonthill was on the road. We overtook and passed him. Our mishap on the track through the pass had a curious result. It allowed us to arrive here several hours before Mr. Fonthill possibly could arrive."

"How's that?" Lloyd asked.

"Well, you see, Mr. Fonthill was wiser than we. He left his car somewhere before reaching the pass and he and his man took to horses. They meant to come here by the road up the pass; but when they reached our stranded car it occupied the full width of the track, and no horse could possibly squeeze by. They had to go back to the end of the valley and find some other way."

"You seem exceptionally well-informed about Mr. Fonthill's proceedings, if I may say so."

"I know no more than anyone else would have known who saw what I saw," said Tolefree. "Farrar and I, when we had decided to walk on, observed Mr. Fonthill and his chauffeur examining our car. We did not then know whether he'd driven his Daimler up to that point or not. Anyhow, he couldn't pass, and he returned. Later on, getting a view over the valley, we saw them on horseback going down. We also saw Mr. Fonthill signalling to somebody somewhere. Probably to one of the farms, should you think?"

"Probably," said Lloyd, quite calmly. "Well, Mr. Tolefree, you will now perhaps tell us why there is no point in Mr. Fonthill's visit to us because you have arrived before him?"

"Willingly, in general terms," Tolefree responded. "It is because he was coming to prevent me from ascertaining what I have now learned."

"General terms is pretty apt, I am thinking," Lloyd said, drily. "I would like you to be more particular."

Tolefree said he had no objection to being particular to the last detail. "But is this the time? – I mean, are these the circumstances?" he asked, with a glance round the table.

"We have no secrets from one another, if that's what you mean. You can speak freely. I intend that you shall speak freely."

Tolefree raised his eyebrows at the tone of the last sentence. "Very well. I'll tell you all I think essential. It shall be what I told Mr. Fonthill this morning – the thing that caused him to get out his car on the instant and make for Bwlch-y-Groes. I think you know some of it already. The rest, I should warn you, will not be pleasant hearing."

That seemed to make Lloyd cogitate. But when he answered, it was to say,

"Never mind. Let us hear it."

"Fonthill," said Tolefree, turning to the young man, "do you agree?

"It's a matter of complete indifference to me," Fonthill replied.

His voice startled me. This was the first time I had heard him say more than one word since he groaned, "But you can't!" in the police office at Westport. He was as different now in tone as in appearance and manner. Tolefree had said,

"You may not be so indifferent presently." He turned to Lloyd. "The reason why Farrar and I came here was to discover whether, as we believed, young Mr. Fonthill was here. We had no intention of inflicting ourselves on your hospitality. A little talk with Mr. Fonthill himself would have sufficed."

Said Lloyd, with a look round the tribe, "No person has ever come to this door without being offered rest and refreshment. Disregard it, Mr. Tolefree."

"I can't quite do that. I should have said nothing of these matters except to Fonthill if you had not insisted. You know that we took charge of Mr. Fonthill on the night of the blitz and carried him away to a place of safety in the country?"

Lloyd nodded.

"But do you know how we first met him?"

"They don't," said Fonthill, "and I see no need for you to tell them."

"If that's so, I have finished," declared Tolefree.

"Indeed you have not," Lloyd said decisively. "We wish to know everything. It is not for Bill to decide what I shall be told."

The tribal Chieftain spoke.

Mrs. Fonthill chimed in, "Bill, you must see that we've got to know."

Tolefree still looked to Fonthill. He shrugged his shoulders and said, "All right."

"Very well. Then, we first met you in the lobby of the hotel at Westport not many minutes before the blitz began. We fell over you in the darkness of the entrance and turned a torch on you. You'd had a crack on the head, and your temple was bleeding. You were apparently unconscious. We took you to a car, and in the car to the Report Centre of the Air Raid Precaution service, where you had first-aid. If you've not told your family that, I expect you've not told them why you were at Westport, what you were doing in the hotel, and how you came by that injury."

Fonthill was silent, but his was a truculent silence.

"And, if that's so, I expect you've spared their feelings in another way. You haven't said how or why you gave us the slip by getting out of the window at Mr. Rawlings's house and making tracks for home. You have undoubtedly told them you're in peril from the law. That's the reason why you're here, as you supposed, in safety. There's a police call out for you all over the country; but I imagine a policeman is a mighty rare object of the countryside in the Bwlch-y-Groes."

Fonthill still said nothing; but his uncle broke in,

"You speak of Bill giving you the slip, Mr. Tolefree. I do not see why he should not leave you in any way he pleased. What right had Mr. Tolefree to coerce Bill Fonthill into staying in any place where he disliked to be?"

"I had the right the law gives me. But I don't want to insist upon it. I'm not a policeman. We had treated Mr. Fonthill kindly. Perhaps we'd saved his life. Mr. Fonthill deceived us. He was urgently wanted to give information he alone possessed, which was of great importance to the country. He foxed. He pretended unconsciousness when he was quite conscious. Now, Mr. Lloyd, the game's up. Having discovered Mr. Fonthill we shan't lose sight of him again. He had better answer all the questions he's asked, and answer them truthfully."

Fonthill stared past Tolefree to the empty seat at the end of the table and said no word.

"That," remarked Lloyd, "is for Bill to decide. But I think you must tell us why any information he has is important to the country."

"I don't like imperatives," said Tolefree.

"Nor does Bill, it seems," Lloyd retorted.

"But, as I've told Fonthill's father I may as well tell you. I have already warned you that it won't be pleasant hearing. It concerns his friend Blenkinsop, a patriotic man bent on doing a great service to the country."

"What has Bill to do with Blenkinsop's death?"

"What indeed!" said Tolefree. "But he has told you of Blenkinsop's death or you couldn't have known. He made no secret of the fact that Blenkinsop did die at Westport?"

"No. Why would he have any idea of keeping it secret?"

"I don't know. What interests me is the fact that he told you. It is a remarkable fact."

"What's the riddle, Mr. Tolefree?"

"I shall be glad if you can solve it. Just this – how did he himself know that Blenkinsop was dead? The death of Blenkinsop was unknown when Mr. Fonthill escaped. No public mention has ever been made of it since. Yet Mr. Fonthill knew it and was able to tell you."

"Bill — ?"

Fonthill made no response to Lloyd's appeal. His mother stared at him pale with alarm. Mrs. Lloyd shuddered and moved a trifle away from Tolefree towards me.

Tolefree said, quietly, "Mr. Fonthill is indifferent. But his own conduct shows that before we found him in the doorway of the hotel he knew that Blenkinsop was dead. I want him to say how he knew. That is the question the police will ask when they come up with him."

"Bill!"

Lloyd's voice was a little unsteady.

Fonthill said to him, "I choose to say nothing to this man."

"If that's your last word, Fonthill," said Tolefree, "I propose now to tell the family what I told your father. It's the story of what happened in the Imperial Hotel at Westport on the night of the twenty-second of March..."

6

1

Tolefree told his story briefly but without missing a point. At the end the Lloyd family knew as much of the evidence as we did, save that Tolefree hadn't enlarged on our suspicion about the second body. That remained the body of a casual and unidentified man staying in the hotel. Nothing was said to them, any more than to the public at the inquest, of the way in which he came by his death.

But the story as they heard it stupefied them.

I watched Mrs. Fonthill across the table most of the time. Her sensitive face betrayed the paralysis of horror that stole upon her while fact after fact unfolded. Her distress as she glanced from Tolefree to her son at every mention of his name filled me with pity. Hers was the real tragedy that evening.

Fonthill himself glowered. True, he could not keep up the display of indifference. He followed every word closely. But he never interrupted, and at the end was silent.

Tolefree had finished up with our visit to Fonthill's father. He sat back and waited.

Their stupefaction made them dumb. Everyone else looked at Fonthill; but he was as dumb as they. Evidently he had told the family little of the truth: at the most that Blenkinsop had died in the fire (which wasn't true), that he had been the last man to see Blenkinsop alive, and that, for some reason he didn't understand, the police had him under suspicion.

Mr. Lloyd broke the long silence.

"Want to say anything about all this, Bill?"

Fonthill shook his head.

"Mr. Tolefree," Lloyd went on, "yours is a dreadful story. We had no inkling of it, but—"

"Excuse me," Tolefree broke in. "Fonthill hasn't answered the vital question: How did he know Blenkinsop was dead?"

"How can I answer it?"

"At least you can say what you understood from him about Blenkinsop's death."

"I have never talked with him of that," said Lloyd.

"No? Well – his mother. What did you understand, Mrs. Fonthill?"

"I don't think I want to answer any questions." She spoke in a trembled whisper.

"Now this, if I may say so, is all dam' nonsense!"

The loud exclamation startled the table. It came from James Lloyd and was his first contribution since the topic of Blenkinsop cropped up.

"James!" said Mrs. Lloyd, reprovingly.

"Forgive me, Gwyneth. I shouldn't have used an oath. But this is nonsense, nevertheless. Ridiculous! Mr. Tolefree, I will tell you what we understood, because, after all, may it not be the truth? Your evidence is thin. We understood that Bill had a letter from Bob Blenkinsop. He was ill at this hotel and asked Bill to go to him. Bill went. He found Blenkinsop unconscious, and rushed off to get a doctor—"

"One moment," said Tolefree. "Was Fonthill so familiar with Westport that he could rush away at an instant's notice, knowing where to find a doctor? And wouldn't it have been the most natural thing to tell the hotel people?"

"I do not know about that. But he never did find a doctor. He was knocked out by some person in the doorway whom he never saw. When he came to he found himself in custody – of yourself and others, at a police station, not knowing what you suspected of him—"

"Ah – a bald and unconvincing narrative," said Tolefree, with a side glance at Fonthill, sitting dumb. "Don't you see that this was before I or any of my friends knew anything had happened to Blenkinsop?"

"Yes – I see it now. But I couldn't have known it, could I? I give you what you asked for – the truth as we understood it. Bill found that you suspected him of something. He'd form a pretty sound opinion of your business and your status, wouldn't he? He panicked and took his chance of escaping from that house."

Tolefree shrugged. "The Lloyd family, if it will permit me, has a great deal of intelligence. Too much intelligence to understand anything so fantastic. Why does a man panic if he's merely on an errand of mercy? How could Fonthill have acquired any knowledge or opinion of our job. Do realise that, from the time when we picked him up in the doorway of the hotel till he vamoosed several hours later, he hardly said a dozen words, and we certainly said nothing in his presence which could have given him the faintest notion of our job?"

"Bill is not without intelligence," said James Lloyd.

"But he doesn't credit us with any," declared Tolefree. "I put a very simple proposition. The evidence shows that he was in the corridor close to Blenkinsop's room when Blenkinsop died. You now tell me that he did see Blenkinsop – that he himself thought he was the last man who saw Blenkinsop alive. I propose that he should now disclose every circumstance of his visit to Westport and tell us exactly what he saw in Blenkinsop's room – why he said nothing of it then – why he took the first opportunity of haring away."

"I think he should do so," said James Lloyd.

"But — !" The head of the house exploded the word. "But I do not know, James, that you are called upon to speak for the family." Mr. Lloyd, recovering his composure, began to assert his authority. His brother made a gesture of impatience and said, "Very well. I have spoken for myself."

"I am a magistrate, Mr. Tolefree," Mr. Lloyd continued. "I know that if Bill has decided to answer no questions and make no statement, you have no right to coerce him."

"Absolutely none," Tolefree agreed.

"Let us bring this to a head, then. Are you making any charge against him?"

"None whatever. It is not for me to make charges. But Fonthill is putting himself in a false position. He could help to clear up the fate of a man who died just when he was about to do the country a great service, as I said. The story he's told you can't be true, or rather it tells you a small part of the truth. It's quite certain that he knew before we found him that Blenkinsop was dead. I believe that's why he ran away. It's why he's here. I make no accusation. I ask him to give us valuable information which he possesses."

"Bill?" said Mr. Lloyd.

"I had nothing to do with Bob Blenkinsop's death, and that's all I'm going to say."

It was the longest speech I had heard from him. He addressed it to Lloyd.

"You knew how Blenkinsop died. You knew he'd been murdered. He was your friend."

Tolefree rapped out these short sentences. They had no effect on Fonthill. He continued to stare gloomily down the table at the empty chair.

"You had on you a photograph of Blenkinsop's wife which she gave to him soon after they were married. Where did you get that?"

Fonthill turned on Tolefree a look of anger and hatred, but said nothing. Tolefree sat back and fell silent. Mrs. Lloyd gave a look to her sister and rose. I went to the door and held it open as they went out. Lloyd made no sign. I returned to my place.

"We shall not sit up late, I think," Lloyd said. "Just a glass of port. James – will you pass it round? Impossible for you two gentlemen to get away tonight. I've arranged rooms for you."

Astonishing man! Not the least hint of annoyance or resentment, though Tolefree had as good as asked his nephew to defend himself against a suspicion of murder. His was hospitality in the grand manner. Tolefree murmured thanks – said we were being treated much better than we deserved.

"Not a bit," said Lloyd.

"You have your job to do," said his brother. "Your first visit to Welsh mountains?"

Thus abruptly did the talk shift away from Blenkinsop. A cigar followed the port. Fonthill refused a cigar, excused himself, and went away. Just as abruptly the talk came back to Blenkinsop.

"You've given us some surprises tonight," said Lloyd, addressing Tolefree. "All that business at Westport was unknown to us. Bill seems to be playing the fool – Heaven knows why. But he's a difficult boy. Not that I would believe for a moment he had anything to do with Blenkinsop's death. I assure you they were great friends. And, moreover, Bill's incapable of murdering anybody."

"We all think we are," said Tolefree, sententiously. "But I was inclined to think that too. And Farrar was certain of it, weren't you?" He turned to me.

"I couldn't see a murderer-type in Fonthill," I agreed. "I know you say there's no such thing as a murderer-type. But I felt as sure as Mr. Lloyd about this."

Tolefree said the whole idea was hateful to him; but he stuck to his point.

"Blenkinsop was murdered. I believe Fonthill knew he'd been murdered. There's some reason why he stalls about telling what he knows. He hasn't the shadow of a right to keep it back. I'm right in supposing that he's seen his father – and came here for sanctuary?"

Mr. Lloyd baulked at an answer. He sat looking at the burning tip of his cigar for a time.

"The Lloyds are clannish. Let's drop that part of the subject," he said at last. "Your story was terribly interesting, Mr. Tolefree. One part of it especially. You don't seem to set much store by the most striking thing in it – or what seems so to me."

"Oh? And what part is that?"

"Jackson," said Mr. Lloyd.

I started. Tolefree said, "Indeed? What of Jackson?"

Lloyd riposted with another question: "Do you know anything about Jackson?"

"Very little. Except that he's in the soft goods trade, and like everybody else in it is having a thin time at present. But you, Mr. Lloyd – it seems quite unlikely you'd know anything about Jackson."

"It does. But let's consider what we both know..."

I opened my eyes wider and wider as he went on till I was staring at him. He had Tolefree's narrative quite pat – all the points in it. He went over them one by one. Jackson, he said, was the least explained person of the piece. He turned up at Westport casually, and a few hours before the murder. The very fact that Tolefree had mentioned – that he was in a business which languished – made his visit to a distant provincial town remarkable. There was no evidence that he knew anyone in Westport. It was improbable that he had anything to sell. Did Tolefree really credit this soft goods story?

"I'm listening to you," said Tolefree. "Develop the argument. It interests me profoundly."

"Ah? Well, I disbelieve the soft goods story. If it isn't true, then you had better be getting after Mr. Jackson. He's the man you want – not Bill. He's the man who heard the shots, and apparently the only one. He's the only man on that corridor left alive, and he was there for – what was it – about three hours instead of a hurried few moments, like Bill. Did it ever occur to you that the reason why he heard them might be that he fired them himself? I should guarantee one of two things. Either he isn't called Jackson but is now masquerading as Jackson, or he's secretly connected in some way or other with the Blenkinsop affair."

I was about to speak. Tolefree gave me a warning glance.

"It's a theory," he said.

"Worth following up," said Lloyd. "There's another point. According to you, Bill rushed through the corridor. What was the word? – pounded through. Yet Jackson, sitting quietly in his room, writing, didn't hear anything. It is not possible, Mr. Tolefree," he ended with slow emphasis.

"I don't know about that," Tolefree protested. "In an hotel there's a lot of tramping about. You don't take particular notice of sounds outside your room if you're absorbed in work."

"You will not have it that way, evidently."

"Won't have it is too strong. I'm open to all ideas. There's one of yours which might be sound. I fancy we shall find Jackson is Jackson and not somebody else. But your second point – that he may have had some connection with the Blenkinsop affair. You mean that he may have known Blenkinsop was at the hotel?"

"Why not?"

"It's difficult. Blenkinsop went there secretly. He'd only just returned to England after five years abroad. So far as we know the only people who had any communication with Blenkinsop after he went to Westport were Farrar and Fonthill. Unless one of those two told Jackson, and Farrar certainly didn't – you see?"

"There's the other man – the one Blenkinsop picked up in Pernambuco."

"If there's any connection there we shall find it," said Tolefree. "It hasn't come in sight yet."

"I should have thought," said Mr. Lloyd, deliberately, "that a connection was particularly clear."

"Ah?" said Tolefree. "What do you see?"

"I see the second corpse you found in the ruins."

"Do you, indeed!" Tolefree was startled. He gave our host a wary look.

"You won't tell me you've never speculated on that Mr. Tolefree, will you?"

"One's speculations—" Tolefree spoke in a tone of contempt for speculation. "We had better stick to evidence. That man is quite unidentified, Mr. Lloyd. There was nothing left by which he could have been recognised by his own mother."

"Well, I shall not credit you with absolute indifference to a suggestive circumstance. In my opinion Bill's story explains Bill, whereas you have two men who are quite unexplained – Jackson and the second corpse. Now that you have found your way to Bill, we shall be quite content to wait upon events, Mr. Tolefree. Another glass of wine? If not, you must be greatly fatigued. Your rooms are ready for you. The ladies have gone to bed."

He rose and put an end to the remarkable symposium.

He stood up. Tolefree said, "We can't thank you enough for your courtesy. Could I stretch it another inch? I should like to telephone."

"Unfortunately we have no telephone," Lloyd answered. "There are no lines near. One of the penalties of living in the Bwlch-y-Groes. We aren't even in reach of the grid – have to make our own electricity. In the morning I could send a message for you to Bala."

Within ten minutes we were sitting in Tolefree's bedroom. The hospitality of Mr. Lloyd had run to the length of fires in both our rooms, which were side by side, and to a display of pyjamas and slippers. Tolefree filled and lit a pipe. We stretched in long chairs by the fire. Despite the blackout, which meant closed windows, the mountain air was keen.

"The clan Lloyd," said I, "is a close-knit organisation."

"You'd understand it, being a Scot. It's something new in my experience, Farrar. We're going to be done down if we aren't as sly as mountain cats. That old boy – did you ever — ?"

"Has his head screwed on tight," said I. "But he strikes me as a kind and honest old chap."

"Kind – yes. But his honesty has tribal limitations, don't you think? They'll fight like tigers for anybody with an ounce of Lloyd blood in his body. What strikes me is his cool astuteness. How he picked up the point that we hadn't explained the second corpse, as he called it!"

"You hadn't," I objected. "Why?"

"I don't want our friend Black in the foreground of this picture," Tolefree declared. "You'll have noticed that I didn't identify him to the lord of the manor. Nor to Mrs. Wollaston."

It had not occurred to me, but in fact he had not.

"And Jackson, too! It might have been Horridge himself talking. There are no flies on Mr. Lloyd."

Tolefree got up and walked about the room. He showed a little excitement.

"Suppose," he said, "Lloyd does know something of Jackson? When I suggested that to him, he didn't give a straight answer. He's as wily as they come."

I thought this was excessive. Tolefree said it might be, but he was taking no chances. He looked at his watch. "There are five or six hours of darkness in front of us. I hate the idea of leaving the clan Lloyd alone in the dark."

Suddenly he went to the door and switched off the light.

"Hi!" said I.

"A minute or two. I want to get my bearings," said he.

I heard him fumbling with the blackout curtains and the window. Presently a dim grey oblong showed in the wall opposite the door. I joined him.

"As I thought," he whispered. "We're at the back of the house."

Peering, I saw the vague outline of the hill rising steeply in front of us. Perfect silence. We might have been alone in the world. Tolefree closed the window and drew the curtains. He switched up the light again.

"It wouldn't be impossible," said Tolefree, "for these Lloyds and Fonthills to sell us a pup. Smother us in hospitality while they make plans for our undoing. While we slept there might be—"

"Dirty work at the crossroads!" said I. "Tolefree, you've got the jitters! Be yourself."

"I'll try. Look here, Farrar – bet you that the lord of the manor's right here now, at this moment."

"But – how — ?"

"How do I know? I feel in my bones – I felt it at the time – that message from a farm. It wasn't reasonable, was it, that somebody should ride up the gorge several miles in the dark with a message from a farm which would have done just as well in the morning? Farrar – I'm not going to buy a pup. I'm going to know every single thing that happens in this house tonight!"

"You're fey," I told him. "Letting your imagination run away with you."

"If that's so, I'll come back. But," he repeated, "I'm taking no chances. Having tracked down Fonthill, I don't mean to let him give us the slip once more."

"Can't understand you," said I. "You don't think, and I don't think, Fonthill killed his friend Blenkinsop. Yet you're getting after him – relentlessly."

"What I think about Fonthill is that he's up to the neck in it. He's scared of his life; but he's defying us, and the family's holding up his arms. Every single thing Fonthill's done since we picked him up in the hotel porch shouts his fear that he'll be found out. We've got to find him out, and he's as slippery as an eel."

I still felt that Fonthill, difficult as he was, didn't fill the bill. But it was useless to try to divert Tolefree in this mood. I had to confess to myself that the big point he made in the argument with Lloyd was sound. Fonthill had no business to know that Blenkinsop was dead; but he did know it, and he'd told the family. It was inconceivable that he hadn't told his father. The lord of the manor had lied, as Tolefree said, thirteen to the dozen. He lied with circumstance when he affected surprise at the news of Blenkinsop's death. He lied direct when he denied that he'd seen or heard of his son since the Westport affair. So I said,

"I admit Fonthill mustn't get away with it. What are you going to do?"

"Wait till the lights are out and then go prowling," said Tolefree. "If they try anything it won't be till they think we're asleep. If? – I'm certain they will! The young man's going to vamoose again with the connivance of the clan. It was in the air, Farrar – you could smell it."

I couldn't. However, I said merely, "You'll have your head, anyhow. What am I to do? Not prowl too?"

"Certainly not. Snore loud enough for two if you like. But one prowler's enough."

It was just after one in the morning when Tolefree, stealing into the corridor and to the head of the stairs, found that the lights were off. He took his pencil torch and disappeared.

I had waited half an hour in a room dark, but for the glow of the fire, before he was silently by my side again. He had on his arm the coats and carried the hats we had left in the washroom.

"Then — ?" said I, looking at them. He handed me mine.

"Yes – they're at it, Farrar. It's an escape." He spoke under his breath; it gave his news an added excitement. "Family conclave in a little room behind the dining room – Lloyd's study or his gunroom I guess: couldn't get a look. The two Lloyds, the lord of the manor, as I expected, and Fonthill. Can't make out exactly what they plan. But there are no horses in it. They're going on foot. Somewhere into the hills. There's a pack in the hall. Had a peep at it. Mostly food. A few other things – toilet things. Only one piece of any importance – and that's a pistol."

"Good Lord!" I muttered.

"Makes you think, eh? Can't imagine why Fonthill wants a pistol in his kit. But time will show. He's going at two o'clock.

They reckon we'll be sound asleep by that time. I don't know whether they're all going, and I don't know where. But it can't be far, because the tribal chief has to be back here to greet us in the morning. The idea is that we shall then get our congé, very politely administered of course, and that Fonthill will be having his breakfast in bed. They did consider whether he should be ill. But they came to the conclusion that it would be quite natural for him not to wish to meet us at breakfast."

"They know their job," I said.

"They certainly do. Not very flattering to us, I may tell you. It's not our noble selves they fear. But they think the police will have been put on the trail, and they don't want Bill to have to face the law in uniform."

I didn't see exactly what we could do about it.

"If they've made up their minds to get him away," I said, "how can we stop 'em?"

Tolefree admitted that we couldn't. "But we can see where they take him. You're game?"

"Of course. But you're not making too light of the job, are you? This is uneasy country for scrambling about in the dark."

"I know. But if we can't keep up with two old boys like Lloyd and Fonthill—"

2

It was never easy to divine Tolefree's mind. He had his own processes of imagination as well as of deduction. But I think he hadn't fully discounted the hazards of mountaineering in the dark in strange country.

He plunged into this escapade as eager as a boy. It was to him not only a step forward in his job; it was a lark. He chuckled over the idea of transferring the keys from the inside to the outside of the bedroom doors, locking up, and putting the keys under the mats. In the same sense that Fonthill was to have breakfast in his bed we were to be asleep in ours.

At a quarter-to-two the tiny spot light of his torch had guided us to the head of the staircase and down into the well of darkness which was the hall. His plan was to get outside the house before the expedition started. He had already unfastened the big door. I had a nervous shiver when, as we reached the foot of the stairs, a door opened, a segment of light appeared, and we heard voices. Tolefree shut off his torch. He whispered, "In here!" and guided me behind the big chesterfield nearest to us. In three seconds we were crouching there, out of view from any point in the hall. Somebody was standing holding the door and talking. It was Lloyd himself.

"I am quite willing, Henry," he was saying. "But I repeat that it's dangerous, and I cannot quite see the sequel. That man Tolefree is astute."

The lord of the manor answered from the room,

"All the more reason for keeping Bill away from him. He's not astute enough to see the truth – or he showed no sign to me of seeing through it."

"I would not be too sure, Henry." This was James Lloyd. "He does not wear his heart upon his sleeve, that man. He has evidence. I do not think he has disclosed all he knows."

"Perhaps not, James. But I shall go on with it. I won't put Bill in a position where he would have to explain. Let them solve it themselves."

"Very well, Harry. He's your son," said Mr. Lloyd. "Now I will go up and make certain that they're asleep before Bill leaves."

The door closed. A light sprang up in the hall. I caught my breath. We heard Lloyd's footsteps crossing to the foot of the staircase. He would pass up almost over our heads. The back of the chesterfield cast a dark shadow on our hiding place. But, if he chanced to look down —

He moved silently up the carpeted stairs. No challenge came. He passed across the gallery.

"Now!" said Tolefree, in my ear. "Outside!"

Half a dozen stealthy strides across the lighted hall, and we were in the open. Tolefree softly shut the door. We stood a moment or two on the step under the porch to accustom our eyes to the darkness. One invariably did that in the blackout. Everybody was developing a cat's eyes. Tolefree did not put on his torch. We waited till the outline of the terrace came clear and then crossed it, taking cover behind the low cupressus hedge which fronted the house.

"Just in time," said Tolefree, almost gleefully.

Our vigil was not long, but long enough to let us feel the chill of the night coming with the light draught that blew up the gorge. It might have been three minutes or five when the door opened and the light from the hall shone out for a split second before somebody switched off. In that instant we had seen three figures. Afterwards they were invisible, but we could hear them talking in low tones. In the dead silence of the world every word reached us. They were waiting for Lloyd. Presently he joined them.

"All is quiet," he said. "The rooms are locked, both men sleeping. Well, Bill – good luck. You'll lie low till you hear from us. That will not be till the day after tomorrow, perhaps not then. You will easily get there in two hours from now. Don't use your torch unless you must. It could be seen from their windows. But they've not moved the blackout curtains. I went round to the back to see. Now, get off with you."

Mr. Fonthill's voice: "You're not likely to see anyone, Bill. But don't show yourself. You've got clever men after you. Think over what I said just now. It might be the better way."

"No. I'm sure it wouldn't work. Too risky. I'll manage. If you don't see me again—"

"No nonsense. We shall see you in three days at most. Think of your mother. Goodbye."

"Au revoir, Bill. I think you're wrong, but good luck." That was James Lloyd's voice.

One figure detached itself from the group. We saw it move as a shadow along the front of the house away from the entrance. The others went in. The door was shut. We heard the key turn in the lock.

"Give him one minute," Tolefree murmured. "I'll count."

We had not foreseen this lay-out. We had assumed that one or more of the tribe would go with Fonthill. It would have been far easier to track two or three men than one This as it turned out, was our chief snag. Following one man who knew his way, moving alone in silence, we must keep at a distance lest he detected the sound of our own movements. Many times in that two hours' nightmare of a walk we lost him. Indeed only the difficulty of the way saved us from failure. He was forced to use his torch at some points and that occasional gleam kept us on his trail.

But heaven save me from another five miles climb around a Welsh mountain in the small hours of the morning!

The path from the house which we took when Tolefree had counted his sixty turned to the left at the end of the terrace. There it passed a wicket gate to reach a rough lane ascending through the wood which had made the green patch we saw from the other side of the gorge. It led towards the neck between the mountains.

With a minute's start Fonthill was out of hearing before we moved, but there could be no doubt about direction. The lane was sunk in a combe and a stream rattled down beside it. Dark as it was in the wood, with the help of Tolefree's torch well shaded we were able to keep on the beaten way. While the road lasted, the ascent was not severe, and when it issued beyond the trees the light which never deserts the sky save in time of thick cloud, proved sufficient.

It was shortly after passing this point that we had a shock. A bright beam shot out not more than fifty yards ahead of us.

We stopped in our tracks.

The beam circled slowly like a ship's searchlight moving over the water. Before it could catch us, we had crouched at the side of the lane and hidden our faces. It passed us, completed the circle, and was then extinguished.

For a time we thought Fonthill had either heard us, or suspected us despite his uncle's assurance that we were in bed and asleep. But still and silent ourselves, we heard him move on, and shortly we followed.

In the first fifty yards or so the sudden appearance of the torchlight was explained. The lane came to an end at a field gate. In unfastening and opening it Fonthill had used his light and it had swung round during the process. But beyond this our real troubles began. We were on the open hillside: the gate kept sheep or cattle out of Lloyd's grounds. On the other side of it was no road, but only a track through grass and scrubby heather, hard to distinguish without a light which Tolefree would not use. For fully a quarter-of-an-hour we could not glimpse Fonthill. He was invisible against the dark background of the mountain. He had moved faster than we, for when his torch shone for a few moments again he was far ahead of us. Marking the direction as well as might be, we hurried along as quickly as the more steeply rising ground allowed, and came upon the reason why Fonthill had shown a light. We had reached a region of scree, the rock-debris of the mountain. On our starboard bow we could pick out the outline of the peak of Aran Benllyn against the sky. Else, all was a misty confusion. The track continued through it, but was now a mere path between boulders, twisting and wandering.

It would be tiresome to relate the details of that journey. Time and again we checked and felt lost. We had to use the torch much more than Tolefree liked; but I thought there was little danger that Fonthill would see it even if he turned to look back, since it was but a tiny spotlight and Tolefree directed it only on the ground. Time and again the bright light shone out above us as Fonthill climbed. We learned later that he never saw us while we were below him.

We must have climbed a thousand feet and covered about two miles in the first hour, when the ground began to get less difficult. We were on the shoulder of Aran Fawddwy, who towered on our left, with his neighbour Benllyn across a deep valley. The going was easier, but that made it less necessary for Fonthill to show his light and less likely for us to go astray. We did not see the light again till we were over the neck and had started descending on the other side. We simply stuck to the worn track and hoped for the best.

We soon found ourselves in the scree again, and the track had petered out. We stopped. It seemed hopeless.

But our divagation was really a phenomenal bit of luck. We had stood peering into the dimness for several minutes when we were dazzled by the beam of a torch shining up from below and almost abreast of us.

"Ah!" sighed Tolefree.

Fonthill had evidently taken a lower path which was longer but easier. At present he was in the scree and finding it difficult, for his light began to show frequently. Then we realised that he was coming towards us, climbing.

We moved behind a big boulder and waited. A symptom of dawn came into the sky behind us.

Fonthill came steadily on. He passed us within ten yards. We waited still, but not long. Tolefree was determined to keep on his heels this time. We were not twenty yards behind him when we came out from among the rocks on to a patch of grass. Tolefree put his hand on my arm and we stood on the edge of that clear space. Fonthill too had come to a halt. It was four in the morning. We could see his figure as a shadow. He seemed to be looking over the edge of a rock and was perfectly still.

There had been no sound up to then except the little hiss of the breeze. But now we heard a familiar noise, a low hum which in less than a minute had become loud.

"Plane!" I whispered.

"More than one," said Tolefree.

For a moment some fantastic thought of an escape by air flashed into my mind. It was absurd. No plane could land anywhere within many miles.

The noise became a roar. The first plane passed overhead at a great height and faded away towards the sea twenty miles to the west. It was just a reminder. I had heard no planes since the night in Rawling's house. Doubtless they were going out on the Atlantic patrol. I was looking into the sky – an irresistible temptation to look for planes at night, but the vainest of all endeavours.

"Ah!" breathed Tolefree, and pulled me down on the turf.

Fonthill had put on his light. It lit up the wall of a stone hut built against the hillside. He was unfastening a padlock on its door. He pushed the door open. He disappeared.

"And not such a bad hide-out," said Tolefree. "A shepherd's hut, I suppose? The lambing season's over. Nobody will come here for months."

Very likely. And now what should "A" do? It seemed to me that we'd tracked Fonthill to a place where we could do nothing at all with him.

Tolefree said, "I don't want to do anything with him. I merely want to have a few words with him, after which we will conclude whether or not he's anything to answer for at Westport, and act accordingly. If that young man is culpable, he'll never get away from his maternal mountains, Farrar."

"How're we going to stop him?"

"We aren't. But there are others who will. You don't think I left Stowford for the Bwlch-y-Groes without bringing some connecting link with the outside world? No, I don't think he'll get clear to lead us another dance. But he might have stayed here quite a while without risk if we hadn't got after him."

"Good. I don't think he has any culpability – that's an elegant word! – but he's got to talk some time. What do we do now?"

These exchanges had passed in a minute at most. We were still looking across the turf to the hut, now invisible save for the farther corner of the roof which was silhouetted against the sky.

Tolefree said, "We get in there before it occurs to him to put the padlock on the inside."

"You don't forget he's got a gun?"

"No – but so have I."

"You! What the devil are you doing with a gun?"

"Carry it for form's sake these days. But I haven't used a gun for twenty-three years, and I don't propose to use it now. There'll be no gun play. You see."

Without more words he started across the space between us and the hut. I followed him. Giving no warning he threw open the door and flashed his torch inside. Fonthill was standing in the middle of the tiny place, his pack thrown on a rough bench covered with last year's bracken. He had lit a candle which flickered on a box stood on end.

He turned with a cry and shielded his eyes against the ray of Tolefree's torch. Tolefree switched it out.

Fonthill's exclamation was followed by a dead silence. He looked at one and the other of us for a few moments. Then he sank down on the bracken beside his pack. I could not guess whether he was more astonished or more frightened. He looked up at Tolefree with a lugubrious face. Tolefree pushed the door shut.

"Why do you persecute me?" said Fonthill.

"I don't," said Tolefree. "I pay you a call. I want some words with you alone, Fonthill. I couldn't get them at the house, so I've come to your summer shack in the mountains to have them."

"I've nothing to say to you. I don't want to hear you."

"Afraid you'll have to, unless you stuff your ears with wax. My words aren't going to be soft words. I want to know how your friend Blenkinsop died and I mean to find out. Even if you had anything to do with his death—"

"I hadn't," said Fonthill.

"Even if you had, I'm not going to tackle you about that. Not my job. I want to ask questions which only you can answer. They're important because Blenkinsop was important. You heard what I told your mother and your uncles, and you know why he was important. Think that we're going to allow you to get away without explanation, when we're convinced that you can explain? If you do, think again. If you don't explain to me, you'll explain to the police tomorrow. Don't be an ass, Fonthill. You've played the guilty man from start to finish. Farrar, at Westport you didn't believe Fonthill was guilty—"

Fonthill looked at me, more alert than he had been all the night.

"I didn't think he was the man you were seeking, Tolefree," I said.

"And he wasn't. But his conduct from the first moment we saw him was foxy. He foxed at the Report Centre. He foxed in that bedroom at Rawlings's house while I was looking through his papers—"

"A dirty thing to do!" cried Fonthill.

"Moderate your language, young man. Would you think it a dirty thing to examine the papers of a man who might have been a dangerous spy? With your background of Stowford, you certainly wouldn't. When you saw me at it, why didn't you protest? Instead of foxing? Instead of clearing out when my back was turned? Why did you go into hiding? Why are you here in this primitive shanty?"

Fonthill opened his mouth, but shut it again without speaking.

"I'll tell you," said Tolefree. "You'd done something that made you fear to face us and still more to face the police."

"You know nothing about it," Fonthill declared.

"I know that Blenkinsop was murdered. I know that you were in the neighbourhood of his room at the time. I believe you were in his room, Fonthill."

"Go on believing. You can prove nothing."

"I can prove by your own statement that you visited Blenkinsop. I can prove by Jackson's statement that the shooting took place about that time. I don't want to prove that you shot Blenkinsop. I want to know what you actually did and saw and heard, and it must be a more convincing story than the one your uncle told. Otherwise—"

"How could I have shot Blenkinsop? I carry no gun. I have never—" He bit off the sentence short.

"Fonthill, there's a gun in your kit at this moment," said Tolefree.

"It's not mine. It's my uncle James's. He had it in the last war. He thought I ought to have one here."

"Why?"

"Because these are queer times and queer people may be about."

Whether our presence and his lone condition intimidated him, or whether Tolefree's insistence had broken down his reserve, Fonthill was beginning to talk.

"How did you know I had a revolver?" he asked.

"It's my business to know all I can learn," said Tolefree. "No doubt you've guessed that we were out of the house before you. We heard a conversation at the door. Your uncles and your father think you're wrong in your judgment of the best thing to do. I think so too. Why not come clean, as the saying goes?"

"I can't trust you."

"You can if you've committed no crime."

"I can trust nobody. You have no evidence. I'm not going to give you any."

"Not even if another man's put in peril because you won't?"

"What do you mean?"

"Jackson."

A nervous spasm seized Fonthill. He buried his face in his hands in much the same attitude of despair we had seen at Rawlings's. Then he looked up at Tolefree.

"Absurd!" said he. "How could that man be in danger?"

"If you don't see that, my friend," said Tolefree, "it must be because you won't. I'll give you a break – a start towards candour. Tell me all you know of Jackson."

"I know — ? How could I know anything? What d'you think Jackson could have to do with me? – a casual visitor to the same hotel?"

Tolefree looked at him for a few painful seconds with a sort of pity in his eyes.

"You can't bulldoze me, Fonthill," he said. "You do know Jackson. The fact's shouting at me. I was watching you when Jackson's name came into my story at the dinner table. Better make a clean breast of it. You don't want another man to suffer because you're a stubborn, pig-headed fool, do you?"

"Of course not. But how can he suffer?"

"Ah – that's better!" said Tolefree. "Let's get to reasoning it out. Did you tell your father or your uncle anything of Jackson?"

"Certainly not!" Tolefree smiled. "I mean, how could I tell him what I didn't know?"

"Don't try to keep up the pretence," said Tolefree. "You and I and Farrar are quite well aware that you knew Jackson. Jackson was there because you were there, or vice versa. Otherwise the coincidence would be too pat. My dear fellow, wriggling's no good. You're in a jam. You don't want Jackson to suffer for your sake – but, believe me, your uncle does."

"Good God! – no!"

He started up from the bracken and looked wildly at Tolefree.

"Yes – I assure you. One of the last things he said to us. He seized upon the fact that Jackson was in a room nearby for hours, whereas you're supposed to have been in the corridor only a few minutes. I think he's quite prepared to consider Jackson a murderer."

A look of horror came to Fonthill's face. He stood with frightened eyes staring at Tolefree. He groaned. He collapsed to the bench again.

"Let me think," he muttered.

I never saw a stranger scene than that rude interior in that moment, its naked walls of stone, the slates showing above the rough rafters of its roof, Fonthill crouched in the depth of despair on a couch of bracken, as one of his remote ancestors might have crouched in the Bronze Age in some such hovel, Tolefree sitting on the upturned box regarding him, and the whole lit by one guttering candle. There was utter silence but for the gentle hiss of the breeze along the roof. The silence had lasted perhaps three or four minutes when Fonthill looked up.

"All right," he said. "I'll tell you," and as he spoke he started to his feet. A breeze had come into the place and made the candle flicker.

"I think not," said a voice behind me.

I jumped round. The door was open. Mr. Fonthill stood there, and behind him the two Lloyds. The chief of the tribe came in. James remained in the doorway. Tolefree seemed too astonished to speak.

"I think not, Bill," the lord of the manor repeated. "Not here, and not in these circumstances. Mr. Tolefree has no rights here. You're under no obligation to tell him anything."

The old gentleman spoke quite calmly, without raising his voice. It was his vantage and he knew it. Tolefree, still sitting on the box, said,

"You gentlemen must have had a rough walk. What's the idea? Sort of commando raid?"

"We keep our ideas to ourselves, Mr. Tolefree," said Lloyd. "In a long life I have found it to be good policy."

"It is," Tolefree answered. "One I nearly always follow. But tonight you strayed from it for once, Mr. Lloyd. You imparted to me your ideas about Jackson."

The elder Fonthill made an impatient gesture. "We didn't come up Aran Fawddwy to chop logic with you, Mr. Tolefree. There will be no more discussion. We shall take my son home, and you can do what you like about it. You haven't a leg to stand on. Bill, pick up your knapsack and join Uncle James. You gentlemen stay where you are."

"Eh?" I exclaimed, and made a step towards the door. Lloyd stood in my way. Tolefree said, "Better not, Farrar," and I stopped.

By this time, Fonthill was outside. Lloyd backed away to the door. The elder Fonthill followed. Before we realised their plan the door was pulled to, the hasp of the padlock clicked, and we were alone in the hut.

I seethed. Tolefree, who had not stirred from his box, burst into laughter.

"The old heroes!" he said. "The Lloyd blood's boiling."

"It's a damned outrage!" I cried.

"He who plays bowls must expect rubbers," said Tolefree. "Tit-for-tat, Farrar – and one up to Wales. I daresay you might have bowled 'em over, but I intensely dislike a rough house."

"Tchah!" said I.

3

Rough-housing gets you nowhere, Tolefree averred, and I daresay he was right. But that bit of anachronistic feudalism rankled. If there was Lloyd blood, there was also Scots blood which could heat itself to boiling just as fast.

Tolefree went on laughing at my tantrums. I told him that we'd had a desperately uncomfortable night for nothing, and, with Fonthill now away again, he was further off his solution than ever.

"In the words of the lord of the manor – I think not," said Tolefree. "First, Fonthill will not get far. I've seen to that with the help of Colonel Franklin."

"Stacked the cards again," said I.

"You are in a temper, Farrar! Must be this exciting mountain air. But you didn't imagine that, having located the bird, I was going to let him fly once more? Next, he's told us so much by inference, that short of a confession, which wasn't likely, he could hardly have told us more. I begin to see daylight. The trail leads back to Jackson."

But when Horridge had produced the Jackson theory, Tolefree hadn't thought much of it except for its ingenuity. I reminded him of that.

"I believe I said I was keeping my mind open or some such thing."

"You'd better keep on keeping it open," I retorted. "I bet you again that Jackson's a perfectly honest fellow – hadn't a thing to do with the Blenkinsop affair."

"And yet Fonthill was on the point of telling us what he knew of Jackson when the lord of the manor flung the spanner into the works. If Fonthill went down to Westport because Blenkinsop was there, if Fonthill knew Jackson, and if Jackson was there at the same time – my dear fellow, do hedge on your betting. You see, it's obvious that, like Fonthill, your perfectly honest fellow was deceiving us from the first. However, between Horridge and the Colonel, we have 'em both on a string."

It was, indeed, puzzling when Tolefree put it like that. But, if I could judge a man, Jackson was decent. However, I let it go.

"All very well to sit on that box dissecting people," said I. "But how do we get out of here?"

"Yes, how? You're the practical man, Farrar. How's it done? I'd like to know, though I haven't the least notion of stirring till daylight. Four or five miles of mountaineering in the dark is enough for one night."

But it would soon be broad daylight outside the windowless hut. We had been there an hour or more. I borrowed Tolefree's torch and examined the door. With a hefty screwdriver and a hammer it would have been a simple job. The staple that secured the padlock was clinched by turning over its ends inside. We had neither hammer nor screwdriver. Searching the place, the best instruments I could find were an old nail and a broken stone. With these I made enough noise to wake Dolgellau – or so it sounded. It took ten minutes to prise open the ends of the staple and another five minutes, crashing the stone against them, to drive them back through the plank.

Then a pocket knife levered the door far enough from its jamb to get fingers into the opening and a hard pull wrenched the padlock away.

A burst of golden light hit us in the eyes. The sun was coming up over the neck between the two mountains.

We drew in big breaths of the exhilarating air and stood silent, looking down two thousand feet to the floor of the valley. A thin mist hardly hid it. Ten miles to the east, the landlocked estuary of Afon Eden gleamed, beyond the roofs of Dolgellau, and further still the sea; to the north-east we looked across lesser mountains to the Snowdon range against the sky.

Tolefree sighed. "I begin to understand the Lloyds," said he. "Don't you feel a bit above yourself, Farrar? Don't your native contempt for lowlanders and their laws and customs come to the surface?"

I said what I could most easily bring to the surface at that moment was a yawn as wide as the valley. We were pretty tired. The twenty hours that stretched between our last beds at the Stowford Arms and the hut on Aran Fawddwy had been filled with much excitement and many exertions. Tolefree confessed that he could do with a bath and a spell of inactivity.

"And there they are," he added, pointing to the distant view of Dolgellau. "What is it? – ten miles? All downhill. We'll be there in time for breakfast."

And then? Perhaps a few hours' sleep. And then? There would be a train to London.

I was astonished. "You're quitting? Leaving Fonthill to es- cape again?"

"He won't. Or it's improbable. With the knowledge that he's somewhere in this bailiwick, the police can pick him up any time – if they want to."

If they wanted to? Was he telling me we'd had those killing twenty hours for nothing? He wasn't. Was it nothing to have seen the sun rise over the mountains? Hadn't we had an entertaining time? Perhaps not so restful as fishing in the Gloucestershire streams, but anyhow not dull.

"Come off it!" said I. "Does Fonthill get away with his parent's bluff?"

"No. We do. And we start now. Bet you that by tomorrow we know every single thing that happened in Westport. And above all the thing that matters to me – whether Mr. Black's in the land of the living or the place where he belongs."

"And who killed Blenkinsop?"

"That, too, I shouldn't wonder."

I reminded him that we'd left a car blocking the road in the Bwlch-y-Groes, and our baggage in it. He said there'd be a telephone at Dolgellau and he'd get Colonel Franklin at the other end of it. We couldn't shift it, so why worry? Tolefree was obviously on a keen scent which led away from the Welsh mountains. He'd had enough of the tribe of Lloyd. We cast about for the best way to start down towards any road that passed through the valley.

But we had not said goodbye to the Lloyds yet. Before we'd walked a dozen yards across the ledge where the hut stood, I saw a man on horseback looking black against the sky over the col. He was moving fast towards us. Tolefree took out his glass and picked him up. He passed the glass to me. At the distance of a mile in that clear air he was plainly distinguishable.

"James Lloyd!" I exclaimed.

"The famous Lloyd hospitality," said Tolefree, "coming to enquire what sort of night we've had."

He couldn't have had time to do much more than walk home, saddle a horse, and ride back. Eaten with curiosity, we waited for him, sitting on a boulder at the edge of the scree. He was within hail in a quarter-of-an-hour, waving his riding-stock in greeting. The horse picked an unhesitating way through the rough ground and was pulled up beside us. James Lloyd alighted.

"So you got out?" he said, offering his hand.

"Good morning," said Tolefree, taking it. "Yes – thought the air outside was better. No reflection on the accommodation you so kindly provided for us, of course. But I'm afraid we owe you the price of a staple. I'll send it on. What a glorious scene this is!" He waved an arm across half North Wales.

James Lloyd was nonplussed.

"You take it well," said he. "I brought the key to release you. I brought a few sandwiches and a flask as well. If you would care — ?"

"We certainly would," Tolefree told him. "Lovely air, but it has a nip in it. I hope you got back without mishap? And Mr. Fonthill and his son, and your brother? – they are well and happy?"

Lloyd was unwrapping a packet and fishing a flask out of his pocket. He passed them to Tolefree.

"We had no mishap," he said. "They are well. But happy? Not very happy, I think, Mr. Tolefree."

"Ah, that's a pity. But the world's a vale of tears, is it not?"

"I would like very much to talk seriously with you, Mr. Tolefree," said Lloyd, earnestly. "You must have gathered last night that I did not agree with the family in the method of dealing with Bill's predicament."

"I remember that there was a certain difference of opinion, a rift in the lute," said Tolefree. "Or should I say the harp? If I can quote you correctly, I think you said it was dam' nonsense."

"Well, I do think that. I am sure the tactics pursued by my brother and brother-in-law are unwise. But I am only one. I cannot be disloyal to them. What I wanted to say was that I do not believe Bill is capable of doing anything so vile as you suggest."

"Ah," said Tolefree. "But you go too far. I haven't suggested anything vile. I merely assert what is unquestionable, Mr. Lloyd – that young Fonthill is withholding from us things he knows which we must get to know. Whatever the reason for his obstinacy it's to be broken down. It's a matter of vital importance. Young Fonthill prevents us from settling a question we must settle. I told Farrar a moment ago what it was: whether a certain person is alive or dead. Your nephew knows. In fact, he was on the point of telling us last night when his father came into the hut and stopped him—"

"Unwise! Again unwise!"

"However, you've nothing to regret, Mr. Lloyd. It's strange to me to find Fonthill under tutelage at his age. But he is. I suppose ordinary laws which bind us mortals don't run above a certain altitude. So I put it down to the mountains. I make allowances for people who breathe such a rarefied air. And I suppose tribal laws are far older than the Statute Book – and in these parts there's a great reverence of antiquity."

Lloyd's dark eyes twinkled at that. "I don't know quite how to take you, Mr. Tolefree. Some tribal laws are very good – superior to the inventions of Parliament. The basic law of the tribe is loyalty. But that goes for loyalty to the country. And I'll guarantee that Bill, being half a Lloyd, hasn't consciously done anything whatever to the detriment of his country."

"Consciously? Perhaps not," said Tolefree.

"And another tribal law is the sanctity of friendship. I'll guarantee that Bill has never dreamed of doing any harm to his friend Blenkinsop."

"You knew Blenkinsop?"

"Yes. Once he came here with Bill. I've met him sometimes at Stowford."

"But you didn't know Jackson?"

"I heard him named for the first time last night. No, I didn't know him."

"Well, Mr. Lloyd, we're grateful to you for the sandwiches and the flask," said Tolefree. "I could wish that your brother and Mr. Fonthill took the same line. But they don't, and that's that. They may live to be sorry for it. In this way. If Bill had been allowed to tell me what he wanted to tell, and if he had no responsibility for anything that happened on that terrible night, he could have continued to enjoy his uncle's hospitality without interruption. As it is, wherever you have now concealed him, he'll be dug out, and put to the question by people who'll treat him less tenderly than I've done. I'm leaving it to them."

Tolefree got up from the boulder and handed back the flask.

"I hope we may meet you again in a less agitated atmosphere. Now, we're off to Dolgellau and to London. I shan't soon forget the pleasure of seeing the Lloyd family in their native surroundings. You might tell Bill's father that if he thinks better of it, a message will reach me at 57, Half Moon Street, St. James's. Goodbye."

"I fear my brother-in-law doesn't easily alter his views," said Lloyd. "Goodbye, gentlemen."

We watched him over the horizon. Then we set out for Dolgellau.

7

1

"Rather an attractive bunch of brigands," was Horridge's verdict, accompanied by a broad smile for rider, when Tolefree had given him a short narrative of our adventures in Wales.

We were in his flat in Half Moon Street, eating a late dinner, on the day which began with our long tramp to Dolgellau.

"Tolefree," said Horridge, "you'll have to get the local police busy right away picking up Fonthill. That young man's deeper in the mud than you think."

"Do I perceive that you have news?" Tolefree asked with a smile.

Lashings of news. First, Horridge had complete justification of his Jackson Theory. Next, Fonthill and Jackson were fellow-conspirators. "So I can tell you what your lord of the manor so dramatically prevented Fonthill from saying. Probably tell you more truthfully."

Tolefree seemed surprised. "You must have been really busy!" said he.

Horridge said that with help he'd covered a lot of ground in three days. "Take it from me that Jackson and Fonthill are partners in crime. They went down to Westport in company. Fonthill's a curious bloke – sort of willing to wound and yet afraid to strike, I should say. But down there he found that his partner meant real business. Either saw him do it, or knew of it. Got tremendous wind up. And the rest follows."

"One moment," said Tolefree. "Let's clear up as we go. You admit, then, that the man is and was known as Jackson in London?"

"Undoubtedly: probably just one more of his aliases."

"English or German?"

"Hard to say. You can judge better than I. You know how perfectly English some of 'em can get to be."

Tolefree said it was important. "The difference between an honest spy and a filthy Fifth Column man."

"I agree. Well, let's give him the benefit of being a German if you like."

I shot in a remark: "I'll bet you he's just plain Yorkshire!"

"Doesn't matter to the argument."

"But it means," said Tolefree, "that you've revised your theory. The picture you gave us of Black or Smith, or whatever he's called, shooting an innocent man, sneaking his belongings and stealing his identity – you blot it right out."

"Yes. It goes by the board. I give you that. But it doesn't alter the prime fact that Jackson and Black are one and the same person."

"Let's say the assumption, shall we?"

"Have it so if you will. But I'll give you evidence which makes it more than an assumption. I'm afraid, Farrar, it puts your friend Fonthill in the soup."

"Tolefree's already thrown him in," said I.

"I'll push him in further. Here's what we've dug up. In the first place, I've heard from Barrett. He says that in going through the debris at the hotel the searchers have found a second bullet. It's identical with the one that killed Blenkinsop, same markings and all. So we know now that one man shot both."

"Let's say the same gun shot both," said Tolefree.

"Sceptic! Really, I don't see your point."

"I like to stick to evidence and make it carry no more than it will."

"I think it'll carry what I said. But that's by the way. You'll see. I haven't a doubt that Jackson shot both. Listen to the record of Mr. Jackson. He comes into view just after Dunkirk. In September last year he turns up at No. 14, Pitt Street, Bloomsbury, which is a boarding-house. He has a yarn which nobody tries to verify – and we can't verify it now – that before the raids early that month he had a house in Surrey and an office in the City. Both were blitzed, his office one night while he was at home, and his house the next night before he got home. Most unlucky man, wouldn't you say?"

"I would," said I.

"If the tale were true," said Horridge.

"But it's not an impossible one, Horridge," Tolefree observed, "and not singular by a long tally."

"Where's your scepticism now, Tolefree? Anyhow, Jackson says he's an agent in the soft goods trade. He hasn't anything to prove it. His papers and everything he had were destroyed, except the clothes he was wearing and his balance in the bank, poor fellow. So he gets a little printer in a back street in Clerkenwell to print some cards with his new address. We've seen the printer: he did the job at the end of September."

Tolefree was making a few notes on the back of an envelope. I saw him write the word September.

"He's a quiet chap," Horridge went on. "Writes many letters. Is away for days at a time. Not long after his arrival, enter Fonthill—"

"Any date?" asked Tolefree.

"End of the second week in September. Fonthill's a young man of shifty moods. One of his eccentricities is to keep on shifting his lodgings. When he turns up in Pitt Street, it's just at the height of the fire-watching campaign. Both he and Jackson become fire-watchers. They happen to be on duty on the same night each week. They're supposed to get to know each other this way. They arrange to sit at a table for two in the dining room. They're soon as thick as thieves."

"You might," said I, "have used some other figure, if they'd been two other men."

"I must tell you, Horridge, that Farrar won't have Jackson as a criminal at any price," Tolefree interjected.

Horridge smiled. "Farrar, what a trusting soul you are! You won't have any criminals at all. Well – perhaps, if they'd been two other men... Anyhow, they get thick, inseparable. A duet that never joins in the boarding-house chorus. Remember, Farrar, that Jackson denies he knew anybody who was in the hotel at Westport that night. But that's putting the exhaust pipe before the radiator. Now, at the beginning of November, exit Jackson."

"Exit?" said Tolefree.

"Yes – he goes out. He goes out for a long time. He keeps his room on, but he doesn't turn up till March, when something strange happens. Meanwhile Fonthill has changed houses again. Probably he finds Pitt Street sans Jackson a desert. He takes a flat in the West End – in Half Moon Street – in this very house!"

Horridge sat back to witness our astonishment.

"I know," said Tolefree. "His father told me."

Horridge laughed. "My bomb's a dud! So – well, what did his father tell you?"

"He has a different version of the move. He says Bill has been wandering about London from lodging to lodging in a miserable state of mind, and he suggests a bachelor flat – and I expect he raises the allowance accordingly. But you may be right. Jackson's absence may have had something to do with it, if on the one hand they were as thick as thieves, or if on the other Fonthill had at last picked up a friend who suited him."

"Ah?" said Horridge. "But listen to the rest—"

"Before you go on, do you know why Fonthill might be miserable?"

"Yes, I think I do. And if he were a straight man I should sympathise with him. Nobody more. There was an idea at Bloomsbury that this sad-looking young man was peeved because the recruiting office had turned him down. I turned the War Office medical records inside out – or got 'em to do it – and it was true. He went before a Medical Board in London, and they threw him out pronto. Wonky heart—"

"Interesting. His father told me a few fairy tales, but this was a real one. Sorry to interrupt."

"Where was I?" Horridge frowned. "Oh, about Fonthill coming here. It's almost as hard to get into a flat in Half Moon Street as into Buckingham Palace, but he managed to snaffle this one, on the top floor, two storeys above us. I've spent no more than two weekends here for the last six months but I could identify Fonthill from the porter's description. He described a young man I passed in the lobby twice. He was the same lonely figure here, just wandering about. Nobody ever came to see him. Tolefree – I've done a bit of dirty work—"

"Not the first by many – all in a good cause, of course. You searched his flat?"

Horridge nodded. "He's careful. I found nothing fishy. Unless it was two letters from Jackson. The first written from Liverpool. Here's a copy. I'll read it. The original's in a pretty good business hand. He's at the Queen's Hotel. It's the 14th of November. He says:

"DEAR FONTHILL – I'm sorry you're moving from Pitt Street. Your West End touch is a flight above me. But no doubt we'll meet when I get back.

"I'm on a long tour, as I told you. It may be longer than I thought. Travelling isn't easy these days and it costs a lot of money to go long distances, so I shall cover as much ground as I can before returning to London.

"You sound nervy and downhearted to me. There's no real cause to worry. You'll be all right on the night. Hope you won't get any bombs near you.

"The business I told you about you will keep to yourself. Never mention it. After Liverpool I can't give you an address. I shall be constantly on the move. But I'll write now and then.

"Yours sincerely,

"J."

Tolefree asked for the copy and studied it closely.

"Fishy?" he said.

"Perhaps not. But – difficulty of travelling? All right on the night? The business never to be mentioned?"

"If it was our business, Horridge, I wouldn't have referred to it in a letter even to Farrar. Would you?"

"Well, no, I shouldn't. But don't jump at it till you've seen the second letter. It's just a note, but mighty significant to me. Southampton this time. Note the date – 20th March."

"Ah? – yes," said Tolefree, making a mark on his envelope.

"He says: *'Dear Fonthill – I'm back. Shall be in London tomorrow. If you care to come round to Pitt Street I shall be very glad to see you.'* That's all."

"Nothing fishy in that," said Tolefree.

"Except the date and the place and the strange thing that happened. Mr. Jackson is at Liverpool in November. Mr. Black is in Pernambuco about Christmas. Mr. Blenkinsop and Mr. Black meet there. In January and February they are in New York together. In March Mr. Black and Mr. Blenkinsop reach England. In March Mr. Jackson is at Southampton. The space of time which these dates cover is precisely the time Jackson was away from London and out of touch with Fonthill. On the 22nd March, Jackson, Fonthill and Blenkinsop were in the same hotel at Westport – and we know what happened there."

Tolefree scanned the marks on his envelope.

"There is a coincidence of dates," said he. "But coincidences are common enough. This one isn't so surprising as Fonthill's tenancy of a flat in this very house."

"Scepticism reappears," said Horridge. "It'll take more to convince you. But I'll provide more, Tolefree. Much more. Correspondence for one thing. I'll beg you to note how careful Fonthill was to leave no compromising letters in his rooms."

"That's putting the exhaust pipe bang in front of the radiator!" said Tolefree. "You haven't got the first term of your syllogism. You don't know that he ever received compromising letters."

"Don't I? Well, how's this? One day some time ago – may be two months or more, George the porter gave him in the hall a letter with foreign stamp and postmark which had just come in. The porter can't remember what sort of stamp and he didn't notice the postmark. But he noted the circumstance because the letter had been opened and sealed with a label 'Opened by Examiner Number something or other'."

"The fact that the letter was delivered doesn't suggest anything compromising," said Tolefree. "The postal censors are dead nuts on codes."

"But listen," Horridge urged him with a touch of impatience. "Fonthill stared at the envelope for a few moments, and then at the porter. He was going out, and he opened the letter in the hall, read a page and went white about the gills. The porter ventured, 'No bad news, sir, I hope?' Fonthill crammed the letter in his pocket, said, 'Eh? No.' And he rushed out."

"A pity George didn't notice the stamp. If he could have said whether it came from the United States—"

"Ah, but he could. I asked him that. He said no, he knew American stamps well enough – but this one was in some foreign lingo."

"Yes – and then? You haven't really compromised him yet," said Tolefree.

"But I will. The porter remembers one other letter which came under similar circumstances, by the second post, just as Fonthill was going out. This wasn't a foreign one. But it excited Fonthill in much the same way. He read it and bolted – that's George's word for it. Fonthill generally strolled in an aimless way. When he rushed or bolted, George noticed it. He observed that this was the second explosion of activity. And he remembers the date. It was the 21st March."

"Why does he remember it?"

"Because Fonthill went away the next day, saying that he might be back in two days or three, and George was to see that his rooms were cleaned, for which purpose he left him the key. And Fonthill hasn't been back since."

"Useful fellow, George. He should be in the Department, Horridge. But still you haven't compromised Fonthill."

"Wait. He gets that letter at eleven o'clock. Before noon he's at No. 14 Pitt Street, asking for Jackson. The soft-goods broker is out for the day, but will be there for dinner. At seven in the evening, Fonthill's back again, and he dines with Jackson. What about that?"

"I should have expected it. Jackson had written from Southampton the day before, asking him to call round. It may have been Jackson's letter that excited him – though I hardly think so. Well – he dines with Jackson. Go on, Horridge."

"The next morning he leaves. In the evening he and Jackson are in the same hotel at Westport. That's my tale, Tolefree. Have a cigar?"

Tolefree smiled. He said he'd prefer his pipe, loaded it and lit up.

"Horridge," said he, "'tis a good tale and useful. But you haven't really established anything yet. It looks to me as though the letter which roused Fonthill out of his accustomed boredom must have been the one he received from Blenkinsop at Westport. There's good evidence that Blenkinsop wrote to him. Fonthill told his family so, and there was no reason for deceiving the clan. It's a perfectly good explanation of his journey to Westport."

"But not of Jackson's."

"Certainly not. Why Jackson went down we've still to discover, if we don't accept the soft goods explanation."

"And you don't, you know, Tolefree. You simply can't."

"If it's untrue I can think of another – even for a reason why he pretended. But let's stick to your theory for a moment. If Jackson is the crook you make him, and if Fonthill's in the swim with him, what happened at Westport is fantastic. Barrett finds Fonthill rushing in and out of the hotel in an apparently demented state. Jackson, who on your showing must be the man Blenkinsop met in Pernambuco, sits tight waiting for a chance to commit murder in a place where his fellow-crook is doing his very best to advertise them—"

"Oh, come!—" Horridge began.

"And yet another point. If Jackson is this crook, he'd been in Blenkinsop's company for many weeks, and they'd just landed after a perilous escape from Lisbon. Contemplating the murder of Blenkinsop, wouldn't he be far more likely to get about the job quietly without inviting or allowing Fonthill to draw attention to him in London, in the train, and at the hotel?"

"And," said I, "is Jackson the sort of man who'd have gone to Westport on the day of a raid apparently foreknown to him?"

Horridge stared. "Eh! – that's a new one on me."

"But I thought it was implicit in what happened before the raid," I insisted. Horridge went on staring. "Wasn't the idea that he knew Blenkinsop's body might be burned?"

"Always a shadowy idea," said Tolefree. "When the shooting became known it evaporated."

"But," I exclaimed, "Barrett and his doodling! Barrett certainly knew."

"That's a different matter, Farrar. There are ways of getting to know things. Less said about 'em the better,"

Tolefree declared. "Well, Horridge, you've done a good job of work – lighted up some corners. But I can't say you've made the right case against Fonthill. I can't see him in the plot. But he observed, or knew, or did something at Westport which threw him into fits of terror strong enough to frighten an unbalanced young man into the eccentricities which have led us such a dance."

"Tolefree," Horridge said, "you evidently aren't going to have Fonthill in it at any price. I don't understand you, I've a slavish respect for your judgment—"

"Which means you're about to spring something on me!"

"And for your intuition—"

"And for my grandmother and all my ancestors back to Adam. What is it, Horridge?"

Horridge laughed. "I expected you to see through it before now. Yes – I have something to spring on you. I shall prove that the poor devil who went to his death with Blenkinsop wasn't a spy or a Fifth Columnist, but some innocent man who just happened to be unlucky."

"But not Jackson," said Tolefree. "Well, that was always a possibility. The proof will be interesting, but I should say not easy. Do you know anything? Or are you guessing? Or a little of both?"

Horridge muttered a damn. "Tolefree," he said, "you're a wizard! What made you say that?"

"You had a look on your face which said to me: Horridge has up his sleeve a bit of news from Westport to knock you off your perch, and it's carried his imagination soaring to the stratosphere."

"But how did you get Westport?"

"By being a simple-minded person. A man was killed at Westport. Therefore ten to one any information about him will come from Westport. I suppose they've discovered that somebody else is missing?"

"Well, yes – but hang it! You had no business to lead me on. Barrett and Stevenson have been checking in detail the people who were in the hotel that night, especially on that corridor. There were twelve rooms. Odd numbers on the left, 51 to 61; even on the right, 50 to 60. Blenkinsop was in 57, half-way down on the left, and Black in 55, next door to him. Jackson was across the passage in 54 and Fonthill next in 56 – exactly opposite Blenkinsop. Look here – I made a diagram—"

Horridge opened a note-book and showed a page. "Barrett says the round-up the next morning was hurried. The clerk and the maid seemed vague about everybody but Blenkinsop, or Perry, as they knew him – they wouldn't forget a man who'd been ill for two or three days – and Jackson whom they'd seen that morning."

"Yes – it was pretty vague," said Tolefree.

"Well, when Barrett persisted in demanding a closer tally, allowing for the two bodies, they found that one other man wasn't accounted for. After they'd sifted the names they had and the people who'd escaped, they were short of one. Then the maid remembered that there was a middle-aged man in No. 60, who'd been there two days. She thought he was a commercial traveller. He's not been seen or heard of."

"That was significant," Tolefree admitted. "But it's not proof, Horridge. You have something else?"

"Only inferences. But if two men are missing, and one of them's dead, isn't it far less likely to be Black than the other man?"

"Because he's trained in the art of looking after his own skin? Yes. But we mustn't forget one thing which satisfied Barrett and the police about Black – the box with the remains of his passport in it."

"It's a snag. And yet—"

"You prefer to think he escaped?"

"I seem to recall that, when we were discussing this with Stevenson at Westport, you yourself preferred to think so."

Tolefree shook his head. "I hadn't got that far. I fancy what I said was that I'd rather have had him escaping. Farrar, your memory's as good as a dictaphone. What did I say to Stevenson?"

"You told Stevenson you'd prefer him to have escaped, and you thought there was a chance that he had escaped. You said something about the mistakes that are made about dead bodies."

"That's it. There was a chance. There is a chance now. I've always allowed for it. The box and the passport seem to yell that he's dead; because if he'd got away he wouldn't have been likely to leave a sort of trail. That's why we've never let go the bone, but have worried it ever since. The evidence doesn't carry the conviction of certainty. If he wasn't in the hotel when the fire started, he wouldn't be able to get at the box. If he was in the hotel, he'd very likely calculate that the fire would destroy his stuff and he'd decide not to burden himself with a heavy suitcase. My own guess is that, if we found Horridge right, and this body was the unfortunate commercial traveller's, Black had already left the hotel. With murder on his shoulders he'd hurry up for his alibi."

Horridge cried, "Cheers! You're coming along with me, Tolefree."

"Not far, indeed! You've no proof of anything. You want Jackson to be the Macbeth of this piece. I'm not convinced. He made no dash for an alibi. He stayed where he was – a few yards from the corpses."

"Ah – but nevertheless you'll come the rest of the way. Wait till I spring my last surprise. In ten minutes time, at nine o'clock. I asked a man to call round then, and he's got something interesting to say. Meanwhile, shall we talk of other things? Or perhaps you'd like to hear a gramophone record?"

"So long as nobody starts crooning in the middle of it," said Tolefree.

Horridge put a portable gramophone on the table. It had a record already mounted. He started the machine. "A little One-Act Play," said he. A round of scratches and the record began:

"Come in!"

The sound of a door opening and shutting.

"Ah – here you are. Well, what's the news?"

The sound of a chair moved and a match struck.

"I've spent a small fortune in telephones."

"Never mind so long as the news is good. I've told you the sky's the limit."

"But I'm afraid it isn't good. It's grim. I got on to his father. Caught him just as he was leaving. He says there are two men after him – picked up his trail somehow. Been in touch with the police. Chief Constable sent them to the old man. Secret Service men. One's called Tolefree and the other Farrar."

"That's bad. I know 'em both. What are they up to?"

"Getting hold of the youth right away. The old man's got wind up. They've been to see Blenkinsop's mother, and he's afraid she'll put 'em on the track of Wales."

"What sort did he seem?"

"Oh, a toff. Very slow-spoken and polite about you. But I'd say anyone who touches the cub is going to be scratched. He was just off to Wales when I got him on the phone. Expects to be there first and shift him somewhere else."

"He'll have to be smart to outwit Tolefree. Did he say what line they took about Bill?"

"Only that they know a darn sight too much. They'd got hold of the notion that the mother might be hiding him."

"Wait a minute. Let's think."

Scratching lasts a few seconds.

"If he don't get away from Wales they'll catch him. He ought to be in London. He was a fool to bolt. How can we get him back?"

"You can't. There's no phone at that place. It's why the old man was haring off in his car."

"If he has any sense he'll get the youth back to London. Only place where he can really go to ground, and he can't get out of the country by sea these days. Did the old man say whether these two fellows made any accusation?"

"No; the usual stuff – wanted to ask him a few questions, especially why he did a bolt."

"Hmm – looks as if we can't do any more for him, doesn't it?"

"Afraid so – and you want to look out for yourself. They're keeping close tabs on you."

"I know. Horridge is suspicious. Saw that first time. But you've managed to dodge 'em, I suppose?"

"Yes. It wasn't easy coming here; still they didn't see me. Wouldn't it be better for you to get out of here?"

"I'm not moving. I can't do my job if I go into hiding. I don't worry. But Fonthill's different. He never does anything else."

"You should know best. I must be getting on. I'll phone you usual time and place if anything happens."

"Right. Thanks for coming. Keep your eyes skinned. So long."

A door shuts. Scratches. The end.

Horridge stopped the machine and turned to us, grinning. He had sprung a real surprise, and I expect my face showed it. Tolefree said,

"Very slick, Horridge. First time I've had any experience of the hidden microphone trick. How did you do it?"

"The man who did it will be here in a moment or two. He'll tell you. But how does it affect our argument?"

"That's to be seen."

"Jackson's voice came fairly well. You could hear his Yorkshire accents," I said. "But who was the second fellow?"

"I believe a private detective employed by Jackson. But we'll know directly. That conversation took place yesterday afternoon at No. 14, Pitt Street. I think it gets our Mr. Jackson in pretty deep, eh, Tolefree?"

"I should like to study it," said Tolefree. "I'll ask you to let me hear it again by-and-by."

There was a ring at the telephone. Horridge answered, and said, "Send him up."

The man who presently entered was of Horridge's own type, big, alert, with smoky, watchful eyes. He said,

"Hello, Horridge – and hello, Tolefree! We do meet sometimes, what?"

"Not often enough, Leeds," Tolefree said. "Horridge dragged you into this?"

"Yes – the old man said I could without butting in on your game. You don't mind?"

"My dear fellow! You've broken out in a new place."

"I've just been playing the record to them, William," said Horridge. "You should have seen their faces! By the way, this is Farrar, Tolefree's friend."

"Howdydo, Farrar? I've heard of you from Tolefree. Think I'd make a fortune as a private Gramophone Company dealing solely in eavesdropping, Tolefree?"

"Quite likely. A short life and a merry one. I'd as lief be a fighter-pilot. But you had a success yesterday. Horridge promised you'd tell us how."

Leeds settled down in a long chair and lit a cigarette.

"Certainly. The old man – by the way, Horridge, the old man's come to the conclusion that he knows who the artist from Pernambuco was – look here, I suppose Farrar's in the know about all this?"

"Absolutely," said Horridge.

"Good. Then this fellow's supposed to be a particularly high-up bloke in their snooping corps. Lots of names, but generally known as Breitmann. In England and America he's

Brightman, which doesn't mean the same thing, but it's convenient – and appropriate. He's a real bright boy. The old man
don't believe Herr Breitmann perished in the Westport fire, and
he's got umpteen people on the look out for him."

"I guess it won't be long before the old man's proved right,"
said Horridge, "and I've got a kind of presentiment we shall lay
hands on him before long."

Horridge nodded. "What do you think? Farrar won't have
Jackson. Tolefree's got a hundred reasons why not, and Farrar's
got one – that he's an honest-to-god Yorkshireman, convicted
of it by his accent."

"I should have said myself he came from Pudsey or Hali-
fax," said Leeds, grinning. "But you never know. These artists
are cute enough to come from Heckmondwike one day and
Whitechapel the next. What was I going to say? Oh yes – about
the record. The old man told me to lend Horridge a hand any
way he wanted it. Horridge told me to keep an eye on Jackson's
contacts. He didn't seem to have many. Solitary sort of bloke.
I wasn't to follow him out of town. Others did that. They did
a dreary round of provincial shops and warehouses and never
picked up a thing. Jackson seemed to be what he said he was – a
soft goods merchant with a hard row to hoe. But in London—"

"To which he pays such high compliments in the record,"
said Tolefree.

"Good little town, London, for anyone who wants to prevent
his dexter hand from knowing what he's doing with his sinister,
what?" said Leeds.

"Holy Writ, revised and inverted by William Leeds," Tolefree
murmured.

"In London, we got the goods on him. I found him one day
paying a visit to an office in a street behind Charing Cross, up
three flights of stairs, where the firm of Fardel and Son oper-
ates."

"Indeed?" said Tolefree. "And what was Mr. Jackson doing
with a firm of private detectives?"

"Since he'd met you, Tolefree, I should say he was going on the principle of diamond-cut-diamond. Anyhow, he had a long session with Fardel senior. Why an honest-to-god Pudsey man should want to consult a private detective was a mystery – don't you agree, Farrar?"

I said I did.

"But it's no longer a mystery now you've heard the record. The second speaker is Mr. Godfrey Fardel, like Tolefree a professional snooper, but on another plane. When I twigged that Mr. Fardel was in the habit of reporting to Mr. Jackson evenings at half-past six, when everybody's too busy thinking about dinner to worry about what other people are doing, I brought a little of my well-known and infallible resourcefulness to bear on the situation. As I dearly wanted to know what Mr. Fardel and Mr. Jackson were saying to each other, by bribery and corruption I procured the room next to Mr. Jackson's. Some other poor devil had to move up a floor, because an extra ten bob a week was too much for the landlady to resist. She may have wondered a little why I admired so highly the view from the window of this room, which looks out on a Bloomsbury by-street. But great is the power of filthy lucre. The evening I moved in, while Mr. Jackson was at dinner, I paid him a visit and hid a little microphone under his writing table, bored a little inconspicuous hole in the two skirtings and led the wire under his carpet and through the hole into my room, where I attached it to a gramophone recorder. The talk you've heard took place last evening. Won't Mr. Jackson be peeved when he hears it later on?"

"I don't think you'll play it to him, William."

"Why not, Tolefree?"

"Oh, just because. I've a totally different conception of Jackson's part in this business. But who's right, time will show."

"Terribly hard man to convince, don't you think, Horridge?" said Leeds.

"Case-hardened. And you waste breath trying to convince him. Well, William – anything more?"

"Yes – and a titbit for Tolefree. I listened in to the snooper and his client again this evening. The snooper had snooped in vain, but the client had some news for him. Bill Fonthill has dodged the police. He'll be in London tomorrow. Mr. Fardel, or someone on his behalf, will meet him at Euston by the train at twenty to nine in the evening, and conduct him to a place of safety. So the rest is up to you blokes."

"Tolefree!" I exclaimed, "you thought it impossible for him to get away."

"Unlikely, I think I said. The unlikely thing has happened. The Clan Lloyd must have underground railways. One up to the lord of the manor, Farrar."

"I suppose, William," said Horridge, "you couldn't possibly have had the miraculous luck to hear the place of rendezvous?"

"Oh yes, I could have. You underestimate my luck, Horridge. Mr. Jackson is to be at No. 24 Caroline Street, Pimlico, at half-past nine, and he will be shown to a room to await the arrival of Mr. Fonthill. So that he shan't mistake the place, he's to understand that it's a refreshment house much patronised by lorry drivers and the like, and the name of the man who keeps it is Balsdon."

2

Tolefree came down to the hall with me when I left the flat to go home to Manchester Square. As we were saying goodnight, it suddenly occurred to him that he'd like a walk, and he went up to get his hat and coat.

It was a dark night, that last day of March. In the narrow alley of Half Moon Street, blackness itself couldn't have been darker. The way across the shoulder of Aran Fawddwy the night before was brilliant by comparison. The first thing Tolefree said when he came down was,

"Which do you prefer in the blackout – London streets or Welsh mountains?"

He himself was country-bred, but he'd lived so long in London that he loved its tricks and turnings, and knew many of them by heart. Years before, after his strenuous time at Pitway House getting at the bottom of the murder of Mr. Harley, when we were in New York he lost himself in admiration of its strange beauty but heaved more than one sigh for the drab of London streaked with London's gold.

Even on this night of blackout he loved it – the velvet softness of the darkness, the glimpse of sky with a searchlight beam wandering across it at Piccadilly, the silence of the byways, the murmur of voices and the rumble of buses in the main streets, the dim flitting of screened torchlights like fireflies. It was a strange London; but we'd become used to it in a year and a half of war.

There were no raiders that night.

"An idea occurred to me, Farrar," said he as we walked across Grosvenor Square, his little pencil torch showing us the kerbstones. "Horridge's plan for tomorrow night – I don't quite like it. Too many in it."

I thought so too. Horridge proposed to have a regular squad of people in attendance on Jackson's rendezvous with Fonthill.

"You could do it better alone," said Tolefree.

"What!" I exclaimed, astonished.

"Why not? I'll work it out for you. It's a mere matter of reporting. You can report better than anybody I know with that memory of yours for things said."

"Flattery is birdlime. What are you after?"

Tolefree laughed. "So Plautus said, didn't he? But you're over suspicious. Let me work it out for you. You used to like play-acting with those nieces of yours. I think you can get a kick out of this. You see, if you're caught out, Jackson believes in you as a champion. But he suspects Horridge, and he's not too fond of me."

"A nice holiday, you old fraud!" I protested. "Why didn't I stay home fire-watching?"

"Confess now – you're enjoying it! Just waiting for the chance to say to Horridge, 'I told you so!'"

"He seems to fancy he's made his case. Has he, do you think?"

Tolefree hummed and hawed. He didn't think Horridge had completed a case. He was in blinkers. Nevertheless he'd certainly strengthened it. Jackson might be a dyed-in-the-wool Eborican, but he was a deep one. If he did all this out of friendship for Fonthill, he was playing a dangerous game with full knowledge of the danger, but thought himself so secure that nobody could touch him.

"What did you mean when you spoke of Horridge's blinkers?" I said. "Horridge has a case. He's keen on it. He always was keen. But this one's got hold of him, and every fact or circumstance that'll fit in with it he adopts, without stopping to see whether it'll also fit into an entirely different case. That's being in blinkers."

"True," said I. "I couldn't see that he'd really linked up Jackson with the man in Pernambuco."

"A beautiful post hoc, propter hoc. And it messed up his conclusions from the talk with the private detective. I want to go through that again; it may be capable of an innocent interpretation – except that Jackson's breaking the law by shielding a man under suspicion. You can say the same about the letters."

"All right then, Tolefree," said I. "Horridge has no real case. But I bet you've got one, and you're keeping it up your sleeve."

"Nothing whatever there," he laughed. "I've no case. Not enough facts. What do we know? We know nothing about the source and origin of all the trouble, the man in Pernambuco. He may be Breitmann; but I'd wager that's only a theory based on two things – knowledge that it's the sort of thing Breitmann might do and the circumstance that they've lost sight of Breitmann. I perfectly agree with you that Jackson can't possibly be Breitmann. The devil who started the business is out of sight.

He's been out of sight all the time. But there's a fair assumption that he was at Westport—"

"And that he was the man in Room 55," said I.

"I think there is. But it's carrying assumption a little far to say that therefore he was the man who died with Blenkinsop. We started with three persons on that floor, didn't we, who might be concerned in the death of Blenkinsop? There were the man in the next room, Fonthill and Jackson. Now we get a fourth man who'd been overlooked – the commercial traveller. If four, why not five? Why not that other hidden person, my hypothetical Possibility?"

"But there's never been a smell of him, Tolefree!"

"No, not a physical smell. At least not one that we could recognise on anybody we've met. But there's a distinct circumstantial smell. The great difficulty's been to reconcile the death of Room 55 with the theory of his death at the hands of Blenkinsop, hasn't it? I don't believe Blenkinsop killed him and then committed suicide. Nor do I believe that he killed Blenkinsop and then made away with himself."

"As Horridge said, you're going his way—"

"No, indeed – I'm not."

"Well," said I, "then I see no other way, unless it's one I've thought of – but you'll think it absurd."

"What is it?" Tolefree asked in a tone of curiosity.

"Probably foolishness. I turned it down in my mind. It occurred to me the other night while Horridge spread himself on that theory of his. Suppose he's wrong about Jackson – completely wrong. But suppose the man in No. 55 really has gone into Blenkinsop's room and shot him. Fonthill comes along, and in a rage shoots him too. How would that work in with what we know?"

We had walked fifty yards before Tolefree answered.

"Yes, Farrar – it would fit in neatly. We shouldn't have to look for anybody connected with the plot. Fonthill's motive, in your picture, is fury at the killing of his friend. Then he gets scared by what he's done in an uncontrollable moment. And, as Horridge says, the rest follows. Is that the idea?"

"Something like that. But, as I say, I threw it out."

"Because I don't believe Fonthill's capable of shooting anybody. When you get to the bottom of this you'll find that he never did shoot anybody."

"Very likely you're right. But the next time we get at Fonthill he'll spill it and tell us what he did. If any one knows whether my fifth Hypothesis can be materialised, it's Fonthill. Well, I'll be getting back. Have a good night."

We parted then to meet again at Horridge's flat in the next afternoon. In the meantime I'd done some thinking on Tolefree's proposal that I should report on the meeting between Jackson and Fonthill. When I left for Half Moon Street I carried a bag full of junk. Tolefree had evidently imparted his plan to Horridge and Leeds, for they gave me an uproarious reception.

"Why the portmanteau?" Horridge asked when I dumped it in his sitting room. "You aren't going to walk out on us?"

"Tolefree wants me to do a bit of play-acting," said I. "I never did believe in Hamlet in plus-fours, so I've brought a costume. No doubt Tolefree's told you about his mad scheme?"

"Mad? – it's grand! What's the character? How're you going to dress before you plunge into the imminent deadly breach?"

"I'm going as a Cockney lorry-driver. I've got in the bag an old suit I used to wear in the days when I was interested in the innards of motor cars, and a pair of rubber soled boots. The clothes have enough garage muck on them to be convincing. I've a very fine moustache left over from my private theatrical days. I can tame my Scots brogue to the accents of Bow. All this against the chance that Jackson and Fonthill might see me. But I don't mean to give 'em that chance."

"Farrar in disguise!" shouted Horridge in loud glee. "Hurrah! We'll tog you up so your own nieces wouldn't know you. I'm a wizard at make-up."

And so he proved to be. Before we had an early dinner the plan was laid out.

William Leeds took the Euston end. Neither Jackson nor Fonthill had ever seen him. Tolefree and Horridge were to drive me down to Pimlico and see me into Mr. Balsdon's premises, where I was to dally with refreshments till something happened. They would stay handy in the car. I should act according to circumstances.

After dinner Leeds set off for Euston to watch the train. I transformed myself into a lorry-driver in Horridge's bedroom with Horridge's help. When he had had his will with me and I looked in the glass, I shouted with laughter at the dirty, rad-dled-looking fellow who stared at me. I marched into the sitting room and said to Tolefree, "Naow – 'ow's thet, guv'nor?"

"I don't know you, do I, my man?" said Tolefree. "Are you looking for anybody?"

He and Horridge went with me to Pimlico enjoying the ad-venture like boys. They dropped me at Victoria, and I did the rest of the journey on foot. Caroline Street was a dim, shabby thoroughfare, mostly warehouses. Mr. Balsdon's house of re-freshment lived up to its surroundings – a dingy, broken-down place, but certainly an excellent hide-out.

With a possible contingency in mind, I had carefully caused myself to smell of whisky – not by drinking it but by spilling it on my clothes. I looked as drowsy as I could when I walked into the long, narrow room past a pewter counter laden with none too appetising food and two steaming urns of tea and coffee. Few people were there. I made my way slowly to the very end, sat at a table with my back to the wall and rapped on it. The one man who sat behind the counter came along. I gave him an order. I toyed with food and a large cup of coffee, smoked my pipe, and waited interminably. No one took any notice of the sleepy-looking, surly lorry-driver. He was probably quite a familiar sight in that place.

Nothing happened for half an hour. Then I stirred. Two men had come in and were talking in undertones to the man at the counter. One was Jackson. The other I guessed was Fardel. They were immediately taken through a doorway in the side of the room. I heard footsteps on stairs. Neither of them so much as glanced at me. The man returned to his place at the counter. He did give me a look as he came into the room. I signalled to him and ordered another "corffee."

"Had a long day, mate?" he said, when he brought it.

"Do wiv a rest an' a bit o' warm," said I.

He went back to his place. Nothing happened for another half-hour. That train must have got into Euston long since. I wondered whether Jackson's plan had gone awry. So, apparently, did Mr. Fardel, for he came through the doorway and made some inquiry at the counter. Then he went back again.

Afterwards, Leeds told me what had held them up. He and his companion were in good time. He soon divined the man from Fardel's office who was waiting for Fonthill. The train came in on the tick. Fardel's messenger met one of the passengers – but it was not Fonthill. A much older man walked away with him to a waiting car. The blackout lighting of the station was so feeble that it was impossible to see his features; but he was at least twice as old as Fonthill, and a dark instead of the fair man who had been described to him as Fonthill.

They went off westward, with Leeds hanging on to their tail-light. But, instead of coming into London, at the end of Marylebone Road they turned north-west by the Edgware Road. It was hard to follow, but Leeds managed to keep them in view till they drew up outside a public house in Willesden. Fardel's assistant got out on the pavement and waited. A young man came along walking, flashing a torch on the ground and whistling "Land of My Fathers." Leeds on the other side of the street heard the whistling stop, and saw the young man get into the car, which was driven away. He followed them into London, and down past Victoria to Pimlico, apparently satisfied that if they had been tailed at Euston they had thrown off the possibility of a chase.

So it was that I had waited nearly an hour longer than I expected before the chance came to put my plan in action. Fardel had re-appeared and was talking to the man at the counter. There was a sound of arrival – a car pulling up outside. Fardel moved to the door and went outside and the man followed him with a torch. It was my moment. I slipped through the doorway at the side of the room, saw a stairway on my right, and instantly began to climb it silently enough in my rubber soles.

It was a ramshackle old place. I went up two flights without seeing or hearing any sign of life, nor did there appear to be a soul in the rooms at the top of the third. The fourth led to an attic floor, and as I stood at the foot I heard a movement above. The stairs were steep and narrow, and unlit. One small bulb on the second landing had given me enough light so far. Here I had to use my torch. Finally I reached a tiny landing under a sloping roof, with a door to the right and one to the left. From under the right-hand door a streak of light showed. The left-hand door stood open. I dodged past it and stood behind it in the room.

A heavy sound of footsteps on the bare boards came up to me. I could see the flash of a torch.

"Careful here, sir," said a voice.

In a few seconds the party had entered the lighted attic and the door was closed. I thought three men had gone in.

I shut the door and flicked my torchlight round the room where I stood. It contained a chair and a small iron bedstead, unclothed save for a mattress. One glance was enough. I went out and stood against the wall in the narrow space between the two doors. The attics were gimcrack structures with thin board partitions papered over. Without straining my ears I could distinguish every word that passed. Fardel's voice I did not know, if it were Fardel's. There were three others – Jackson's, Fonthill's, and, to my astonishment, James Lloyd's.

Jackson was saying as I took my place, "Well, Mr. Lloyd – right thing to bring him here, wasn't it?"

"To me personally," said Lloyd, "none of it looks right. But I abide by the general decision. And, Mr. Jackson, if Bill is to hide he couldn't hide in a better place I'm thinking, though there might be many more pleasant."

"I guess it's the right thing," Jackson said. "He must stay invisible for the time. If it gets known that he's loose and has been in touch with me and Fardel, his liberty won't be worth that" – and I heard a snap of fingers. "Fardel, what do you say?"

"Touch and go," said Fardel. "Best let him stay put. There were two of 'em at Euston, I'm told, but not Tolefree and Farrar. They didn't know anybody but Mr. Fonthill to look for, and the Willesden touch diddled 'em. It would take a month of Sundays to rake London for him."

Lloyd exclaimed, "At Euston! How could they have known?"

"They have their ways of knowing things. Mostly through the police."

"But the police never saw Bill."

"I wouldn't put too much on that, Mr. Lloyd. People like you can't make a move in a country district without somebody knowing, and the police soon find out. Now, Mr. Jackson, I think that's all. I've done my job. I don't want to know the reasons why. I'll only warn you to beware of Tolefree: he's an uncanny guesser. And I'll wish you all goodnight."

Almost before he'd ended I was back in the second attic and crawling under the bed. If it occurred to Fardel to look in and flash his torch around I hoped he would see nothing. In fact he did not look in. If the second door had any attention from him at all, he saw it as it was when he came up.

His light passed out of sight and his footsteps faded away down the stairs.

Fonthill was speaking when I got back to my post.

"I don't know why you take all this trouble for me, Jackson."

"I hate slopping," said Jackson. "But I got to like you, Fonthill. You gave me more help than I've had from anybody else, and I couldn't see you in a jam without lending a hand to pull you out. It was a bad break when you bolted from them at that farm – Rawlings's, wasn't it? Why did you? Just sheer wind up?"

"I suppose so – being hauled off by the police on the instant like that. Finding myself in the hands of two prying devils. Being all shot up by what I'd gone through."

"I know. But when you're in a tight spot it's always better to be normal. Any abnormal trick's bound to mean suspicion. Still, cheer up. You'll be all hunkeydorum here. Not a palace, but you're out of sight and that's the great thing. I'll find a way of getting news to you if anything happens. I expect Mr. Horridge on my tail again before long. He looks at me with a nasty eye. But I can play him. Now, I'd better be off or I shall be missed from my usual haunts. The man downstairs has full instructions about you. He'll feed you well. Sit tight and you're all right till this business blows over. Shall I give you a lift, Mr. Lloyd? My taxi will be here now. If you'll go down, I want a word with Bill."

I was back in my attic in quick time, and in the same hiding place as before. I heard Lloyd going down the stairs and Jackson following two or three minutes after; but he halted at the foot of the first flight. Somebody was coming up, stealthily and fast. Jackson's light disappeared. I imagined that the intruder had neared him when I saw the light flash on again for a split second.

"Good lord, Fardel! What's up now?" Jackson's voice.

"Mr. Lloyd's gone down," said Fardel. "They won't know him. Mr. Jackson, go in and fetch Mr. Fonthill. They've trailed us somehow. Two of 'em outside now, Balsdon says. If they come in, he'll hold 'em up as long as possible. He's told me what to do... Now, both of you, come this way."

Five seconds after they were all three in my attic. I could see their feet from where I lay close to the wall at the back of the bedstead.

For a moment I was flabbergasted. It seemed certain that they must discover me. A single bulb hung from a rafter in the roof, which would have lit the little place brilliantly if they'd switched on. But they didn't – and I saw the reason later: the dormer window of this room was naked. They went about what they had to do with the sole aid of Fardel's torch, and he dared not show that except to guide them about the floor. The circle of light it made flickered across to the wall opposite the bed. There I saw a rectangular crack in the paper pasted on the boarding. Only one sentence was said – Fardel's:

"This leads into the next house. We're going there – and after that we'll see."

He had probably stuck a knife into the crack, for between his legs as he stooped I saw the square of papered board swing back on hinges. Fardel stood aside. Jackson first and then Fonthill bent down and passed through the opening. Fardel followed. The panel closed and I was in darkness, much to my relief. Standing upright again I groped a way to the landing and listened. There was no sound of an approach up the stairs. I went down.

Unseen and unheard, I reached the passage at the bottom, which led through a side door to the street. I went through into a black night. Already Caroline Street was dead – not a step to be heard in it, nor a vehicle. Some twenty yards away, perhaps, the tail light of a standing car showed. As I stood accustoming my eyes to the gloom, a man bumped into me.

"'Ello, guvnor!" said I.

"I beg your pardon," in the unmistakable accents of Mr. James Lloyd. "Can you tell me which way I shall go to get to Victoria Street?"

"Strite on to the corner, boss," said I, "an' turn left. Yer cawn't miss it."

"Thank you indeed," said Mr. Lloyd, and was gone.

I stepped softly to the doorway of Mr. Balsdon's establishment, pushed aside the blackout curtain and looked in. Horridge was at the counter, talking to Balsdon, who was saying, "I tell you there's nobody here. The place is empty. You can go through and see if you don't believe me."

Then I saw Tolefree at the back of the room. He saw me in the same instant and walked towards me. I left the doorway for the pavement, where he came to me.

"All right?" he murmured in the darkness.

In a few words I told him what had happened upstairs. At his suggestion we hurried to the car which stood up the street, and brought back with us William Leeds. Two others who were in the car went to search for the back of the premises.

Tolefree returned to the counter, leaving me outside. Presently he came out with Horridge, and told him roughly what I had seen.

"Post a man here to watch the street," said he, "and keep tab on Fonthill. Don't trouble about Jackson. If he comes out, let him get away. He'll go back to Bloomsbury. Then let's go somewhere to hear what Farrar has to tell us."

Horridge looked up to the skyline of the building. "These two houses must have been one some time," he said. "Partitioned off. And very convenient for Mr. Balsdon, I must say! I've only one man left, Tolefree – the driver."

"All right. Lock up the car and let him watch here. I think we've got 'em cold, as the saying goes."

3

No more convenient place occurring to anyone than Half Moon Street, we took a bus going north-east after Horridge had instructed his man how and where to report. I refused to talk till I had changed my clothes and removed the moustache. Then, over a pipe and a drink, I submitted myself to the question.

I told them as nearly as possible everything that was said in the attic, and described the escape.

"You fellows went off half-cock," said I. "If I'd been able to listen to what Fonthill and Jackson said to each other in confidence—"

It was a pity, Tolefree confessed; but they were anxious. They didn't like the look of Mr. Balsdon.

"But Mr. Balsdon thought I was a half-drunken lorry driver half dead with fatigue. If I'd laid myself out on the floor or the bed to sleep it off he wouldn't have been surprised."

"You did famously, Farrar," said Horridge. "We shan't lose Fonthill now. And Tolefree thinks he can make him talk."

"Oh, Tolefree can make a bit of wood talk," I admitted. "But Fonthill's a tough bit. He would have talked to Jackson."

I learned later on that Tolefree had been for letting Mr. Balsdon's joint alone; but Horridge had insisted that it was a fishy-looking place and I'd been there long enough. They'd watched Jackson's arrival with Fardel and wondered at the long wait, until Leeds turned up with the tale of his chase to Willesden and back. Then, when Fonthill and Lloyd had gone in, they had another prolonged vigil, or so it seemed to them. What made Horridge determined to have a peep at the Balsdon ménage, however, was a taxi that pulled up at the door just as he was strolling by in the dark. He stopped, believing himself unseen and heard the interlocution of the taxi-driver and Mr. Balsdon, who came out to speak to him:

"Bloke told me to be 'ere arf after nine."

"Yes. He's left. Here's a bob for your trouble."

"Bob? – What's 'e take me for?"

"Well, it's all he gave me, and you won't get more, see?"

As no one had left since Horridge and Tolefree arrived, Horridge became suspicious. With very good reason, but it was an unhappy disturbance of my plan. However, Tolefree now said,

"Let's go over what Farrar did hear, and see what we can make of it. It's plain that Jackson brought Fonthill to London, with the approval of the Lloyd clan except James. Uncle James is more practical than the other denizens of their Welsh mountain. What about this, Horridge? Undiluted affection on Jackson's part? Or a wish to have Fonthill under his eye?"

"You know my answer to that one, Tolefree."

Tolefree sighed. "I wish I could be so sure. Fonthill asks why Jackson's taking all this trouble about him, and Jackson says he owes him a helping hand now that he's in a jam—"

"It all backs me up," said Horridge. "Somehow and sometime or other, Fonthill's pulled Jackson out of a jam, and now Jackson's returning the compliment – and doing himself a good turn at the same time by getting Fonthill where he wants him, under his eye – and his thumb."

"I see. And the same motives apply to what he said about the bad break Fonthill made by bolting from Westport?"

"Of course. But now, with Fonthill safely hidden, he can play me! Gosh! – I'll play him," said Horridge. "Good heavens, Tolefree! – you aren't going to argue that there's nothing crooked in all this, are you?"

"Certainly not. I only want to make sure that we hit on the right kind of crookedness," said Tolefree.

"Well, what does the very latest escape mean? – going into hiding in a rabbit-warren like Caroline Street? Anything in the world to avoid us, doesn't it?"

"Perfectly. The point is we don't really know why they're avoiding us. It may be as you say. But, as I was suggesting to Farrar yesterday, all this could carry what would be, from our point of view, an innocent interpretation."

"Innocent my aunt!" cried Horridge. "I don't understand you, Tolefree."

"Often enough I don't understand myself," said Tolefree. "But I've an uncomfortable feeling that we're in danger of switching on to the wrong track. Let's make a plan for getting at Fonthill tomorrow. How I wish I knew where Mr. James Lloyd went when the lorry-driver directed him to Victoria, Farrar!"

It seemed a vain wish. "Why d'you want him?" Horridge asked.

"Oh, because. I said just now he's the only practical man in the Lloyd family. I'd like to make one suggestion to him."

Tolefree really was, as Fardel had called him, an uncanny guesser. At half-past eleven, I was on the point of going home when the telephone bell rang. Sitting close to the receiver, I picked it up. The voice of the porter in the lobby:

"A call for a Mr. Tolefree, sir. Is he with you?"

"Horridge," said I, "this is a call for Tolefree," and held out the receiver. Horridge nodded. Tolefree took it.

"Who's speaking? ... Oh, put him through, please... Yes, Tolefree here.... Really? One moment." He put his hand over the receiver. "Horridge," said he, "somebody wants to come round and speak to me. That all right?"

"Of course."

Tolefree spoke into the telephone. "Yes – certainly. Very pleased. Where are you now? ... Better take a taxi. Ask the porter for Mr. Horridge's flat.... Yes, Horridge – two Rs for Robert.... You've got it?... It'll take you ten minutes, not more... Oh, been here before? Of course... Then that's simple. I'll be waiting."

"Talk of the devil!" said Tolefree.

"Not Jackson?" Horridge growled.

"No – James Lloyd."

"Well, I'm damned! Now we'll all see what the practical man makes of it – that is, if it's not to be private, Tolefree?"

"I should say not. A round table. You'll probably like him. Farrar, don't go."

I had no wish to go, but a keen curiosity to see James Lloyd after what must have been for him a bizarre and disturbing experience. When he came in, looking worried and fatigued, he shook hands heartily with Tolefree and me, and gave Horridge a little bow.

"Our host, Mr. Horridge," said Tolefree. Lloyd held out his hand. Horridge welcomed him, set a long chair, and gave him a drink. He sipped it gratefully, apologising for disturbing us so late. "There was something I wanted to say to Mr. Tolefree," he began and hesitated.

"Horridge is one of us," Tolefree told him. "He knows all about our business and our meeting with you. He lives at Westport. Horridge will leave us if you like."

"I couldn't hear of it," said Lloyd. "I will not evict a man from his own room. Stay, Mr. Horridge, if it please you. I heard your name tonight. I heard that you were within fifty yards of me, and that Mr. Tolefree was there too. So you know all about it – a horrible place!" He shuddered. "I am deeply disturbed. I imagined no such thing when I agreed to come with Bill to London to see his friend, Mr. Jackson. When we parted yesterday morning, Mr. Tolefree, you hoped we might meet again in a less troubled atmosphere. We meet before I expected, and the atmosphere is more troubled than ever. I want to get Bill out of it. I came to ask you if there is any way. You know my opinions. I do not agree with my brother-in-law's attitude. I have thought much about it this evening. I am unable to rest. Is there a way, short of handing Bill over to the police?"

He spoke in desperate distress, but with dignity. Tolefree said, "Mr. Lloyd, there's a divinity doth shape our ends. Half an hour ago I said to Horridge and Farrar that I wished I knew where you were, because I had a suggestion to make to you."

"Ah! Yes?" Lloyd looked eager.

"It was this: that you should put us in the way of meeting Fonthill again, to take up the talk his father unwisely interrupted. Don't answer for a moment. I believed that when you found where this last escapade had landed him, you would regret it—"

"Indeed, indeed!" said Lloyd.

"And that you might be inclined to almost any plan which would put an end to the unpleasant absurdity."

"If there is such a plan—"

"There is. But it has conditions. You've already seen, no doubt, that this situation was absurd from the moment when you found yourself off on a wild chase round London to end up in a hole like the eating-house in Pimlico. I expect you now realise that the place is under surveillance, and that it's impossible for Fonthill to get away."

"I imagined so."

"Perhaps you don't know what happened after you left. Fonthill and Jackson were taken into another garret in the next house, in the hope that their escape would not be discovered. But it was discovered almost as they moved and before you'd left the street."

Lloyd looked horrified. "The way out of it all! The way out, Mr. Tolefree!"

"Candour, Mr. Lloyd, and nothing else. Candour is the first condition. The next is our assurance that, apart from his concealment of knowledge, Fonthill has committed no crime. The next is that he holds himself at our disposal for any inquiries we may want to make. I hate to break in on a close family alliance, but Fonthill's a man of mature age and a responsible person. If he has to fly in the face of the family, he must do it. He'd have done it two nights ago but for his father. He undoubtedly has knowledge most vital to us – and to you and everybody. He's got to bring it to light. That's the way out, Mr. Lloyd."

Lloyd looked around at us all. He pondered Tolefree's words. Then he spoke slowly, pausing between sentences:

"I do not believe that Bill has committed any crime – in the moral sense. I do not understand his relation to Mr. Jackson. He is a moody, restless young man – and the reason for that is no disgrace to him. I think something or someone has misled him into this – conflict with the law. I know he is very loyal to his word. That is why I am sure he has done no great wrong thing."

He made a long pause then.

"Mr. Tolefree – I will try to do what you say, to put you in real touch with him. But I do not know the ways of Pimlico. You must help me—"

"Of course. No difficulty there."

"Then I will do it."

"And something more?" said Tolefree. "Will you try to persuade him to be frank? It would be easy enough for the police to get him for us. But I don't want that. He is, I know, under some terrible pressure to hold his tongue – some fear. It had already driven him frantic when we first saw him at Westport. It has never left him. Tell him that if he's done no wrong he needn't be afraid. Make him see it. If you can't nobody can. And you could make the alternative clear to him – that he will have to answer to the police."

"I shall go there in the morning, Mr. Tolefree. I do not know how to set about it—"

"We'll deal with the keeper of the house, Mr. Lloyd. He shall produce your nephew to you."

"Then I am glad indeed," said Lloyd, "that I came to you. The atmosphere begins to clear already."

I left with Lloyd. I grabbed a taxi for him and put him on the way to his hotel. Then I walked home.

It was hard for me to believe that the last time I saw Lloyd was some thirty-six hours before as a silhouette against the sunrise on Aran Fawddwy. He was a very different James Lloyd in the London blackout.

I pondered the situation Tolefree had now created. He must be pretty sure of himself to take the risk he ran in his implied promise to Lloyd. True, he had said that one of the conditions on which Fonthill and his family could extricate themselves was that Fonthill should have committed no grave crime. But I knew that Tolefree wouldn't have taken that line unless he were convinced that Fonthill had not, at any rate, done murder. Therefore he had in his mind the approach to a conclusion. I knew the symptoms. I couldn't guess even faintly what it was; but I hoped that tomorrow would disclose it.

For I, who felt convinced that Fonthill was innocent – for reasons of character and not of evidence – had to concede that his conduct all through looked more like guilt than innocence.

Tolefree believed him guilty of something which was not murder. It would be quite like Tolefree to prove the major innocence by means of the minor guilt.

We had agreed to meet at Horridge's in the morning. Before we packed into a car with Leeds we learned from Horridge that Jackson had tired of his incarceration in Mr. Balsdon's annexe and come out by way of the shop. In accordance with Tolefree's instruction he was not challenged, though he seemed to expect it as, in the light of early morning, he faced Horridge's watcher, the only man in the street at that time. Afterwards, Fardel ventured out. He too passed without interference.

I wondered whether in some way they had contrived an escape for Fonthill; but that proved to be wrong. They were so confident that if and when the place was searched no Fonthill would be found that they left him for the time lying as they supposed perdu.

This was obvious when the five of us walked into Mr. Balsdon's shop, to the surprise of the three or four customers there drinking his execrable coffee. Mr. Balsdon himself was in shirtsleeves behind his zinc counter. He played his hand coolly. He stood looking at us as though awaiting our orders.

Horridge said, "Good-morning. I described to you last night three persons out of four who had entered your house and not come out. You said there were no such persons on the place. You were badly misinformed. One of them came out last night immediately after. Two others came out this morning. There is still one here. He is a young man with fair hair and grey eyes, about twenty-eight or thirty years old—"

"No such man here," said Balsdon.

"Wearing a brown suit with a blue tie, a soft collar, and dark brown shoes. Please produce him."

"I can't produce a fair-haired toff at a moment's notice," said Mr. Balsdon. "I know nothing about him. You're barking up the wrong tree."

Horridge said quietly, "You'd do better not to be impertinent. You're not telling the truth. Fetch him down, or we'll search the place."

"You're welcome to search. Though I don't know by what right you come into my place and—"

"If you insist, I'll give you our authority. But you won't like it. If you'd prefer to have half-a-dozen men from Scotland Yard, you can."

Mr. Balsdon looked as if he hated Horridge intensely, but he shrugged his shoulders and said,

"Search away."

"Very well." Horridge turned to me. "Farrar, you take Mr. Lloyd and go through the place with a small tooth comb. Leeds, you go outside. We two will stay here and keep Mr. Balsdon company."

The customers looked with excited curiosity at us as I led Lloyd to the door in the side of the room. We heard a buzz of voices break out while we were going up the stairs. We passed a woman doing some cleaning on one of the landings. She stared at us but said nothing. I went straight to my attic, and, as Fardel had done, prised open the low papered door with the blade of a knife. We found ourselves in an exactly similar attic, giving on to a similar landing. There was nobody on the top floor. We went down to the next and, switching on the light in one of the two bedrooms there, we came upon Fonthill. He was lying in bed fast asleep. His face looked less troubled than I had ever seen it. A small suitcase lay open on a chair. Our entrance did not wake him.

"Tired out," said Lloyd, looking with distaste at the meagre room. I went to the window and pulled back the blackout to let in the light. Lloyd switched off the bulb.

"You'd better wake him," said I.

Lloyd's touch on his shoulder caused Fonthill to turn and spring out of bed in a fright. His nerves were shot to pieces.

"Uncle James!" he cried, "what—"

Then he saw me and stopped. He groaned and sat down on the bed, with head in hands much as I had remembered him at Rawlings's farm.

Lloyd said, "Bill – don't be alarmed. We've come to get you out of this filthy hole. We're going to get you out of your troubles altogether. Do you understand?"

Fonthill looked up. "No – I don't. Where's Jackson?"

"Jackson has gone home. You're coming with us."

"To my hotel. I've promised Mr. Tolefree that you'll see him—"

"I won't see Tolefree!" cried Fonthill.

"But you will. You must. He's going to put you right with things."

"A trick. A trap!"

"Nothing of a trick or trap whatever, Bill. You should know me better."

"Mr. Lloyd," said I, "I'll go outside. You can speak to Mr. Fonthill more freely. I'll wait for you."

Without staying for yes or no, I walked out and shut the door.

I had smoked through a pipe on the landing before Lloyd came out. He was perspiring.

"The boy has no nerves left whatever," said he. "But I've persuaded him. He will come with us."

"He has good cause to be grateful to you," said I.

But Fonthill showed no gratitude to either of us when he came on to the landing, carrying his case and an overcoat, and wearing his hat. His expression had gone back to the furtive sullenness it had shown all through. He followed me up through the two attics and down to the shop. Horridge and Tolefree stood there by the counter. The customers looked up. One of them called out to Balsdon,

"Wrong for once, George!"

A burst of laughter followed. Balsdon's surprise was well acted. Horridge said, "Go on to the car, please. I want a word with Mr. Balsdon."

What the word was Horridge did not say when he joined us, but he was smiling contentedly.

Leeds pushed the car along without delay to the door of an hotel in a West End backwater where I had never been before. It was the Cymric Hotel, and was a bit of Wales planted in London; the accents of staff and guests left no doubt of that, and Mr. Lloyd was received with much respect.

He had a sitting room on the first floor, and it was there that Tolefree began to develop his ideas of the Blenkinsop mystery. Lloyd, recovering from his bout with his recalcitrant nephew, insisted on having coffee served and did his best to strike a friendly note. Fonthill was, however, still difficult – silent, morose, suspicion in every glance he threw at Tolefree.

Lloyd, when the maid had gone and he had dispensed coffee, said,

"Bill, all these gentlemen have helped me to get you out of that place. They all want to be friendly. Mr. Tolefree, I have told Bill about our talk last night. He has promised to answer your questions."

"That's good," said Tolefree. "I hope we shall arrive at last. Did you tell him that he's on no account to incriminate himself?"

"I did. He spoke of a trap. But I assured him you were laying no trap."

"Thank you," said Tolefree to Lloyd. And to Fonthill, "This is no trap for you. It's a shot at getting you out of a tangle and discovering what you know about a matter most important to us. I put that to you at your uncle's house, I thought in an unmistakable way. But the conditions there weren't favourable to confidences, and I'm not harking back on that. I don't accuse your family in any way. I believe you hadn't told them all the facts. That's so, isn't it?"

Fonthill nodded.

"So I'm going to begin where we left off the other night on Aran Fawddwy. You were about to tell me of your relations with Jackson when – well, when something happened to stop you. Let's get it out now. But before that, I want to clear up your relations with another man – poor Blenkinsop. You were once his rival in love, but you remained his friend. If there was a plot which placed Blenkinsop in danger, you had nothing to do with it. I accept that. You were probably unaware of it until Blenkinsop told you in a letter, didn't he? – a letter from Pernambuco about three months ago?"

Fonthill nodded again.

"I should like to know what exactly Blenkinsop said."

Fonthill faced with visible nervous tremors the first words he'd been asked to say. He looked round at us all, shrinkingly, then suddenly made up his mind to take the plunge. He shook his head and straightened up.

"Bob Blenkinsop's letter," he said, "gave me the biggest shock I remember up to then. I'd heard from him a time or two while he was in the States, and had one letter from Brazil before the war. Then, nothing, until that day when George gave me a letter in the hall. Bob had been a long way from the war. He didn't realise, it seemed to me, what he was up against. He wasn't very explicit, but he gave me the idea of playing with fire. You know all about it, of course?"

"Blenkinsop wrote to us," said Tolefree, "but under another name."

"Was it Perry?" said Fonthill.

"It was."

"He told me he wasn't going to show his real identity to this fellow and was passing as Perry. He said—"

What he said was more or less what he had written to Mrs. Wollaston. Tolefree nodded as he checked off the points. Fonthill added that Blenkinsop mentioned his decision to let the British authorities know what the spy was up to, but did not supply him with any details.

"And after that, any further letter from Blenkinsop?"

"Only one – the one I told you about. It came from Westport in the morning of that day. It told me that he'd gone to Westport to watch the fellow—"

"Nothing about his adventures after leaving America?"

"No, not a word. Did he have adventures? This was a letter written in bed in the hotel, saying that he was down with a stinking bout of malaria and felt helpless and anxious. Would I like to come and see him? That sort of thing. What were the adventures?"

Tolefree told him briefly the story of the S.S. *Bridgend* and the escape from Lisbon. Fonthill listened with his mouth agape. "My God! – what awful luck!" he muttered when Tolefree had done.

"Well, Mr. Fonthill, we'd got as far as the letter from Westport, the S O S. What did you do?"

"I rushed off to see Jackson. He agreed to come with me, and we took a taxi to Paddington and caught the 10.30."

I gave a start and looked at Tolefree. He said, "It's a pity we weren't acquainted then. Farrar and I were on that train."

"What!"

"Farrar was on his way to Westport because Blenkinsop had asked him to go. The captain of the *Bridgend*, who was lost in the disaster, was a friend of Farrar's and had given Blenkinsop a message to pass on to him. I was going to see Blenkinsop because of a letter he sent to us. Had we met you, and had we acted together, there would have been a very different story to tell." Fonthill groaned and sank down in his old attitude of despair. "However," said Tolefree, "that's an idle fancy. Now, let's come to Jackson. That's where we left off three days ago. First, why did you hide your acquaintance with Jackson from everybody but your father?"

"How do you know I told my father?"

"I think you did, and that you didn't tell your uncles – or perhaps your mother. That's so, isn't it?"

"Yes," said Fonthill in a whisper.

"And I think you confided in your father and in him only, what you're going to tell us now."

"My father—" Fonthill began.

"I think also that I understand why," said Tolefree. "Let's leave that. You and Jackson had been acquainted ever since you went to Pitt Street to live. You became apparently fast friends. Without explanation, that might seem to some people a little strange. You two weren't much of a piece."

"That's wrong," said Fonthill quickly. "We were of a piece. We were both lonely and suffering men. We got acquainted in long nights of fire-watching on the roof in Pitt Street. Perhaps you can't understand what that sort of companionship means," he exclaimed passionately.

"Perhaps I can," said Tolefree. "Farrar certainly can. He's done a lot of fire-watching."

Fonthill looked at me. "Then he'll know what it is to have a companion, if the night's quiet and lonely or if bombs are bursting and guns barking."

"Yes," said I; "I know."

"Jackson," said Fonthill with the same unfamiliar note of passion, "is the salt of the earth. He's incapable of a meanness. He's loyal. He's brave. He's a commercial man. He mayn't have much ornamental education. But he's a fine man in a tight corner, and I know it – how I know it!"

8

1

Fonthill looked round the room as if challenging us. I saw Horridge regarding him with half-closed eyes and an expressionless face.

"Then," said Tolefree, "you think he's a man who'd certainly have nothing to do with a plot—"

The very whisper of it made him furious. "He's a Yorkshire Englishman – as patriotic as they are. He himself suggested going down to Westport with me to see whether we could help Blenkinsop."

"You wouldn't care, I suppose, to tell us whether it's true that Jackson had some secret in his life that he's confided to you but wants you to keep to yourself?" said Horridge.

Fonthill stared hard at him. He stared for several seconds

"Ah! – I've seen you before," he said. "You're the man that keeps a flat at Half Moon Street and comes there now and then – presumably to read other people's correspondence."

Horridge turned pale with anger. Tolefree broke in quietly,

"It'll be better to stick to the point, Fonthill. Answer Horridge's question or not, as you like."

"Oh, I'll answer it. Jackson had no secret. But there was something in his life he couldn't bear to think about. There was something in my life too that didn't bear thinking about. But for that, Jackson wouldn't have mentioned his tragedy to me. I was in a bad mood one day, and he said if I got it off my chest, whatever it was, I'd feel better. I told him. I couldn't get into any Service because the doctors wouldn't have me. They'd doomed me to go about for the rest of my life mooning around doing nothing because I had a heart. Jackson said the doctors were often wrong, and I shouldn't worry. Then he told me what had happened to him. In the raids last year his office in the city went up one night. The next night, before he reached home, his house in Surrey was hit and they were taking the bodies of his wife and his little girl out of the ruins when he got there. He said they were all he had. He wanted to think about it as little as possible and never to talk about it, and he asked me to mention it to no one. I've broken my promise, damn you!" he said to Horridge.

"Fonthill," said Horridge, "I'm sorry."

"Bill," said Lloyd, "I'm sure your friend won't mind. He won't consider it any breach of faith whatever under the circumstances—"

The old fellow had tears in his eyes.

"It's all right, Uncle James," Fonthill answered, swallowing hard.

Tolefree resumed. "Let's clear up all the questions about Jackson before we go on. He went away from London in November, and was away for some months, wasn't he?"

"Yes. Doing a long round of the country, seeing his clients. I think he did it because he couldn't endure sitting in London and being reminded at every turn of what had happened."

"It's suggested," said Tolefree, "that he went abroad. Can you say, one way or the other?"

"Certainly. He never went outside the country. He couldn't, could he, without some very special reason? But he didn't. I had letters from him every now and then, written in various places from Scotland to Cornwall. The last was from Southampton, the day before I got Blenkinsop's."

"Horridge will admit," said Tolefree, "that he examined the letters in your flat. It was his duty to do anything that might help to get at the bottom of a dangerous business. Some expressions in one letter didn't exactly explain themselves. You've explained the allusion to the subject you must never mention. There was another phrase – to the effect that it would be all right on the night—"

"Was there? I'd forgotten. Very likely: that's a pet saying of his when any trouble crops up. You don't mean that you thought it some mysterious – My God! – Westport!" he almost shouted. "But you couldn't—"

"I didn't," said Tolefree. "Don't fly off the handle. You say it's just a tag that Jackson uses. Very well. I can understand why you were excited by Blenkinsop's first letter, the one from Pernambuco. But Jackson? – you speak of his offer to go down with you at an hour's notice that morning to help a man he'd never heard of—"

"Oh, but he had," Fonthill put in. "I showed Bob's first letter to him and asked his advice. He was the only friend I had. He'd known about Bob and me and Vi Arscott. He was sympathetic about Blenkinsop."

"Then you both bolted off to Westport to hold the hand of a man suffering from malaria?"

"Nothing of the kind. I'm afraid I missed out the most important part of Blenkinsop's letter asking for help. He was lying ill, sometimes in delirium. He was afraid the fellow he'd met at Pernambuco would discover him there helpless. You see, they'd parted when they landed in England; but Blenkinsop wouldn't lose sight of him. He trailed him to Westport—"

"Ah?" said Tolefree. "That might account for one thing we couldn't understand?"

"It would," Horridge answered. "But it was dam' silly all the same. A word to us, and we could have trailed him better."

"Sorry, Fonthill." Tolefree turned to him. "Go on. You were saying he trailed the man to Westport. And then?"

"Blenkinsop began to get ill in the train. He was almost out of action when he got to the hotel. He said he'd written some letters to London but was afraid of collapsing altogether. One of the letters was to some Branch or other."

"The Special Branch?"

"That was it. You know about it?"

"We know that the letter never came."

"Could have been abstracted from the post," said Horridge.

"If Black was in the hotel at the time, yes. But that's a mystery can never be solved." Tolefree resumed: "You and Jackson reached Westport late. The train didn't get in till after six o'clock There was a crowd at the station and another in the hotel lobby. What did you and Jackson do?"

"They told us it was hard to find rooms, but they had two left on the second floor. They gave us 54 and 56. We went right up. It was a bit of luck being on the same corridor with Blenkinsop – or so we thought," said Fonthill with a wry face. "As soon as we'd dropped our bags, I went across to No. 57. I knocked at the door and there was no answer. I went in. I had a shock. Blenkinsop was looking dreadful. I hardly knew him. He was so weak that he could scarcely speak. He shook hands, and said, 'Good old Bill', and then he seemed to go to sleep. I went back to Jackson and he came along with me to have a look at him. Jackson said not to disturb him; perhaps he'd be better for a sleep."

"Did you notice anything about the door key?"

"It was on the outside of the door, if that's what you're driving at. I saw it while I waited for an answer to my knock."

"Ah, yes," said Tolefree. "Well — ?"

Fonthill said they'd been told that dinner began at seven. Just before that they went to No. 57 to see whether Blenkinsop was still asleep. On a small table beside the bed was a tray with food which hadn't been touched.

"Blenkinsop lay broad on his back, with his eyes staring open and a ghastly look on his face. He was bathed in sweat and breathing at a terrific bat. He raved—"

"Did you catch anything he said?"

"He was almost – well, inarticulate. I caught a word or two: 'There he is! Catch him!... He's gone – my God!' That sort of thing. Once he seemed to catch sight of me, and said, 'Bill, get after him!' I said to Jackson that he was in a bad way. Jackson said we ought to get a doctor. There was a glass of lemonade or something on the table. Jackson raised Blenkinsop's head and put it to his lips. He drank and fell back. We went down to the lobby to see about telephoning for a doctor. There was a long queue at the telephone boxes, people complaining that they couldn't get numbers. Jackson said it would be quicker to fetch one. He knew Westport, and he told me of a doctor about fifty yards up the street from the hotel. He suggested that I should go and rout him out and he'd stay and keep an eye on Blenkinsop—"

"Curious!" said Tolefree. "If he knew the town and you didn't, why didn't he suggest going himself?"

"No – I don't think it was curious," said Fonthill. "Jackson was cooler than I felt all through – seemed to keep his head better. I believe he thought I'd be more useful moving about and doing something than watching poor Bob."

"Very considerate of him," said Tolefree. "And then—"

"I went out in the blackout. I couldn't find the doctor's house Jackson talked about. I inquired of passers-by for the address of another doctor. It was harder to find. When I got there he was out too. I tried a third and had the same luck. By this time I'd gone a long way from the hotel. I thought I might lose myself. I groped my way back, meaning to get Jackson to do the hunting while I looked after Blenkinsop. I'd been away about twenty minutes. I found Jackson in his room. He said Blenkinsop had quieted down and was sleeping. Then we set about the doctor business again – went down to the lobby to wait for a call. It was a quarter of an hour before our chance came—"

Tolefree interrupted. "I've been calculating the time. It must then have been half-past seven – or later, perhaps?"

"You're probably right. I wasn't taking much account of time. Anyhow we couldn't get a doctor."

"Did you speak to the hotel people?"

"No – there were such crowds in the lobby and so few servants. I suppose we didn't think of it."

"Because," said Tolefree, "a doctor had been attending Blenkinsop. He was there at six o'clock. The hotel manager could have told you."

"Could he? But the confusion was so great—"

"All right," said Tolefree. "And after that — ?"

"We went back to Blenkinsop's room—"

"And you found him lying dead on his bed. Now, Mr. Fonthill, think carefully before you go on. I don't want you to accuse yourself or Jackson. That's understood?"

A spasm passed over Fonthill's face.

"I'm going to tell you the whole thing. I've made up my mind. I want to get it off my mind," he answered.

He was a pathetic young man as he sat facing the four of us in his confessional; but the most affecting figure in the room to my eyes was Lloyd. He suffered under a terrific strain. Tolefree had held up a warning hand.

"Have you ever told this to anyone before, Fonthill? Your father — ?"

"Yes, I told him everything. Nobody else."

Tolefree sat back and waited. Fonthill began in a staccato, stumbling way. But as he went on the story came with a rush.

"It wasn't quite as you said. I opened the door. Jackson was behind me. The room was in darkness. The light over the bed had been on when Jackson left. We thought Blenkinsop had put it out. I fished for my torch as I stepped in, saw Blenkinsop dead on the bed. Then, in the same instant, the beam hit a man kneeling on the floor by the foot of the bed. His back was towards me, but he'd turned his head and was looking over his shoulder, dazzled. He had a suitcase on the floor, and some of the things in it were tumbled out. Immediately the thought of

Blenkinsop's enemy flashed through my mind. He wore what looked like a black shirt and trousers, and he had a black cap on his head. He put up his hand to keep the light out of his eyes. I saw a gun on the floor and he was reaching, fumbling for it. I dived down and got it, and leaped back. It all passed in two seconds. Jackson switched on the light from the door. The man had scrambled up. He stepped backwards and raised his right arm. I fired and at the same moment something hit me on the head and I dropped. I heard Jackson cry out, 'My God! – what have you done?' Then I felt blood streaming down my face. I got up. Jackson was bending over the man on the floor. He said, 'You've killed him.' I glanced at the bed. Blenkinsop was lying half out over, with a hole in his forehead and his eyes glazed and staring."

Fonthill collapsed, put his arms on the table and sank down, face in hands. I knew why he'd shown us that attitude so many times.

Horridge reached for a sideboard, poured whisky from a bottle, got hold of Fonthill and said, "Here – drink this."

Fonthill's teeth chattered against the glass. He spluttered and coughed. Then he said, "I'm sorry. It's been a nightmare." Lloyd sat looking at him with a horror-stricken face. Horridge said,

"Cheer up, Fonthill. You did a good job."

"Good job!" he exclaimed hoarsely. "You don't know what sort of job it was. But I'm glad it's had to come out."

"Take it steady," said Tolefree. "Have a rest, Fonthill. We'll leave you with your uncle for a bit if you like."

"It's all right, Tolefree. Better tell you the rest now. There isn't much. We were left there with two dead men in the room. We couldn't do anything for poor old Bob. Jackson said it was a bad business. We had to get out quick. Nobody seemed to have heard the shot. I threw down the gun. He picked it up and wiped it, and he put it down on the floor near the man. I had a look at him, just a glance. Then I saw on the floor a photograph of Vi Arscott – I mean Blenkinsop's wife. I picked it up and put it in my pocket. Jackson hurried me out. He locked the door and we went to his room. I was all in – hadn't an idea in my head, and it was aching like a sore tooth. I told you Jackson kept his wits about him. He said somebody might turn up at any minute to go into Blenkinsop's room. He told me to wait while he fetched my bag. He brought it to me, and we took everything out of it that had my name on it and put it in his suitcase. He returned the bag to my room. Then he said he'd fake up a story somehow, and I was to get out of the hotel and stay away for two or three hours – go to a cinema or something. I went down and outside. I found I'd left my torch somewhere, probably in Blenkinsop's room. I couldn't go anywhere without a torch, so I rushed back and Jackson lent me his—"

"That," said Tolefree, "was when Barrett saw – but you don't know about that. Never mind. Go on, Fonthill."

"Well, I went down again and got as far as the door. Everything went giddy, and I don't remember any more till I found three men standing over me – and you know all the rest."

We did. There was silence in the room for a minute which seemed like an hour.

Tolefree broke it. He said gravely, "This is a confession, Fonthill."

"I know it is."

"Confession be damned!" cried Horridge. "I told you it was a good job."

"Half a moment, Horridge," Tolefree said. "It's a confession to us, and not official. I think there's something more Fonthill wants to say."

"He's said enough. If Jackson confirms it, Fonthill's put paid to the account of a dangerous enemy," Horridge persisted.

"But," Fonthill said in an agonised voice, "that's just what he wasn't."

"Not the man? Who then?"

"I can tell you," said Tolefree. "He was an air-raid warden. That's so, isn't it, Fonthill?"

"Yes," Fonthill groaned; "he was."

2

This utterly new slant on the events of the night in the hotel staggered us all. Lloyd gasped. Horridge exclaimed. I sat gaping at Tolefree.

He rose. "This has been trying for you both, Mr. Lloyd," said he. "We'd better leave you now. You won't go away from London without letting me or Horridge know?"

"Indeed I should like to leave London at once," Lloyd answered, miserably.

"No doubt. But it would be convenient if Fonthill stayed within reach until we've had a chance of thinking over what he's told us. You must see that this makes a great difference to us."

Lloyd said he did see. He agreed that Fonthill should stay with him at the hotel till Tolefree communicated.

In ten minutes he and I were on the way with Horridge to his flat.

The simple story Fonthill told had thrown a big stone in the pond. It stirred up an entirely new lot of mud. But it explained the conduct which had seemed at times so mad and at others so desperate. Fonthill had been snared in a tangle of circumstances. Tolefree had said more than once that his behaviour meant overwhelming fear. Now we knew what he feared – what had led his father to such extremes while there seemed to be the faintest chance of concealing him till the storm blew over.

Tolefree attributed the lord of the manor's unlordly conduct at Bwlch-y-Groes to his belief that we had no definite knowledge or evidence of what happened at Westport. The Lloyds, who knew nothing either of the event itself or of Jackson, followed Mr. Fonthill's lead out of sympathy for their sister and against the better judgment of one of them.

All of us, even Horridge, had listened to the tale of Fonthill's ordeal with horror and concern. But what of Jackson? I had to admit that nothing in Fonthill's narrative explained him. Tolefree agreed.

I raised the question of the air-raid warden. What was he doing in Blenkinsop's room? How did Tolefree know he was a warden?

Tolefree said that couldn't escape anyone who heard Fonthill's description of the man's clothes. He wore the uniform of a district warden: the dark blue would look black by artificial light.

"Then," said I, "he brings your Fifth Hypothesis to life?"

"He may," said Tolefree.

"Hypothesis?" Horridge exclaimed in scorn. "What does it matter? The spy got away. He's loose now! That's our headache. My Jackson Theory's coming true after all."

Tolefree said, "I've been thinking of that. A good deal in Fonthill's story might be used against Jackson."

"A good deal? Why, Tolefree, everything Fonthill said yells at you that Jackson was in the plot. He was the man at Pernambuco. He was the man who came home with Blenkinsop on the steamer."

"Everything? Hardly. The letters Fonthill had from him, for example?"

"Those letters? Easy, my dear fellow. He'd only to get them posted from various places at various dates."

"There's also the fact that Jackson was in London with Fonthill when the man from Pernambuco, according to Blenkinsop, was in Westport."

But Horridge had an answer for that.

"Blenkinsop had been in Westport several days – ill, unable to keep tabs on the man. Jackson didn't reach London till the day before the raid. There's nothing in that, Tolefree. I maintain my Jackson theory. You'll find it coming true. Not the details, but the essentials. With slight differences it meets all Fonthill's facts."

Tolefree asked him to work out the parallel. He began with the times. He had to account for the hour between seven o'clock and the moment when we picked up Fonthill in the hotel door-way.

"It was seven when you left Barrett to go in to dinner, wasn't it? At that time Jackson and Fonthill were upstairs considering what to do about Blenkinsop. And note what happened, Tole-free. Did you hear anything in Fonthill's account that specially bears out my theory?"

"Several things. But – you particularise, Horridge."

"Well – this: Blenkinsop was raving, but he wasn't too deliri-ous to see Fonthill in the room, Jackson either – especially Jackson."

"How's that, Horridge?" I asked.

"Tolefree wanted to know if Fonthill could remember any-thing Blenkinsop said. He remembered something like this: 'There he is! Catch him! Bill – get after him!' What about that?"

"It's a point," said Tolefree.

"Then, Jackson's own behaviour. He didn't behave like a close friend of Fonthill—"

"No? I rather thought he did."

"I know you think I'm obsessed. But see! – Jackson wasn't distracted by grief for his friend's trouble. He kept his head. He kept it well enough to seize the skirts of happy chance. Things played into his hands. He caught them. He sent Fonthill out chasing doctors. It was his opportunity. It gave him time to do his business on Blenkinsop. You saw that yourself, Tolefree. You picked it up on the instant."

"Yes," said Tolefree; "I saw that."

"In fact he had plenty of time to do a job that could be done in two minutes. Fonthill was away twenty minutes: the devil favoured Jackson. And how well he played his hand! That farce of telephoning for the doctor – what gorgeous evidence, if he ever needed evidence, that he'd nothing to do with what happened in No. 57!"

I said, "Then, Horridge, he murdered Blenkinsop while Fonthill was out. He left the room unlocked for anybody to go in, and sat calmly in his own room waiting for Fonthill to come back."

"He's a calm customer – cool. Cool! – he's cold as steel and as hard, if he's Breitmann – and I think he is. The unlocked door? – why, my dear fellow, he'd have given himself away if he'd locked the door."

I admitted that. "But suppose Fonthill had wanted to see Blenkinsop immediately he came in?"

"Why not? Though Jackson had probably given Fonthill a wrong direction for the doctor, he couldn't know that Fonthill wouldn't find another. The discovery might have been made any time. But if Fonthill could be persuaded to waste another quarter of an hour on the doctor question, so much the better. It worked in with his plan. The air-raid warden in the room when they got there upset his own scheme for rushing down to announce the discovery—"

"You're guessing," said I.

"Isn't it obvious? It's what he was bound to do. When Fonthill shot the warden, that made things awkward. But he's a dab hand at plans. He had another instantly. It sent Fonthill out looking for any trouble there might be and left him sitting quietly in his room, a picture of innocence. You know, but for the accident that Fonthill overlooked his torch, Barrett would never have seen him. You realised that, Tolefree?"

"It was so," said Tolefree.

"So while you were up knocking at Blenkinsop's door he was dead, and Jackson was inside his door listening, and cooking up the yarn he'd spin whenever he had to spin one – the yarn he did spin to you next day."

"He might have spun a much simpler one," said Tolefree. "How?"

"If he'd said nothing about hearing a shot – or two shots—"

"Only shows how hellishly clever he is. He'd be expected to hear a shot if there was one. Even if the police passed that, he knew there was a bullet in Blenkinsop's head. He wasn't to know Blenkinsop would be burnt to a cinder. So far as he knew, he was the only man on the corridor. If he heard shots and talked about 'em – see?"

"Yes – well, that's diabolical ingenuity, certainly."

"Ask Barrett whether Breitmann is as ingenious as the devil. Tolefree – I've accounted for the times, haven't I? It all happened at the times when it must have happened, and it was all over before Barrett saw Fonthill rush through the lobby to go upstairs."

"The times fit very well," said Tolefree. "Of course, it all depends on the truth of the theory. If Jackson is Breitmann, yes. If he isn't—"

"He must be," said Horridge. "The fact that Fonthill killed an unhappy warden and not Blenkinsop's enemy clinches it. There's nobody else."

"About the warden, Tolefree," said I. "I wanted to know about the warden. Why was he in the room? And why did he act as he did?"

Tolefree said that was a secret buried in the ashes of the Imperial Hotel.

"I don't know about that, Tolefree," Horridge declared, "I think you could deduce from the facts an answer to Farrar's questions."

"Could I? You do it," said Tolefree.

"All right. The warden couldn't have gone in because he heard the shot. He'd have given the alarm at once. But he must have had a suspicion of some sort. Perhaps he knew there was a sick man in the room. Perhaps he'd seen Jackson sneaking out, did a round of the hotel, got back to that corridor and decided to have a look. He must have had a suspicion. What created it is buried in the ashes."

I protested that if Horridge had got the warden into the room, he hadn't explained why he acted as he did.

"Well, think Farrar. He opens the door, finds a blacked-out room pitch dark. He switches on his torch. He sees a dead man on the bed and a gun on the floor. He wonders whether it's a suicide. Then he sees the suitcase spilling things all over the floor, and he wonders whether it's a robbery and murder. He kneels down to look at something which makes him curious – perhaps the photograph. He hears somebody at the door. He switches off the torch – which is no doubt what he flings when Fonthill gets hold of the gun."

"Well, Farrar," said Tolefree, "that's an interesting reconstruction, eh?"

"Very," said I.

"We'll find out what we can about the warden by inquiry at Westport. No doubt more than one were missing that night. Meanwhile, for our next objective – a heart-to-heart talk with Mr. Jackson."

"Hooray!" said Horridge, reaching for the telephone. "Now we're getting somewhere, Tolefree – at last."

He spent five minutes with the receiver at his ear. He established the fact that Jackson, as Tolefree divined, had returned to Pitt Street, that he was still in the house, and that a man was watching the door. He looked at his watch and said, "Ring me at two o'clock – or before if he leaves... Now, you two, what about some lunch? We'll take it here, it's quicker. We have three-quarters of an hour."

The aged servitor brought us a good lunch. We ate it. And at ten minutes after two Horridge's car brought us to Pitt Street. A characteristic Bloomsbury stretch of straight-fronted tall, narrow houses. No. 14 was at a corner. Tolefree and I sat in the car while Horridge had a word with a man who suddenly turned the corner on the other side of the street. We then walked up the steps and Horridge pushed the bell-button.

"Mr. Jackson?" he said to the maid who answered.

"I'll see, sir. Please step inside."

We stood in a hall which was hardly more than a passageway, and there overheard a colloquy in the gloom beyond.

"Three of 'em?" an incisive voice said.

"Yes'm."

"All right. I'll have a look myself."

A figure appeared out of the gloom, tall, straight, in a black dress with golden hair which had apparently not aged with the face. Nevertheless, the landlady of No. 14 Pitt Street was a shrewd woman, with no other nonsense about her.

"You want to see Mr. Jackson?"

"If you please," said Horridge.

"I don't know whether he's in. He was here at lunch. He may be in his room. Ella!" she called. "Go and see whether Mr. Jackson's in his room."

The maid came out of the gloom and trudged up the stairs. She returned in two minutes and said,

"No'm."

"Mr. Jackson appears to be out. Any message? What name?"

"Forgive me," said Horridge. "There must be some mistake. He can't have gone out."

"Can't he? Why?"

"I feel sure he's not left the house since luncheon," said Horridge.

"You seem to know more about the house than I do. What are you? — the police?"

"Certainly not," Horridge replied, with a suggestion of annoyance.

"Oh – well, as you know so much. Anyhow, Mr. Jackson's not at home."

"We should like to make sure for ourselves," said Horridge.

"You mean you want to go to his room? No, thank you – unless you're the police. Mr. Jackson's not here. I wish you good-day."

The tall figure crowned with its golden mane brushed past us to the door and held it open. Horridge hesitated.

"If you don't move out," she said, "I'll soon fetch some real police and we'll know what's what."

Tolefree took a hand. "We'll save you that trouble," said he pleasantly, and passed her raising his hat. I followed. There was nothing for Horridge to do but to come as well. The door banged behind us. Horridge was enraged.

"Enter Minerva, exit Pallas," Tolefree laughed.

"Stop grinning like a Cheshire cat!" said Horridge, and crossed the road to the corner. Upon which the man to whom he'd spoken suddenly re-appeared. Tolefree and I walked over, and we all passed into a side street. Horridge said, "You're sure he didn't leave the house?"

"Positive," said the man. "Haven't had an eye off the door for five seconds."

"The woman's lying and bluffing!" exclaimed Horridge. "Probably in cahoots with him."

"She didn't seem to me that sort of person," Tolefree said.

"But if he hasn't come out of the house he must be still in it," Horridge insisted angrily.

"If he hasn't been seen to come out of the house, which is the more precise truth," said Tolefree, "he yet may not be in it. Who did come out?"

"Very few – three women and one man, and it wasn't Jackson," said Horridge's watcher. "He was an old fellow with one foot in the grave, limped down the street on a stick with a brown paper parcel under his arm. Besides them only a servant. She came out twice before lunch and went to buy something at a shop round the corner."

"Any way out of the place except that door?"

"No – we looked around days ago. There's no back entrance and the side wall's a blank. You can take it from me he's not come out."

"Excuse me, Horridge," said Tolefree. "I've just thought of something. I'm more likely to have luck with Minerva than you," and he went back to the house. He was away two minutes. He came back.

"Mrs. Pardoe says—"

"Who the devil's Mrs. Pardoe?" Horridge growled.

"Otherwise Minerva. Says that no old gentleman with one foot in the grave is numbered among her clients. And I believe her, Horridge."

Horridge and his watcher looked sadly at each other.

"Damn!" said the watcher.

"What time did the poor old fellow crawl away?" Tolefree asked him.

"Half-past one."

"Mr. Jackson lunched early at 12.30," said Tolefree.

3

Horridge walked dejectedly to the car. "Cheer up," said Tolefree as we got in. "It rather backs up your theory, you know."

"Gosh – so it does!" said Horridge, brightening. "Disguise – therefore confession of guilt."

"At any rate it's an admission that he saw the place was being watched and didn't want you to know where he was going. And that might be – where?"

"Fardel's?"

Tolefree said, "Perhaps – or Balsdon's more probably."

"Why more probably?"

"Because – but first, ask your man what sort of overcoat and hat the old gentleman wore."

Horridge popped out of the car like a man emancipated and went, quickly for him, to the corner. He returned with the news that the old gentleman wore a thick black overcoat, had a grey muffler round his neck, and a black felt hat on his head. "Why do you guess at Balsdon's?" he asked.

"Because when Jackson left Balsdon's this morning Fonthill was still there. He can't have got news of Fonthill since, unless from Balsdon. If he did it must have been alarming news for him. He'd be very likely to go down to Pimlico to pick up any traces he could. There's one other chance – that he may have risked going to see Lloyd at his hotel."

"How would he know Lloyd's hotel?" said Horridge.

"He certainly would know, either from Lloyd or from Fonthill."

"Ah!" Horridge started the car. "We'll settle that at the next telephone box."

He found one in Russell Street and was away five minutes. He came back shaking his head.

"He's not been there, Tolefree; but he telephoned twenty minutes ago asking about Fonthill. I spoke to Fonthill himself. Jackson told him he heard that he'd left Balsdon's with his uncle, hoped he wasn't being annoyed – by us, I suppose – and felt glad he was with Lloyd. Fonthill didn't mention anything to him about our session this morning."

"Anything else?" Tolefree asked.

"Fonthill said he'd probably be going to Stowford shortly. Jackson said he was likely to be away for some days, but he'd write to Stowford."

"Well, well! So let's get back to the flat and pack our bags, and then to Manchester Square for Farrar to pack his," said Tolefree.

Horridge pressed the starter button. "What's the idea, Tolefree?"

"Westport, undoubtedly."

Horridge had a jerk and the car swerved. "Are you in your senses? Talk of frying pan and fire! Why in Heaven's name would Jackson go to Westport?"

"Might be one of two reasons, depending on the real character of Jackson. If he's an innocent man, the only thing he'll think of is the plight of his friend Fonthill. He'll go to Westport to see how the land lies, whether the police know anything, and whether they've any idea of running Fonthill down. And then to judge what his next step should be. If he's an innocent man, he can go straight to Stevenson."

That hypothesis didn't interest Horridge. He wondered why Tolefree wasted a word on it with Jackson's tacit confession under his very eyes. Tolefree smiled at this fervour.

"All right," said he. "I'm only trying to get him to Westport, you know. You can have him there as a tottering old man if you like. But I think a guilty Jackson, if he's our man, would go there for much the same reason – to see how the land lay and to judge his next step, which might be to carry on with the business that took him there in the first place Farrar – what do you think?"

I didn't know what to think. My first conception of Jackson persisted. He was, to me, a sturdy, keen-witted tyke – certainly not a Breitmann. But I'd been shaken badly by Fonthill's story and Jackson's present escapade had given me another jolt.

Horridge exclaimed, exulting: "He's done for himself! Tolefree, if you go to Westport after him it'll be wild-goose chasing."

"I think not, Horridge," said he. "Of course I don't want to drag you down—"

"My dear fellow, nothing I'd like better than to get home. But you'll agree that we should leave word here for a sharp lookout? I should at least tell them my theory of Jackson."

"Tell 'em anything you like, Horridge – as long as we catch the 3.30 train. It's now half-past two. We can do it if we hurry."

We did hurry, but we didn't catch the 3.30. Horridge, who had the air of humouring Tolefree in a foolish move, was so certain Jackson would hide in London that he took a long time making his dispositions to catch him. We just missed the train – as it turned out, a sizeable bit of luck for us. We travelled by the 4.15, a much slower affair, which did not run into Westport much before midnight. It had unaccountably crawled for many miles, but we learned the reason on arriving: another big raid had just ended. The town was in an uproar. Many fires raged. We saw again on a smaller scale the scenes of that first night of ours in Westport. Crowds were streaming out of the air raid shelters in the station subways. This time the raiders had hit suburban parts. The ruined centre was dark and deserted save for fire engines and ambulances racing through.

We could not get a taxi. We dumped our bags and walked the mile and a half to Horridge's. Nothing had happened in that region, and by this time the fires in the distance were dying down. If we had come by the earlier train we should have been "just in time for the show", as Horridge said. But one such show had been enough for me.

Horridge fixed us up with make-shift beds in his living room, since neither of us would hear of occupying his bedroom. I did not sleep for hours – then went off soundly. When Horridge woke me the sun was shining in through the long window. Tolefree had gone out before Horridge was awake, he said, having packed up his bed and left everything shipshape.

"Energetic beggar! If you'd like to get up, Farrar, Betsy will give us breakfast in twenty minutes. This is the only place I have to feed in. Bathroom across the landing – the white door. Water's hot if you want it."

Tolefree had not got back when Betsy bore in a vastly laden tray and greeted me with a curtsey and a "Good-morning". She must have made grave inroads on Horridge's rations, I thought, to give us bacon and eggs, toast and marmalade ad libitum, and tea of a better colour than I'd seen for a long time.

"I've been away for a week," he explained. "The rations have accumulated. We're having all this richness in consequence." He switched off to the raid. "It was pretty bad last night, Farrar, the paper says. Quite a lot of people killed in little houses out to the west. You don't have much luck with your visits to Westport. Have you a private hoodoo?"

"Unless it's Jackson—"

"Ah – Jackson, yes. I can't make Tolefree out. He's a wizard, I know, but I don't believe he's conjured our friend Jackson back here. Not for a moment. A mad idea."

I said there was generally some method in Tolefree's madness and Horridge left it at that. He seemed to me to have missed the significance of Tolefree's double reason why Jackson would be likely to return to Westport if either he was an innocent and harmless or a guilty and dangerous man.

And when Tolefree came in a quarter of an hour after we'd started breakfast, Horridge had the surprise of his life.

"Sorry to be late," he said, as Horridge reached the bell push. "I rose to catch the early worm, Horridge. A pity we didn't get the 3.30 yesterday. Jackson was on it."

"Eh!" Horridge stared, with a finger of toast poised halfway to his mouth. "How — ?"

"Well, Stevenson has all the trains watched. Jackson came in at eight o'clock – seen by one of Stevenson's men."

"You mean, of course, an old man with one foot in the grave and a brown paper parcel came in."

"No – Jackson in person, in his habit as he lives. A dark coat and hat, certainly. But no older than usual, no stick, no limp. The only likeness to the poor old chap in Pitt Street was that he had a muffler twisted round his neck. You know, Horridge, I don't think Jackson was made up at all when he left Pitt Street. He tried the old trick of simulating age, and brought it off. He had only a few yards to go before he was out of sight of your sleuth."

"Dammit!" was all Horridge could find to say. Tolefree gave him a pleasant grin. "Cheer up," said he.

"The brown paper parcel – had he a brown paper parcel?"

"No – a small suitcase. Picked it up at Balsdon's no doubt. He must have been there when he phoned to Lloyd's hotel."

Horridge nodded gloomily. "No chance that Stevenson's got him, I suppose?"

"Not a chance. Why should he? Remember that to Stevenson Jackson's just a witness. He wouldn't be concerned. You know, Horridge, your own suspicions of Jackson didn't come on very early – not seriously."

"You put 'em into my head yourself, Tolefree. You asked me to keep an eye on him."

"I did. But I mean you didn't produce the Jackson Theory till we'd been in London a day or two and you'd got Jackson to come and dine with us. Anyhow, here's Mr. Jackson in Westport—"

"You do have hunches, Tolefree, don't you?"

"Not often. I'm cursed with a damnable curiosity about people's eyes. I can generally tell when a man's got a secret – some reserve that he's guarding as if it were the Koh-i-noor. It seemed to me when I first saw Jackson, the morning Barrett was getting his story, that he had a desperate secret hidden behind his apparent frankness. That was why I wanted him watched. However, here he is, and – the mischief of it! We've about as much chance of lighting on him as Goering has of getting into heaven through the eye of a needle."

"If he's an innocent man," said Horridge, with intention, "as you said, he'll go and see Stevenson."

"Oh, come, Horridge! The irony would be keener if I'd said it. What I did say was that he could go to Stevenson if he was an innocent man. But there are more likely ways of finding out what the police are doing about Fonthill than asking the Superintendent. That's not our difficulty. It's the raid. It began just after Fonthill's train came in. It lasted hours. The police are up to their eyes in work. Who's to worry about Jackson?"

"Nobody for the moment," said Horridge. "But all the same, he's ditched himself. He can't get out of the country. When the police once find his trail they won't take long pulling him in."

Tolefree reminded him that the police hadn't scored a great success with Fonthill.

"That's a different matter. They weren't particularly interested in Fonthill. They'll be interested enough in Jackson when we tell 'em, Tolefree."

"Tell what? The Jackson Theory?"

"They'll get a Jackson theory themselves in two shakes of a lamb's tail when they hear Fonthill's story."

"And who's going to tell them Fonthill's story?"

"Aren't you?"

"Fonthill spoke to us with a certain understanding, you know. You took the lead in that yourself. It was a confession to us in the interest of the truth we wanted to get at, and not official."

"But—"

Horridge protested.

"There's no but," said Tolefree gravely. "We can go for Jackson as hard as you like, but we keep faith with Fonthill."

"Of course," said Horridge, but with a certain reluctance.

How to set about going for Jackson? Searching for him in a big town in the aftermath of a raid was hopeless. The police had something else to do. It was up to us, said Tolefree. Jackson would be found by trying to put oneself in his place and guessing how he would act – remembering that Astuteness was his first name.

I tried to imagine what the Jackson of my first conception would do – the Jackson who was a decent Yorkshireman getting into a scrape by trying to help a friend. Horridge wouldn't join in the discussion. His conception was of Jackson as a wily spy, who could only have come to Westport to do dirty work; he'd assume some other character to do it, and then disappear from the town immediately. If we weren't to put the police on him, we might as well throw in our hand.

Tolefree said no. He didn't believe Jackson would disguise himself in Westport. There his established personality, the casual witness, was his best security. Horridge was forgetting that Jackson didn't know Fonthill had told his story. He believed that none but he and Fonthill knew what happened at the Imperial Hotel, and that his own unveracious account still stood.

These differences of opinion reached me only subconsciously. My own prejudice had started a train of thought which led to a possibility. I chewed it long before venturing to suggest it.

"Will you listen to an idea?" I asked.

"Trot it out, Farrar," said Horridge.

"You probably won't like it," I warned him. "It flows from the supposition that Jackson is Jackson and nobody else, and that he's here, as Tolefree says, to see if he can do a good turn to Fonthill."

"All the same, trot it out," Horridge insisted.

"All right, then. In the few minutes when they were alone in the attic after Fardel left, Fonthill must have told Jackson what happened to him after they parted in the hotel. When I was able to hear them again, Jackson began to talk about the escape from the farm. Last night, things in Westport were pretty much as they'd been that night. What more likely than that Jackson would do of his own free will just what Fonthill did under compulsion? He'd guess that Rawlings might know as much as anybody about the police view of Fonthill—"

"Golly, Farrar!" exclaimed Tolefree. "You may have hit on it."

Horridge didn't think so, for the simple reason that he refused to accept Jackson's possible innocence.

"I hadn't quite finished," said I. "I try to put myself in Jackson's place. He's landed in the middle of a raid. It's unlikely that he could get in anywhere. He might have gone to the air-raid shelter at the station for a time. When things quietened down—"

"He'd think of Rawlings's farm and find his way there?" said Tolefree. "That's not impossible, Horridge. We can soon find out. That is, if Rawlings's telephone's working."

But the same thing had happened again. The telephone system was deranged. Tolefree could not get through.

"Twenty minutes in a car," said he. "What about it, Horridge? Let's get hold of Barrett."

9

1

We spent the whole morning trying to get hold of Barrett – or Horridge did. The confusion and excitement were not so great as before, at any rate in the middle of the city, but any official person was elusive. Everybody seemed up to the eyes in the work of re-organising, feeding refugees, finding billets for them. Horridge finally ran him down in a distant suburb, working like a navvy in the wreckage of a street.

No man was ever more astonished to see anybody than Barrett to find us looking at him. After a few words from Horridge he wiped the muck off his hands, and we walked with him to the place where he'd parked his car.

All his comment on what Horridge told him was,

"Jackson? Well, I'm damned! Sure you haven't got the bull by the tail?"

Horridge's explanation and Tolefree's sober nods persuaded him that there was reason to suspect Jackson. He came with us willingly enough, and we pulled up outside Rawlings's farm gate about one o'clock.

The scene there differed little from the one we saw the morning after the first raid. The yard and the outbuildings were full of refugees, mostly women, children, and old men.

We followed Barrett, threading his way through them to the door of the farmhouse. A great buzz of voices came from within. Barrett went forward to the kitchen. The buzzing declined when this man in uniform appeared in the doorway.

We heard the accents of Rawlings himself:

"Why! Come in, Cap'n Barrett. Purty full, but room for a few more, I reckon."

Barrett beckoned to us. We entered. A long table stretched down the middle of the big, stone-floored place. People sat about it, feeding. More were in the window-seat. As in the yard, all old men, women, children.

Barrett told Rawlings of our quest.

"A middle-aged man, you do say? Round about forty or may be fifty? No, Cap'n – no such man here. As for his name, I wouldn't know it, would I? Liberty Hall today again."

There was certainly no Jackson in the room, and nobody with the least resemblance to him. It looked as though this hunch of mine was a wash-out. Barrett thanked the farmer, admitted we were looking for a needle in a haystack, and we backed out. When we reached the yard, Tolefree had disappeared.

Horridge had a brainwave. He suggested that we should split up and go round the place looking for an old man with a crocked leg, a muffler and a black overcoat. If Tolefree was right about Jackson's supposed disguise yesterday, it might be possible that he had used the same trick today, especially if he had seen us enter the yard. One more old man among a crowd of refugees – what was it, and who would take any notice? And, indeed, what good to ask questions?

We separated, after a thorough scrutiny of the people round us. I took a big barn which stood near the tower. Feeding was going on there too. A field kitchen had found its way into the yard, and relays of helpers carried hot stew to the waiting crowd. I stood just inside the door. I counted eleven men – old men all. Not one of them had the slightest resemblance to Jackson. Not one of them could have been Jackson. My gaze was too much for one old fellow.

"Think you'll know me again, mister?" he asked.

I retreated. Neither Barrett nor Horridge had any better luck. We had apparently drawn blank. I looked round for Tolefree. He was nowhere to be seen.

"It would be like Tolefree," said Horridge, "to turn up directly with Jackson eating out of his hand. But I guess his luck's out today. We'd better find him and hare back to Westport."

Tolefree did not turn up directly. We had been kicking our heels for a full ten minutes when he did arrive. And then he walked in at the gate with Jackson, not eating out of his hand, but in earnest talk with him. And it was Jackson as we knew him – no masquerader in the character of a grandfather.

We greeted them silently. Said Tolefree, "Well, Farrar, your intuition came off, you see. And here's Mr. Jackson. I've asked him to give us half an hour or so of his time, and he's agreed. Where shall we go? Barrett, do you think Mr. Rawlings would lend us his room in the tower?"

"Excellent scheme," said Barrett. "Of course he will. I'll ask him."

In that high place, whence I had seen the most awful spectacle in my experience, we had our critical session with Jackson. We carried up chairs. We sat in a rough circle, Jackson between Horridge and Barrett, both looking grim. Tolefree, too, displayed an unaccustomed severity. When he began at once to speak we knew why.

"It was fortunate," he said, "that the idea of taking a stroll occurred to me. I'd observed an elderly refugee leaving the yard out there, who had much difficulty in walking. I thought it would be a kindness to lend him an arm. I overtook him and grasped his arm to help him along, and I was astonished at the likeness between the old gentleman and Mr. Jackson here. In ten seconds I discovered that it was Mr. Jackson here, and I thought it was better to bring him back to rest his gammy leg. So here we are."

Jackson sat facing Tolefree and didn't turn a hair.

"Mr. Jackson," said Tolefree, "appears to have been suddenly afflicted with this disability about the same time yesterday, Horridge. It is evidently one which works itself out in twenty-four hours for, as you perceive, he was able to climb those steep stairs as nimbly as any of us."

"Yes, Tolefree," said Horridge, "that's all very well. But I think we should get down to it right away and ask Jackson what the hell he means by it."

Tolefree sighed. "Just as you please. Ask him."

Horridge said, "No. I think Barrett, who got Jackson's evidence from him the other day should take him on now."

"What do you say to that, Jackson?" asked Tolefree.

"Nothing," Jackson replied. "You've got me in here by weight of numbers. Get on with it any way you choose. You're all off the rails, you know."

"Are we? Well, you put us on again. Barrett, do you agree with Horridge's plan?"

"All right," said Barrett. "But you clear the ground a bit first. Ask Mr. Jackson the reason for his extraordinary conduct these last two days."

"Very well. Jackson – I ask you that."

"I don't have to explain my conduct to you? Or do I?"

"You don't have to, of course; but we can draw our own conclusions from your silence."

"Come to any conclusions you like. I don't mind. They're certain to be wrong."

Jackson spoke quite easily. He was as cool as a refrigerator.

"We were hoping, or I was hoping," said Tolefree, "that you'd be willing to correct our mistakes and prevent us from going wrong again. You know, your conduct has been surprising. You went to great pains to avoid talking to us in London. Now you've been at still greater pains to avoid talking to us in Westport. One natural conclusion from that would be that there's something you want to conceal from us."

"I can think of another," said Jackson. "Just that I don't like you, and that I don't admit your right to question me or my duty to answer you."

"A pity," said Tolefree. "I have no natural repulsion from you. Rather the other way. But you're in Queer Street, and it depends on what will happen now whether you get out of it, or go on walking in it till you come to a very unpleasant precipice. We've made up our minds to get at the truth behind the lies you sprayed over Barrett at Westport. Barrett, just remind him of what he did say to you."

"I will," said Barrett. "Mr. Jackson, you told me you'd come to Westport from Bristol that day on your business as a commercial man. You weren't within fifty miles of Bristol any time that day. You left London by the Westport express in the morning. Isn't that so?"

"You're telling me. I'm not telling you."

"You said you weren't aware of any other man who booked a room on the same floor about the same time as you did. But you were quite well aware of him, weren't you?"

"Finish your yarn. I'll say what I have to say all in one piece," said Jackson.

"You indicated that the first time your attention was drawn to any other room than your own was when you heard a bang. That you heard another bang, which you thought was a shot, but you didn't investigate it except by listening outside your own door. But you had in fact been in another room more than once; you knew there had been two shots; and you knew the results of both. Isn't that so?"

"Any more questions?" said Jackson.

"At present, no. They'll do to go on with."

Jackson looked around at one after the other of us.

"You gentlemen," said he, "are trying to trap me into giving you evidence you don't possess. I've nothing to say. I gave my evidence to the police, and to you, and to the coroner. Let it stand – till you can produce something better."

Horridge had a look of champing at the bit, but Tolefree took up the tale.

"Jackson," he said, "you're playing with us. I'll bring you to close quarters. Do you know Bill Fonthill?"

"Very well indeed."

"Did you come down from London that day with Fonthill?"

Jackson delayed an answer. Then he said,

"May I ask you another question?"

"Of course, but whether I answer it—"

"If you don't undertake to answer it truthfully, I shan't put it."

"If I give you an answer it shall be truthful," said Tolefree.

"Have you seen Fonthill in London in the last two days?"

"Yes."

"What did he tell you?"

"He told us that you did come down from London with him."

"Very well. I did."

"Therefore the evidence you gave to Captain Barrett and the police and the coroner doesn't stand. Are you going to put anything in place of it?"

Jackson considered. "I still think you're trying to trap me into saying what I never will say under any circumstances. All of you except Mr. Farrar are in the Secret Service. You think you have something against me. You'll have to prove it without my help. That's a fair warning. Now I'll answer any questions that I wish to answer."

Horridge could contain himself no longer.

"Jackson," he exclaimed, "you're false from top to toe! You've done nothing but lie ever since you began to speak on this. I've seen through you. Your evidence, as you call it, was a tissue of lies. I know your type. I've seen so many of you. You get a man like Fonthill into your clutches and you work your will with him. You were with Fonthill at the hotel. Fonthill was the man who was heard running along the corridor. I asked you in detail about that. You insisted that you didn't see the man, and knew nothing about him except the footsteps you heard going away in the distance. Lies – all lies! And why, Jackson? Tell me why!"

Jackson refused to be excited. "Let me remind you," said he, "that I was your guest at dinner. You asked me a number of questions which went outside the scope of my evidence. I answered them as I saw fit."

"Tchah!" said Horridge. "We've got you, Jackson. Make no mistake. All your wriggling won't do you a bit of good."

"And all your vehemence leaves me perfectly cold," said Jackson.

Tolefree broke into the wrangle.

"I think you should be told," he said, "that since we saw you at Horridge's we've collected much information. We know all about your association with Fonthill from the time when you first met at Pitt Street, some of your correspondence with him, your long journey in the winter, your return in March, and your visit to Westport together. All this comes not from Fonthill but from other sources. Your evidence is full of discrepancies with our exact knowledge up to the point of the shooting at the hotel. I leave that on one side for the moment. After that we have exact knowledge also of all you've done since you travelled to London with us and we parted at Paddington."

"Snooping so soon?" said Jackson.

"If you like. The important fact for you is that there would have been no snooping but for considerable doubts from the first moment about your – let us say your veracity."

"And what you've discovered by snooping is that I did everything I possibly could to keep Fonthill out of your – let us say your clutches, Mr. Horridge."

"You'll know all about our clutches before you're much older, Breitmann!" Horridge declaimed.

"Brightman? That's not my name, Horridge. You are mistaken. Do you accuse me of masquerading under a false name?"

"Yes, I do, Breitmann!" Horridge retorted. "Several false names – Jackson, Smith, Black, and God knows how many more. But your course is ended. It ends here."

"If I'm supposed to be Brightman," Jackson said evenly, "you might tell me who he is and what he is."

"Mr. Horridge," said Tolefree, "speaks for himself. I will continue to call you Jackson. The answer to your question, Jackson, is that Breitmann is a spy whom we believe to have killed the sick man in Room 57 at the hotel. You can see the importance of this to us."

Jackson turned his gaze from Tolefree to Horridge and gave him a long stare.

"If," said he very deliberately, "I had not so great a respect for your Service, Mr. Horridge, I would say you are a benighted fool. Now we've got something tangible, anyhow. I'm accused of being a traitor and a murderer. Is that it?"

"That's it, Breitmann," said Horridge, with animosity. Tolefree gave him a glance. Then he turned to Jackson.

"We're all going too fast and too far," said he.

"Excuse me," said Jackson. "Too slow and not far enough. If I'm to be accused, I want to be handed over to the police. Put me under lock and key, charge me with treason and murder, and then see what happens."

"Horridge has some ground for his suspicion, Jackson," Tolefree said. "You've given him most of it yourself. I want to put a few points to you. I kept an open mind for a long time. But what's happened lately, unless it can be explained, will tend to make me less open-minded. You don't really want to be handed over to the police on this charge?"

"I'd much rather have to face the police than a private inquisition like this," he answered.

"I'll state the points of suspicion, and you can take them up or not. That won't be an inquisition. The first you've already heard – your fiction that you knew nothing of Fonthill and were a casual visitor to the hotel in the town on business. The second your affectation of ignorance of the man in Room 57. You had come to Westport to see him. You did see him. You sent Fonthill for a doctor whom he couldn't find. Before he returned, the man in Room 57 had been shot. You told Fonthill he was asleep. You spent most time then in a search for a doctor who could easily have been got by applying to the hotel people.... Then you went to the room again. Another man had been before you, had discovered the dead man and was looking at the scattered contents of his bag. A revolver lay on the floor. Before he could reach it, he was himself shot."

Jackson sat silent, looking calmly at Tolefree. He was a little too self-possessed and masterful.

"You have nothing to say to that?" Tolefree asked.

"Nothing whatever – and you know it. Go on stating your points of suspicion. That was the jargon, wasn't it?"

Tolefree said, "You must admit it's a strong indictment. You'll do well to answer it if you can."

"That's your opinion, and you have a right to it. I've a right to mine. My opinion is that I won't be forced to say anything I don't want to say to you. Take me to the police and charge me with something. But you won't do it – and I know why."

"Well – why?"

"You don't want me to tell you what you know already," said Jackson.

Jackson was taking such a curious line that I began to feel shaky about him, and his next remark shook me hard.

Tolefree had said, "You're a most astute person, Jackson."

"Not a bit," he replied. "Just a plain Yorkshireman. You people have always been dealing with crooks till you don't understand a straight man when you see him. You're looking for a crook. You think you've got him. Find out your own mistake. While you waste your time on me, your Mr. Brightman, or whatever he's called, gets farther and farther away."

"You must allow us to know our own business," said Tolefree. "You're astute, but smart Alecs can be too smart. You haven't perhaps apprehended how all this cunning confirms Horridge's theory."

"Oh – Horridge!" said Jackson, with contempt. "I'm talking to you."

"Then listen to this. You took a long journey in the winter. It lasted from November to March. It coincided exactly with the time you would have required to be away from London if you were Breitmann."

"Poppycock!" said Jackson. "If you think I'm somebody I never heard of in my life before, get on with it."

"You're stalling all the time," Horridge exclaimed. "You've got to prove you're not Breitmann and a murderer."

"Really?" Jackson sneered – and I was surprised by Horridge's outburst. "Really? I thought that in English law it was for the accuser to prove his accusation. But you people don't seem to take much stock in law."

Tolefree, with another look in Horridge's direction, intervened.

"I'll make a last effort, Jackson," he said. "There are three or four counts against you. I don't stress your absence from London at a suggestive time. You may be able to put up a perfect alibi, though we know from your talk at Horridge's that you're familiar with New York. As Fonthill showed you his letters, you know what that might mean. But come from suspicions to certainties. They are the deceptions you practised at Westport before the murder; the fact that you were alone in the hotel without an alibi for the time when the sick man in No. 57 was shot; and the deceptions you practised after the murder both in Westport and in London. Add to that your attempt to escape from us an hour ago."

Jackson hesitated. I thought he was going to say "Get on it" again. But something in Tolefree's way of putting it caused him to give a slow and considered answer. He said,

"Horridge calls me not only a murderer but a treason-monger. To be a murderer I must be a treason-monger, for such a man it was who killed Blenkinsop. I don't know why you haven't yet mentioned his name. It must have been such a man, for no one else had a motive. So you have to prove first that I'm a treason-monger – that I am the man from Pernambuco. Horridge says I am. I say, prove it!"

It was a slim argument. But Tolefree countered it.

"You forget," he said, "that even if you prove you are nobody but Mr. Jackson from Yorkshire, that you weren't out of the country in the last six months, that you never saw Blenkinsop before that night, and that you can't be Breitmann, you still have to answer some serious counts: your suspicious conduct in getting rid of Fonthill for the time of the murder and what I called your deceptions before and after the murder. You also forget that a man like Breitmann certainly has accomplices."

"I forget nothing," declared Jackson. "I say, hand me over to the police and make a charge against me. I think Horridge would rush into that out of sheer dislike for me. But I'm sure you won't let him. You astonish me, Mr. Tolefree. There's one question you've never asked me. It's vital."

"I know there is," said Tolefree. "But if I asked it you wouldn't answer."

"Quite right. I wouldn't. That's why I say you won't let Horridge go off the deep end."

"I've had enough," said Horridge. "Look here! – I'll make a proposition. You come to London with us, and see a man who knows Breitmann."

That brought things to a head.

Barrett said, "Good idea, Horridge. What about it, Mr. Jackson?"

Jackson took a full half-minute to consider his answer. I thought he was going to stall again. But he said,

"I should like to know whether Mr. Tolefree considers it a good idea."

"It would be decisive on one point anyhow," said Tolefree.

"Would it be necessary to go into the question you haven't asked?"

"Not on that occasion," said Tolefree. "But it's got to be asked some time – and answered."

"I know that. It'll be when Horridge isn't there. Very well, gentlemen – I'll go to London with you, and see anybody you please – but merely to settle the question whether I'm what I say I am or what Horridge thinks me."

2

We reached London late that night. Barrett was to have ac-companied us, but at the last moment, on Tolefree's suggestion, he stayed behind to make some inquiries at the police office, and was to follow by the midnight train.

"Staying at Pitt Street tonight?" Tolefree asked Jackson, as we were running into Paddington.

"Of course," Jackson answered. "Where else?"

"We'll send a car for you between nine and ten in the morn-ing. You'll be ready?"

"You aren't afraid, are you, that I'm likely to let you down?"

"If you did," said Tolefree, "that would be the *coup de grace* for you."

But Horridge said, when Jackson had left us, that he wasn't going to take any chances. He'd have a man watching Pitt Street. "We aren't going to have any more elderly gentlemen tottering out of the house, Tolefree."

Tolefree agreed.

The precaution, however, proved needless. Jackson arrived at the Piccadilly end of the street at a quarter to ten, and we set off for Whitehall. Tolefree and Jackson entered the Presence together at ten o'clock. Horridge and I waited in an anteroom. We had only five minutes to wait before Tolefree came out. He said the Old Man had detained Jackson for a few words –

probably about fishing in the Wharfe. He gave us a description of the scene which had just passed.

"Good-morning," said the Old Man, and poured a torrent of German on Jackson's devoted head. Jackson either didn't understand a word, or he was the world's best actor. There was another man in the room, eyeing Jackson intently. The Old Man dropped the German, and said,

"Let's see your identity card... thank you." He turned to his companion, who shook his head. "You're not the man I want. Where were you born? Somewhere in the West Riding, I warrant."

Jackson said, "You're right, sir. Can't disguise the accent." But he didn't amplify.

That was all. The Old Man said to Tolefree, "You've caught the wrong fish," and asked him to go out, and he'd send Mr. Jackson along.

Jackson came almost at once. "Dismissed without a stain on my character," he said.

"Good for you," Tolefree replied. "But there's that question still in the air, Jackson. Will you come along to Horridge's flat for half an hour?"

"Horridge's? No. If we're not through, I'd much prefer you to come to my room."

"But I've asked Mr. Fonthill and his uncle to meet us at Half Moon Street. Fonthill's own flat, if you like."

Jackson said, with a tone of suspicion in his voice, "Why do you want Fonthill?"

"I think he should hear what we may have to say to each other."

There was a long pause. Jackson looked like stalling again. Horridge made his amende.

"Jackson, I apologise to you. Sorry I made that mistake, at any rate."

"All right," said Jackson. "I suppose you thought you had to do it, though God knows why."

"We might postpone apologies and protests for half an hour," said Tolefree, "and see whether we need make either."

Then we moved out. We found Lloyd and Fonthill waiting in the flat, and Barrett with them. Fonthill got up and seized Jackson's hand. He exclaimed,

"Frank – I had to tell them. Couldn't stick it any longer."

"All right, Bill. I guessed that yesterday – though I'll say this for Mr. Tolefree: he never gave you away to me. Now I'm for it. You watch 'em put me through the third degree!"

That moment over, Barrett was introduced to Lloyd and Fonthill. Horridge busied himself getting us seated, setting out glasses on a sideboard and offering cigarettes. Tolefree talked to Lloyd and I to Barrett, who was full of suppressed excitement. Fonthill had an absent look, and sad, but seemed less oppressed than I had yet seen him – as if the process of getting it off his chest had restored his self-respect.

Tolefree moved away from Lloyd and sat down at a table.

"We all know why we're here," he said. "We needn't beat about the bush."

"Let's have it straight, whatever it is," Jackson exclaimed.

"I will, Jackson. We're here because Robert Blenkinsop was killed. We all know why he was killed and how. He held the secret of a plot he was on the point of revealing, and he was shot through the head. He was killed either by the man he'd been watching for two months, who came home with him from South America, or by some agent or confederate of that man. And the man from South America wasn't Jackson. We established that this morning."

"You might have established that by checking up on the letters I wrote to Bill while I was away," said Jackson. "In fact we couldn't. The only letters we had were the first you wrote to Fonthill from Liverpool and the last from Southampton. Had you been the man we wanted, even a check on letters would have been useless. What we haven't been able to discover up to now is which of the two killed Blenkinsop – the man we know as

Black because he took that name when he escaped from Lisbon, or someone working with him. I hope we shan't leave this room without knowing."

I was startled. So was Lloyd. He breathed a stifled sigh. Tole-free was going on:

"Two men fell under suspicion. The first was Fonthill. I blame myself for failing to go to Blenkinsop's room immediately we went into the hotel. If we'd gone right up, possibly he might not have been killed – though, if my idea of what happened is correct, we couldn't have saved him. Anyhow we didn't go. I'd seen Barrett in the lobby and I asked Farrar to put off visiting Blenkinsop till after dinner. I wanted a word with Barrett. We had our word. It made me anxious to go outside before eight to look at the weather, for Barrett had hinted at an expected raid. That was when we found Fonthill injured in the doorway. Barrett had seen him rushing upstairs, followed him and missed him. He was a mystery then. His behaviour afterwards and our hunt for him put us on the track of the truth. We were interested in one man only – a highly dangerous person. Fonthill didn't fill the bill."

"I should think not!" exclaimed Jackson. "I wonder you bothered with him."

"Well, I felt that Fonthill was mixed up in the affair in some way, and I went to a lot of trouble to find him. I was rewarded, Jackson, because he led me straight to you. You were the chief witness we had. It was you who revealed the fact that there'd been shooting. Barrett agrees with me that if you'd kept quiet about it Blenkinsop's body might have been buried as that of a victim of the fire—"

"Don't say that made me suspect!" exclaimed Jackson.

"There's a subtle argument that it might have suggested suspicion: I won't go into it. Anyhow, if you were frank about that you kept silent about a lot of other things – that's stating it mildly – and it was only by putting Fonthill through a fierce ordeal that we got at them."

"Bill—" Jackson began.

"Don't worry about me," said Fonthill, and before Jackson could speak again Tolefree went on:

"Now, have I made it clear that our interest in the Westport affair is merely to know who killed Blenkinsop and what became of his murderer?"

"You said so," Jackson answered. "But—"

"But," Tolefree persisted, "there are matters you have to explain. I'm going to ask you to forget all about the evidence you gave at Westport, and your little bouts with Horridge, and tell us the exact truth of what happened that night. I should say that Fonthill's already given us his version. We want to see how the two stories tally."

"Bill," said Jackson, "have you told them the lot?"

"Yes, Frank."

"Every single little thing?"

"Yes."

"And you're willing for me to say my piece?"

"Of course."

"Then, Mr. Tolefree, I withdraw everything I said at Westport. I said it for a good reason. I wanted Bill to be out of it. He never ought to have been in it."

Tolefree said, "I repeat that we're interested only in the man who killed Blenkinsop and in nobody else."

"Right. Well, I don't know the man who killed him. I certainly didn't. And here's all I know about it..."

We listened in almost unbroken silence to Jackson's narrative. It did not differ in any particular from Fonthill's. The only interruption came from Tolefree. He said, when Jackson reached the point at which Fonthill went to look for a doctor,

"Was there such a doctor?"

"Do you doubt it? I happened to have wanted one on a former visit to Westport. I found the nearest one to the hotel. He lives a little way up the hill. His name's Farquhar – a Scot and a very good fellow. Fonthill must have missed the place in the dark, that's all."

"Well, we can test that," said Tolefree. "The other point—"

"Half a moment," Barrett interjected. "There's no need for a test, Tolefree. I know Farquhar. He's actually the medico who attended Blenkinsop."

"Thanks, Barrett. The other point – the delay afterwards."

"It didn't seem like delay to us," declared Jackson. "We felt rather busy – and anxious too. You'll have to take our word for it."

Fonthill said, "Tolefree – that's exact truth."

"I only want to clear up as we go," said Tolefree. Jackson went on with his tale. At the final scene in Blenkinsop's room he checked. He had told of the warden's attempted defence of himself by raising the torch to fling it. Then he said,

"You're not interested in what happened to the poor devil, Tolefree, are you? All you want to know is about Blenkinsop."

Tolefree answered, "As to the warden, you can, if you like, Jackson, use my formula of yesterday. I observed that you didn't miss its significance. You can say that the warden was shot."

"All right. He was shot. Nobody was sorrier for that than we were. But we had to do something about it..."

He completed the story.

"And we're to understand, Jackson," said Tolefree, "that all you did after that, all the lies you told, and all the evasions and pretences, the Fardel business, and the silly escapade in Pimlico – all this was done out of friendship for Fonthill, because you wanted nobody to know about the scene in Blenkinsop's room?"

"That's the fact."

"It must have been a relief to you when the fire destroyed the evidence of what had happened."

"Good God Tolefree! Do you take me for that kind of blackguard?"

"You completely misunderstand me. I mean – it would have been awkward if, say, the waiter coming to take away Blenkinsop's tray, had found two corpses in the room and you the only man left on that corridor."

"I was quite prepared for that – just waiting for it to happen when the sirens went. I think the fact that I did stay in my room instead of bolting, as the murderer must have done, would have counted in my favour. So long as Bill got away, we were safe. He couldn't have stood up to it."

There was a space of silence. Tolefree turned to Barrett.

"You got that information I wanted?"

"Yes – just as you thought."

"Ah! Then we shan't leave the flat without knowing who killed Blenkinsop and where he is. I'll fill in the blanks of your story, Jackson. I calculate that they extend to about five minutes – the last five minutes of the fifteen you and Fonthill spent waiting for a telephone and trying to get a doctor. There was an air-raid warden in the lobby at seven o'clock when we went in to dinner. He went round the hotel and found his way to the corridors of the third floor about five-and-twenty minutes to eight. He went into Blenkinsop's room, and saw him lying asleep or unconscious. He pulled out his gun and shot him dead—"

There was a gasp in the room.

"The warden!" cried Jackson. "But—" A look of stupefaction in his face gave place to the dawning of an idea. "Good God! What a plot!" He shuddered.

"Tell him, Barrett," said Tolefree.

"Yesterday afternoon, when I left you, Jackson, Tolefree asked me to stay in Westport and make some inquiries bearing on an idea he had. I got Stevenson for half an hour in the evening and we went through the records. We found these facts:

"'Three Air-raid Wardens were killed in the blitz and ten were injured.

"'The bodies of all the killed were recovered and identified.

"'No uniformed warden was among the killed.'

"A District Warden in uniform visited the Imperial Hotel every evening to learn how many people were staying in the hotel, to see that water buckets and sand-buckets were filled, and stirrup-pumps in order, and to inspect the shelter.

"He had been through that evening and finished up about six. Stevenson routed him out and I saw him. That gives you what you wanted to know, Tolefree?"

"Couldn't be more precise, could it? It was the first possibility that occurred to me yesterday, when Fonthill told his story. We knew Black had been on the premises. The iron box with his charred papers in it, found by the demolition gang, left no doubt about it. Safe to assume he was the man in the room next to Blenkinsop. He must have watched for a day or two the routine of the real warden, got some clothes that looked like a warden's, taken a room in the hotel and changed into them that evening. A safe bet! He chose his time well – after the warden had finished his round, while dinner was on. I can see him shooting Blenkinsop, dashing back to his own room and waiting on the chance that the shot had been heard. It wasn't heard. You didn't hear it, Jackson?"

"No – we were down at the telephone."

"You said two shots because you knew there were two shots – and as your story involved being in your room all the time you had to hear two?"

"That's the idea."

"Then, nobody heard the shot. The warden goes back to No. 57 to ransack Blenkinsop's papers. He's quite safe. If he's found, people will think what you and Fonthill thought, that he'd discovered the body and the baggage all in disorder and was having a look round before he raised the alarm – and then disappeared in the confusion. He must have had his getaway carefully arranged. But Fonthill upset it and sent him quite another way."

"What a fiend!" Jackson exclaimed.

Lloyd asked anxiously, "How does Bill stand, Mr. Tolefree?"

"Mr. Fonthill will be proved to have shot a scoundrel in self-defence if ever anyone knows that a scoundrel was shot," said Tolefree. "But in my opinion no one will ever know. What do you say, Barrett?"

"I'm sure no one will ever be allowed to know," said Barrett.

Tolefree rose, and the occasion became a festival. Horridge dispensed drinks. He pressed his hospitality more strongly on Jackson than on anyone else.

"Cheerio, Jackson!" he said, raising his own glass. "No ill feeling, I hope?"

"It's rather sudden," said Jackson. "Still, here's all the skin off your nose!"

3

BWLCH-Y-GROES,
14ᵗʰ April, 1941

DEAR MR. TOLEFREE,

My brother James has given me a full account of his adventures in London.

We now have Bill with us, a very different man from the Bill of a fortnight ago. His father is coming to join us next week. We all feel indebted to you for arriving at your goal without involving Bill. James says that we could have avoided all the trouble if his advice had been taken in the first place. But we always act as a family, and numbers were against him.

We wish to make amends for what might have seemed to you a lack of finish in our hospitality. James tells me you glory in the mountain air. Will you come and taste it again under happier circumstances?

If you and Mr. Farrar will honour us with your company for a few days while my brother-in-law is here, he too will be pleased to see you, and will guarantee not to intrude on your privacy or lock you in your room.

My wife and sister join in this invitation.

We will see that you have no trouble in getting here from Bala. Do come.

Yours sincerely,

JOHN LLOYD

P.S. – The police have at last, with great pains, removed your car from the pass. There are some passable trout in our stream.

Tolefree came to Manchester Square one evening to show me this letter.

"What about it, Farrar?" said he. "Do you think a visit to H.Q., tribe of Lloyd, would be fun?"

"I rather think it might," said I.

THE END

The Mill House Murder
By J.S. Fletcher

Q.E.D.
by Lynn Brock

There's Death in the Churchyard
by William Gore

Murder of the Ninth Baronet
by J.S. Fletcher

Dead Man Manor
by Valentine Williams

The Man in the Dark
by John Ferguson

The Dressing Room Murder
by J.S. Fletcher

*Glory Adair and the
Twenty-First Burr*
by Victor Lauriston

The Tunnel Mystery
by J.C. Lenehan

Murder on the Marsh
by John Ferguson

The Fatal Five Minutes
R.A.J. Walling

*The Crime
of a Christmas Toy*
Henry Herman

Death of an Editor
Vernon Loder

Death on May Morning
Max Dalman

The Hymn Tune Mystery
George A. Birmingham

The Middle of Things
JS Fletcher

The Essex Murders
Vernon Loder

The Boat Race Murder
R. E. Swartwout

Who Killed Alfred Snowe?
J. S. Fletcher

Murder at the College
Victor L. Whitechurch

*The Yorkshire
Moorland Mystery*
J. S. Fletcher

Fatality in Fleet Street
Christopher St. John Sprigg

The Doctor of Pimlico
William Le Queux

The Charing Cross Mystery
J. S. Fletcher

Made in the USA
Monee, IL
23 August 2024

64402723R00152